MAYNARD'S HOUSE

HERMAN RAUCHER

DIVERSIONBOOKS

Also by Herman Raucher
Summer of '42
A Glimpse of Tiger
There Should Have Been Castles

Diversion Books
A Division of Diversion Publishing Corp.
443 Park Avenue South, Suite 1008
New York, New York 10016
www.DiversionBooks.com

For more information, email info@diversionbooks.com
For more from Herman Raucher, visit www.hermanraucher.com

First Diversion Books edition May 2015.
Print ISBN: 978-1-62681-890-3
eBook ISBN: 978-1-62681-809-5

For M.K.—
Still with me after twenty years—
Thank you, my friend.

1

The train aimed itself devotedly along, nudging snow from the beckoning rails while the vanishing point ahead kept retreating like a playful Lorelei. On straightaways the engine displayed a joyful confidence, accelerating at times to ten miles an hour. But on turns it grew cautious, and in tunnels it groped, and on bridges it quite simply held its breath.

It was the Bangor & Aroostook Railway—hauler of potatoes and occasional passengers, picking its way over the little spur line that linked Millinocket with Belden, carrying its horizontal red, white and blue stripes into inexorable and wobbly extinction. In a few years it would be no more. All of this in Maine, in the winter of 1972–73.

Inside, turtle-sunk in the parka that had warmed him for one and a half Vietnam winters, Austin Fletcher amused himself by watching the steam of his breath disappear as soon as he created it. The train was unheated and no other passengers abounded. Nothing for companionship but his duffle bag: FLETCHER, A. G., US 51070406. It sat beside him on the seat, embracing everything he owned in the world. As such, and in more ways than one, it was all he had to lean on.

He was a young man, in his twenties, physically unremarkable and possessing no particular characteristic that people might remember—other than his tendency to not smile. Slender, brown-haired and even-featured, he often joked about his ability to go unnoticed, telling all he met that his high-school class had voted him "Most Likely to Be Forgotten" and that his greatest talent lay in his being able to "get lost in a crowd—of two."

The train was tentative but persevering—slowing, stopping, starting, struggling—and Austin admired how, all alone as it was out there, it asked no support and expected none. It simply knew what it had to do and did it. Austin could identify with a train that chugged like that.

Hour after hour the train pushed on, almost merrily, until the merriment went out of it, suddenly and emphatically—his duffle bag flying off the seat as if to cushion his fall, Austin landing hard atop it, full stop and then some.

He looked up to see the mackinawed man ambling casually through the car toward the engine. The man carried a shovel and, noticing Austin on the floor, commented gratuitously, "Snow."

To which Austin said, "Oh," and brushed himself off and got back into his seat, plopping his faithful duffle bag alongside him. If there was one thing he had learned in the Army, it was never volunteer. If any of those crusty New Englanders wanted any assistance with their shoveling, they had better ask for it. Otherwise—forget it.

Through the window he could see a half-dozen men with shovels, all pilgriming their way toward the engine. He silently wished them well, and most effectively, for soon enough the train was jerking forward in small spastic bursts, reiterating its dominance over the elements, willing itself farther north into the innards of Maine.

He was going to Belden. Belden, Maine—wherever *that* was. Somewhere near Mount Katahdin, south of Sourdnahunk Lake, north of Pemadumcook Lake, west of the towns of Mattawamkeag and Millinocket, and east of Chesuncook, Caucomgomok and Seboomook Lakes.

The names slipped around in his head like an Indian chant, a far cry from the Germanic nomenclatures of his native Cincinnati. Austin knew the names from having studied the map, though he wouldn't care to bet his life on how they were spelled. And just what any self-respecting Indian ever did in all that snow would forever be beyond him, for he had always pictured Indians as warm-climate people, dressing only in scanty loincloths, whooping after bison.

The snow was falling so thick and fast that he thought he could almost hear it above the slow *cushing* of the train. And it was falling bright, sharply so, prompting him to put on his dark sunglasses. In so doing he caused the image of Maynard Whittier to jump up before him. Maynard Whittier who *always* wore dark glasses, rain or shine. Dark glasses and an impish, omnipresent smile—he was seldom without either.

Maynard Whittier, the Maine potato farmer. The *dead* Maine potato farmer who had willed to Austin whatever kind of house it was, near Belden, east, west, north and south of all those Indian places.

Austin took the paper from his pocket, reverently, as if it were centuries-old papyrus. Yet all it was was blue-lined notebook paper, dogeared and sweat-stained, hardly the kind one would select to record his last will and testament on. Nor was it centuries old. It was more like six months old.

> I, Corporal Maynard Whittier,
> in the event of my death, leave
> to Austin Fletcher my house
> on eleven acres, eight miles
> northwest of Belden, Maine.
> I also leave to Austin Fletcher
> all that is inside that house.
> I write this while in full
> possession of my faculties, on
> this day, July 23rd, 1972,
> somewhere in Vietnam.

Everything was green and steaming, the jungle lush and overgrown and smelling. They had just come in from a patrol during which nothing was encountered and no one was hurt except Gruninger, who, as usual, skinned an elbow, or bruised a knee, or snagged a nail—or anything that might give him cause to bitch.

The ten of them were flaked out in various positions of death, trying to impress one another with how close to exhaustion they each were. Only Maynard was untainted, sweat and vegetation and gun oil never seeming to find their way to his person. His hair, the color of wheat, was as neatly in place as if he'd just stepped out of a Brylcreem commercial. Even his corporal's stripes were their original vivid yellow. Even his boots, his helmet, his fatigues looked as those things did in recruitment posters. And yet he was the patrol leader, the decision-maker. It was one thing to be cool under fire. It was quite something else to be immaculate. Maynard was something else.

About the same age and physicality as Maynard, it always unsettled Austin to see his own face mirrored twice in the windows of Maynard's sunglasses whenever they talked. It was even more unsettling on that particular day, for Maynard had just sprung his "will" on Austin—and Austin had just finished reading it, to the accompaniment of the far-off whump-whump *of mortar fire.*

"What am I supposed to do with this thing, Maynard?"

"Why, ya keep it," said Maynard in his maddening Maine accent. "Nobody knows anythin' about what's goin' to happen."

"Don't you have a family?"

"Nope. Just my two dogs. Hither and Thither. Left 'em with a couple kids for safekeeping till I get back." He smiled that characteristic smile. "Austin, I'll tell ya, I expect to live forever. But I also expect I might be wrong. In which case you hold on to that thing, 'cause it just may have some value."

"Swell, but why me?"

"It's you or Joe Sharma, or Terry Glover. And since they can barely read, and since you're a kind of loner like I am…Austin, I got books back home. Lots of fine books. And then there's my own notes on the area, got it all catalogued. Even if ya never read none of it, I'd like to know it's in good hands. Thoreau—ya ever read Thoreau?"

"I never read anything."

"Well, ya should."

"I'm not an intellectual."

"Only because ya never took the time. You always seem to act right away and think later, which could get ya killed. Do it the other way around and

you're an intellectual."
    "I barely squeezed through high school. Copied from everybody, anybody. Any paper left uncovered I copied. Once, I was copying some girl's psychology paper. I got so swept up in it, took me two pages to realize it was a letter to some sailor. Weird thing was, I got a B-minus."
    Maynard got to his feet. As far as he was concerned, the issue was closed. "You're my vault, Austin. My Bank of Maine, so to speak. Okay? Now let's get back." He addressed the entire patrol. "Coupla you men need a shower. I don't want to name names, but ya beginnin' to smell inhuman. Let's go. You too, Gruninger. That scratch on ya earlobe—might just be gangrenous."

Austin refolded the wrinkled paper and placed it back in his parka pocket. The train was pressing on, time with it. Belden was ahead. Maynard was behind. Three days after bestowing his will upon Austin, Maynard was no more. Death had come quickly. Incoming mail, just one round. Probably fired off by a Cong infiltrator who came upon the abandoned mortar in the brush and wasn't all that sure how to use it or where he was aiming it. Things like that happened every day. Luck of the draw. Spin of the wheel. Or something like that.

The clerk at the judge advocate's office assured Austin that the will was legal. It had been witnessed and signed by three other men in C Company. Official and binding and uncontestable. Not that anyone was contesting it.

In any case, Maynard was gone. He had been a fairly reticent man, seldom talking to anyone except when he had to, and usually because he had orders to dispense, what with him being the noncom in charge. Austin, of course, being the one notable exception, though he never really knew why. Men took to one another in service, especially under fire. Up until Maynard, Austin had never buddied up with anyone. It was not his nature. Nor would he have been receptive to such an alliance had Maynard not pursued it in such a way as to make Austin totally unaware that it was happening. All Austin knew was that Maynard was his friend. And *how* it came to be was not as important as *that* it came to be.

To say that Austin had time to learn much more than just a smidgeon about Maynard would be an untruth, the longest uninterrupted period the pair of them ever had for rapping being about fifteen minutes. But it was during those few short exchanges that Maynard would unwind. And in those moments, all the inner secrets that Maynard revealed about himself curled into Austin's mind and remained there, the significant and the unimportant, indelibly imprinted and affectionately stockpiled. In Austin Fletcher, the short saga of Maynard Whittier had found a repository for whatever use future historians might have for it.

Maynard spoke of his house and of his dogs. He told of his father who disappeared before he was born, and of his mother who ran off two years later. And of an uncle who was a good guy but hardly a Rockefeller, and of an aunt who couldn't care less and died to prove her point. And of a youth spent in orphanages, with prospective stepparents regularly turning him down despite his smiling like hell through all the interviews—until the smile froze along with his status.

He told of working spring, summer and fall, raising potatoes, saving every penny so that he could hole up in the winter, which he preferred over all the other seasons, in this house of his, where he found more to satisfy him than in all the world of cities and oceans that lay beyond.

And now Austin owned that house. And the least he could do was to go and see it, wherever it was, whatever it was. He'd be doing it for himself too, for he had always thought of being alone somewhere with only nature to contend with. He wanted to learn from nature whatever it had to teach, so that, when it came time for him to die, he would not feel as though he had never quite lived.

Some people went to Mecca, some to Jerusalem, some to the Ganges. Austin was going to Maynard's house. No matter where in life he was to go from there, he was obliged to see Belden first.

2

The train stopped again, this time with a certainty, as though having run into an elephant and pausing to consider its indiscretion. There was a finality to the stop, and Austin sensed that, like it or not, it was the end of the line. Outside, a swarming snow had just about obliterated the sun, and a caucus of men was moving forward to assuage the bedeviled engine.

Austin got to his feet and to the door and, pushing the door open, was met full force by a whirlwind of snow. He pulled up his hood and dropped thigh-high into the thick of it. Slugging, he picked his way toward the engine, maintaining digital contact with the side of the train because he was unable to keep his eyes open long enough to see where his feet were taking him.

Reaching the front of the train, he could see that the forward half of the engine had burrowed itself into a small mountain of snow that straddled the tracks like a Himalaya. Half a dozen men in various plaided mackinaws were studying the situation while leaning on shovels that seemed to have no intention of rearranging the new topography.

The men lit up pipes and waxed philosophical, like consulting doctors confronted with a familiar and deadly virus. They had managed to clear the smokestack so that the little engine could breathe. Beyond that it was up to a higher power.

"What is it?" Austin asked of the nearest mackinaw, red and green with an overplaid of brown.

"Snowslide," said the man, a dour type, leathery and pipe-puffing, uncomplainingly accepting winter's way.

"Ah," said Austin, attempting to appear knowledgeable.

"Be here till thaw."

"What happens now?"

"Got to go back."

"To where?"

"Millinocket."

"But we just came from there."

"Not backwards."

"Backwards?"

"Can't do it frontwards."

"Listen, I have to get to Belden."

"Won't be on *this* train."

"How much farther is it?"

"In miles or in time?"

"In miles."

"'Bout five."

"And in time?"

"April."

Almost on cue, the little engine withdrew its snout from the mountain's gut and slowly backed off to a sane distance, from where it seemed to paw the snow as if contemplating another charge. But Austin knew it was all bluff, that there was no such plan in the train's gasping boiler.

The mackinawed man just stood there, crusting snow filling his facial wrinkles like plastic wood. "Be goin' back in a coupla minutes. No sense in waitin' around."

Austin nodded and then set off to walk around the perimeter of his unanticipated adversary. The damned thing looked to be a mile high. The question, of course, was not how high it was but how wide it was. And at what point on the other side the train tracks would reappear.

To the right of the train was the high, steep slope of a mountain. That was where the snowslide had come from. To the left of the train was monotonous flat snow for about thirty yards, after which came a vertical drop too deep and too foolish to risk chancing.

Austin walked to the left, hoping to circle around to a spot farther along, to where the tracks would delightfully reappear. He made his turn barely ten feet in front of where the vertical drop would have claimed him. And he found it—the opening he sought, the exact place where the tracks came protruding out of the tall snow to point north, as they were supposed to do. Satisfied, he turned and retraced his steps back to the train.

The mackinawed man was still there. But he was the only one. All the others were back aboard the train, and the train was building up steam. "Fixin' on hikin' it?" he asked.

"Yeah. I think so."

"Won't be as easy as it looks."

"Who says it looks easy?"

"Be better if ya could fly."

"No. I'm afraid to fly."

"Get lost out there, won't nobody find ya till thaw."

"I'll follow the tracks."

"Tracks'll wiggle."

"I'll wiggle with 'em." And with that statement of sublime confidence, Austin sloshed back to his car, climbed up and in, stomped the snow from his boots, shook the snow from his parka, zipped the parka as high and as tight as it would go, yanked the hood up as far as he could without lifting himself off the floor, pulled on his gloves, hoisted his duffle bag to his shoulder, and jumped back outside. Geronimo.

The mackinawed man hadn't moved. He was still there, leaning on his shovel like an ice sculpture, when Austin walked up to him. Then he looked up into the sky. "Be dark in a coupla hours."

"Darker than it is now?"

"Twice as." He handed Austin a kerosene lantern that had been standing at his boots. "Won't keep ya warm, but it'll lengthen the day."

"Thank you."

"Name's Nawm."

"Austin."

Norm placed something in Austin's glove. "Chocolate."

"Thank you."

"No almonds. Just chocolate."

"Don't like almonds," said Austin, like a Maine man. And Norm smiled and climbed back onto the train, not saying another word and not bothering to wave.

Austin had been given no off-the-cuff warnings, no dire predictions—just the facts. And a lantern. And a bar of chocolate, no almonds. He liked that. He respected that.

He watched the train pull away backward, retreating in the direction from which it had come. Cowardly, but wise. Then he moved out into his own direction, carrying his lantern and balancing his duffle bag. And even as he trudged the first few yards into the encroaching cold and snow, the thought began to invade his mind that, in all his short and fretful life, this would surely rank as the most imbecilic move he had ever made.

That he had chosen to walk into it so quickly, and with so little thought, troubled him. For he was behaving exactly as Maynard had described him—acting first, thinking later. When would he learn? Why, in the name of all logic, had he gone so offhandedly on this suicidal stroll? What compulsive death wish had taken over the tiller of his ship, steering him on like a character out of Kipling—"To Belden and glory!" Christ, how could he be such an ass?

The questions gathered and bumped in his mind, but failed to deter him. They no longer mattered. He had made his decision and he was stuck with it. Turning back would be more idiotic than plowing on. And standing still would be more self-destructive than either. Standing still would be to die.

The parallel rails knifing ahead were so snow-laden that had he not been walking between them from the outset, he'd never have been able to find them. They were like low-rising, straight-ahead mole tunnels, barely a few inches higher than the snow that housed them, in no way discernible to the naked eye, only to the stubbing toe. And—it was getting colder. A raw kind of cold, and wet. All of it cloaking around him as if an arctic spider were spinning him into an icy pupa.

The light was turning eerie, the sky darkening, causing the snow to look even whiter and the flakes larger, the mix of it milling familiarly, like that Christmas poster he had fashioned in an inspired moment of Yuletide creativity—random cotton puffs pasted on that helpless blue desk blotter, red and green letters slapped over it all with the practiced hand of a palsied Picasso: FRANK'S AUTO SERVICE—CINCINNATI'S FINEST—WISHES TO EXTEND TO YOU AND YOURS A MERRY CHRISTMAS AND A HAPPY 1970.

The radio was playing something scratchily and indefensibly Christmas, while outside it was snowing so heavily that no cars dared risk the road. Frank Brauntuch, a gruff man who always managed to feature a two-day beard stubble no matter how often he shaved, appraised the poster that Austin had Scotch-Taped to the office wall. "I got a three-year-old nephew could do better."

"Can he patch a tire?" asked Austin while doing that very thing.

"The green is wrong. It's got no balance. And my name should be bigger. It should be FRANK'S—big. And maybe with a shiny gold. No, make it silver—for the snow."

"Tell your nephew that's the best I can do." Austin finished the patch and stood the tire on its side in the water trough, to test for air bubbles which were not forthcoming. He had saved another tire. Big deal.

"And how about my last name?" asked Frank, "Shouldn't that be on, too? Big? In silver?"

"It's a poster, not a billboard."

"I suppose you'd like to frame this thing and put it in a museum." Frank was an unattractive man in both body and attitude, pushing forty very hard, at the waistline as well as chronologically.

"I'd like to frame it and shove it up your ass." Austin had had it. He was tired. He'd been working all day. And he no longer could abide the side symptoms of Frank's five-day head cold—i.e., the way the man's nose ran continuously, like a faucet left on, and the fact that he wouldn't blow it, like a gentleman, but rather sucked it back in, like spaghetti.

Frank looked at him with watery red eyes. "Careful there, fella. You ain't indispensable."

"*Then stop knocking my poster. Let's see* you *do one, you're such an expert. And for Christ's sake, why can't you blow your nose like a human being instead of suckin' it all back in? It's goin' to come out your ears.*"

Frank smiled, grimy teeth to match his hands. "*I like the way it tastes. I'm goin' to get Campbell's to put it in cans.*"

"*Jesus, how'd I ever last this long in this place?*"

"*I don't know. You don't know your asshole from a drive shaft. Where you goin'?*"

Austin found himself slipping into his jacket. He was walking out. He was going to quit. Just like that. The idea occurred, took hold, and spurred him on. "*Where am I goin'? Well, I tell you, old buddy, I am resigning my post.*"

"*You quittin'?*"

"*I am quitting.*"

"*Best news I had all day.*"

"*Merry Christmas, you stupid sonofabitch.*"

"*Happy New Year, you ignorant bastard.*"

Austin pulled up his collar so high that his earlobes folded up to close his ears. And, going out, he slammed the door, hard, hoping to break the glass, but all it did was ring the bells and cause Frank to laugh and grunt and reach for a beer.

Stepping indignantly into the snow-blasted night, Austin found it to be unnecessarily cold, colder than should have been allowed, and certainly colder than he had expected. His house was over a mile away, his car in the garage, a taxi a bad joke. He had a better chance of flagging down an Eskimo.

He had not foreseen. Not the severity of the storm or how heavy his duffle bag would become, the snow piling all over it, adding its own weight to the burden. It all seemed never-ending, and the bleakness was visually impenetrable. His feet were dragging and his breath was freezing on his lips. The wind was laying in, the cold was building up, and the name of the game was "Stay Alive." And toward that end his thoughts exploded, the heat of them serving to fuel his furnace, or so he hoped.

"My name is Austin Fletcher. I have two parents. I have logged four years of high school and am saving up for college, though I'm a good bet to flunk out because I'm basically not too smart. I worked eighteen months in Di Paolo's Supermarket, starting at forty-five dollars a week and advancing to eighty, not counting F.C.I. and S.S. and withholding tax and small change. I worked twenty more months in Dugan's Doughnuts, where nothing happened except a hold up where sixty-three dollars was taken and Dugan crapped in his pants. I worked three weeks in the iron foundry, four months at Binder's Dry Cleaning, and one month at Frank's Fucking Auto Shop. It is the year of our Lord 1972 and I am twenty-three years old, six feet tall, one hundred sixty-five pounds, and only two cavities. I have been honorably discharged from the U.S. Fucking Army, my serial number being US 51070406 and my home phone 253-277 fucking 3. My Social Security number is 220-70-069 fucking 4 and I used to know a girl named Alice O'Neale, 35-23-39. I have ten fingers in two gloves and five toes in each of two arctic boots. I have two nostrils sucking wind and one mouth doing likewise. I have two ears turned to dried apricots and two eyes turned to golf balls. I have zero control over my feet and they are going slower than the top of me. I am pitching forward, my head at a ten-degree angle with whatever I'm heading into. It is now twenty degrees. Now thirty degrees. Forty-five will be crucial—and forty-five it is. And all the numbers are leaving my brain like a cash register being cleared. And down I go for the count, like the proverbial bag of shit. And whatever it is I'm carrying I carry it no more…"

The medics at the forward aid station were there almost as soon as he fell, Maynard tombstone-heavy across his back. And he lay there for a moment, gasping for breath and crying, because he knew what the man was going to say.

"He's had it. Do you know that?"

"Yes."

"How far'd you carry him?"

"I don't know."

"Well, we'll take care of him." The medic checked Maynard's dogtags, rather respectfully, considering the circumstances. *"Okay, Maynard—it's all over. No more war for you. Rest easy, kid."* He looked over at Austin, who hadn't moved. *"It's up to Graves Registration now, okay?"*

"What?"

"I said it's over, you can go back to your outfit now. Do you understand?" Seeing that Austin wasn't moving, the medic called off to someone else, *"Hey, Willie? We got a guy here in shock. Willie?"*

But Austin was on his feet and moving off, mourning his only friend but sustained against wracking grief by his soldier's knowledge that death, quick and impersonal, was preferred to death that singled you out, came at you slowly, and hung around obscenely. From that standpoint, and that standpoint only, Maynard had lucked out.

His duffle bag lay in the snow, between the rails, where he had struggled out from under its oppressive weight. And his lantern, which had flown from his grasp when he made his big flop, rested off to the side and down a decline, where it would never be found again.

As to Austin himself, he was mushing on, still keeping between the rails, the snowflakes coming down without end, the wind crowding him, the cold hugging him. He tried to work his fingers into a fist, but his gloves had frozen into boards. With the aid of his armpits, he pulled the gloves off and blew on his fingers. He could see the hot breath but could feel nothing. Time and heat and life were running out, and he knew it. He goddamn knew it.

His legs were pumping forward again, but nightmarishly, slowly and without sensation, seeming to lose ground rather than gain it. He rammed his finger stubs into his parka, groping them about in his inside pocket, where he had earlier cached the chocolate. He found the chocolate and drew it out, losing it twice to the pocket and once more to the snow. He picked it up and held it between hands that had become paws, his fingers no longer able to flex. He couldn't peel the wrapper away, not even with his teeth. And so he shoveled the whole bar into his mouth, wrapper and all, as far as it would go, and he chewed for dear life, his frozen jaw oafishly resisting the entire effort.

Chewing didn't work, and so he concentrated on sucking, reverting to that one primordial instinct that got infants through the night and the species out of the cave. He couldn't taste, not yet, certainly not immediately, but he could feel the saliva slipping from his mouth and dribbling down his chin.

He sucked harder, then able to bring his teeth into play, and he tasted paper—a good sign. He stuffed his fingers into his mouth to rip again at the wrapper. Soggy and thawing, it came free in shreddy bits which he then spat away, and the chocolate was naked and in the clear.

He could taste it, his tongue dancing over it, around it, pushing it, melting it, nudging it back into molar country where those big teeth churned and ground and joined with the tongue and the saliva in the big push toward survival. The chocolate broke and the flavor gushed out, sliding deliciously about in his mouth before diving delightfully down his throat, followed closely by that warm, unmistakable, undeniable feeling of life.

His toes got the news, and tendrils of heat fired the boilers in his boots. His fingers, flexing, grabbed the petrified gloves and forced their way inside, cracking and bending the tough leather into obedient fists.

The banquet lasted but a few moments, Austin knowing he couldn't stay for tea. He foraged about in his pockets for a match with which to light his lantern. But there was no match, and he remembered, all too clearly, that he had used his last match to light his last cigarette, in the last car of what was beginning to look like his last train ride. There was no lantern either, so why all the fuss?

And there weren't any sticks around that he could rub together and thus invoke a flame. Or any flint or steel, or smudge pots, or Zippo lighters, or careless forest fires, or fairy godmothers, or

U.S. Cavalries. Nothing but snow and two railroad tracks pointing endlessly north. And he wondered why the bored tracks, if out of nothing but caprice, didn't turn occasionally left, or indifferently right, or go straight up, or straight down, or separate into different directions, or whistle Dixie, or buy six doughnuts and get one free because it was Dugan's birthday and he did that to drum up business ten or twenty times a year.

His lungs were as full as a blowfish's, one more squeeze still left in the old accordion; one more song to let out slowly before the band went into "Auld Lang Syne." And though he couldn't see the finish line or hear the crowds, instinct told him that if he could just keep pumping, just keep running within the legal confines of his specific lane, clearly indicated by the fucking railroad tracks, he had a chance, albeit a farfetched one, of beating the grim reaper to the tape.

His arms flailed, his spine barely able to maintain its perpendicular, and he saw it, out in front of him like a dangling carrot, flickering and nonspecific but urging him on all the same—some kind of light.

And when he finally got to it and teetered before it in that last shimmer of glacial evening, he wiped the caked snow from his eyes and read aloud the one word in the misty halo beneath the visor-topped bulb; BELDEN. Sweet Jesus. Whomp.

He was dead asleep in the crummy hotel room that had the dimensions of a shoebox and the smell of a green toilet. His duffle bag lay at the foot of his bed where he hadn't bothered to unpack it, let alone open it. And he would have slept another five hours, at the least, had the telephone not rung itself silly. It was the hotel operator, telling him that she was ready with his call to Cincinnati.

"Hello, Mom?...It's Austin, yeah...I've been tryin' to reach you...Oh, bowling. Ahhh.

"I'm in San Francisco...San Francisco...No, I'm not coming

home...I mean, not right away...Maine....Maine...I have a house there...A house!...*Mom? Mom?...*

"Hello, Dad...*I'm sorry I upset her...No, I didn't know you bowled eleven games...No, I didn't know the championship was at stake...I told her I wasn't coming home...Because I have a house...A* house! *...In Maine...In* Maine!*...I don't know; I never saw it. That's why I'm going...I don't know how much it's worth...It's not important...*

"*Shit, Dad—you're drunk....I said, 'Shit, Dad—you're drunk!'...*

"*Listen—Dad? It's kind of a trust...I owe it to a friend to at least have a look at it...Because he left it to me...Because he liked me...Because he's* dead!...*He got* killed! *Goddamnit!...*"

Disgusted, *he slammed down the receiver and plopped back onto his bed, hating himself for having been so abrupt with his parents, hating* them *because they bowled, drank beer and watched Lawrence Welk.*

He turned onto his stomach and fell immediately back to sleep. It was a *warm sleep. All-encompassing. Snug and cozy. A familiar smell slowly filling his nostrils...*

3

It was coffee. Whenever he smelled coffee it meant that he had slept later than someone else. He also smelled mothballs. Smelling mothballs had no significance, other than that it offended his nose. Still asleep, he turned away from the smell, only to find the odor stronger.

He moved on the narrow cot, vaguely remembering that he had pulled himself up out of the snow one more time, one last time after seeing the light suspended on the sky, and had stumbled on into the rickety building where the door had been left unlocked.

He was covered with a blanket, old and rough. It was the blanket that smelled of mothballs. He didn't remember any blanket. He remembered *wishing* there was a blanket, but he didn't remember finding one. Then he remembered finding the cot. The cot was refuge enough and he had plunked onto it. That's all that he remembered.

"Left the door open for ya when I closed up. Just in case ya made it. Left the outside light on, too, though I wasn't too sure how much life was left in that old bulb. Been out there over three years. Long time for a bulb. Longest we ever had a bulb out there was five years, but that was because we never hardly used it. Ya don't use a bulb, it'll last a long time, unless some woodpecker takes a liking to it. Most of our woodpeckers, though, are smarter'n that. Smart woodpeckers up here, even though they don't have to be, since we got trees enough for all of 'em."

It was a Maine voice, nasal and friendly, long-hanging vowels rolling out as small songs, all of it spiced with bursts of vigor that snapped like pine cones underfoot. And whenever a sentence ended with a word like "here" it would curve up into the air and come out "hee-ya."

The voice continued, a man's voice—a big man's voice, deep and resonant. "Nawm called ahead. Said ya might make it but not to count on it. Nawm bet on ya makin' it, so he wins, if I recall him correctly, eleven dollahs and thutty-five cents. Thutty-five cents is from Guerney. Not much of a bettor, Guerney."

Austin shook the fur from his head. "This Belden?"

"Depot, not the town. Town's a quarter-mile up the line. To answer ya next question, it's eight-forty A.M., Tuesday. I should've thought to leave the blanket on the cot before I closed up. Come in at six A.M. and found ya there, half-froze. So I give ya the blanket. Used to belong to a horse, which is why I keep it in mothballs, so's it might forget. Mothballs all over, so careful where ya step. They're white, that's how ya'll know 'em. Also have a distinct smell of camphor, in case ya never come up against 'em before. 'Course, if ya got here and *then* died, all bets'd be off, as that would've been judged a tie. Dead heat, so to speak."

The man was about forty-five and round. Round like a rhino, not a hog, with an obvious strength to him, all of it casually covered by an oversized nappy black sweater that the man's shoulders still pushed to its limits. The navy-blue woolen watch cap he wore looked to be Paul Bunyan's. Even the boots looked to be seven league if they were a league at all.

"My name is Austin Fletcher."

"You in service?"

"Just out."

"Jack Meeker." And he smiled, two dozen facial creases set to work to do the job. It was a good face and honest, like a favorite leather wallet, the eyes so deeply set that they appeared to have no color; the nose and chin slotting perfectly into the framework as if painted on an old barn door by Andrew Wyeth.

Austin raised himself to one elbow and looked over the room that unwound small, square and Spartan, and varnished— everything that mahogany color and all of it ashine. Table and chairs on a swayback floor. Windowsills swollen from rain that got in. A sink, blue-stained. Small refrigerator, circa 1935. Wall clock, loud, energetic pendulum. Telephone on a rolltop desk that didn't rolltop anymore. Two kerosene lamps supplying the light, aided by three bare bulbs dangling on frayed electrical cords. A Franklin stove with a flue driving itself through the roof. A toilet egomaniacally squatting in a corner as if it were a Bernini statue. A square opening in a wall, just above a counter—a place to sell tickets through. A cash register worth thousands if a collector ever saw it. And a dogeared railroad timetable tacked to a wall by three of its four corners, looking for all the world as though it hadn't been changed since Casey Jones blew through.

The black iron skillet balanced light as a Ping-Pong paddle in Jack Meeker's catcher's-mitt hand, the eggs within it dancing like beebees, the bacon curling and sizzling. All of it so tantalizing Austin's appetite that he was soon as salivating as a St. Bernard.

"Two eggs okay, Austin?"

"Two eggs are fine."

"Just a couple days old."

"Great."

"Like 'em once ovah?"

"Yes, sir." Austin swung his legs over the side of the cot and noticed his bootless feet.

"I took 'em off. Looked to be doin' ya more harm than good. Guess ya didn't realize I left the fire goin' for ya."

"I guess not."

Jack was wearing a red plaid shirt beneath his sweater that was not unlike the plaid mackinaws Austin had seen up and down the line since arriving in Maine. Some salesman in that territory could sure sell plaids.

"Must've banked it too much. Didn't care to leave a rip-roarer, 'cause it might burn down the whole depot. This depot burns down they'll never build anothah. Wood's so dry, a bulb'd set it off. Take sugar with ya coffee? We don't have any."

"Just milk."

"Don't have milk, actually, 'cause the refrigerator can't keep nothin' but a secret. Have this dried stuff *pretends* to be milk once it's in the cup. Gives a good color, too. Appetizin'."

"That'll be fine." Austin saw his socks draped over the stovepipe, drying. His boots stood across the room, splayed out, Charlie Chaplin style.

"Boots of yours are all wrong for up here. What ya want is insulated boots and not too tight. And maybe without laces. Laces get wet and shrink they can just about strangle ya feet to fallin' off." Jack plopped the bacon and eggs onto a blue-and-white speckled enamel-surfaced tin plate. For good measure he placed a chunk of sourdough bread alongside, careful to not break the eggs. Austin noticed how the bread was buttered and he smiled—there was a bit of the mother hen to Jack Meeker. "Come and get it, boy," Jack said, rather proud of his culinary accomplishment.

"You *know* it!" Austin wrapped himself in the blanket and fairly flew to the table, mothballs flying like buckshot. He grabbed the tin utensils and dug in noisily and ravenously.

"Travelin' light, ain't ya." Jack was standing, leaning against a far wall. It was the first time that he had looked directly at Austin. Up till then, whenever he spoke, it was pretty much over the shoulder and off the cuff, the words tending to carom off walls before striking home.

"I guess I just…jettisoned everything."

"Bag?"

"Duffle bag."

"Snow-pusher'll pick it up. Providin' ya left it on the tracks."

"I don't know. I think I did."

"Oughta be along soon."

Austin had no true interest in small talk and was incapable of hiding it. He just ate, slopping the food in almost without taking the time to taste it, like one of those dusky, wide-eyed children in the "Help India" ads he'd been aware of almost from the moment he was able to read. He looked up only once, because he felt Jack's eyes frying his head to a crispness worthy of the bacon. They fixed on Austin for the longest time before swiveling away to look disinterestedly through the window.

"Don't stop snowin' soon, won't be nothin' left for the rest of the wintah."

Austin nodded his agreement. The floor beneath his feet was cold, but the coffee was hot, and the eggs were perfection, and the bacon was soon gone except for two thin slivers stuck delectably between his teeth. "Guess I haven't thanked you properly—for all of this. I really appreciate it."

"I'm sure ya do, but it's no imposition. I'm Civil Service. It's on the town. Belden pays."

"Well, just the same…"

Jack pulled up a chair and a cup of coffee and studied Austin for three gulps before beginning his inquisition.

"Something wrong?" Austin asked, aware of the hint of challenge in his voice but unable to suppress it. He didn't like being looked over, especially by eyes that would have set better in the head of a district attorney.

"Three foot of snow, two below zero, and ya walk right into it like Daniel Boone. Now, why would a man want to do a thing like that?"

"I wanted to get to Belden."

Jack nodded and digressed, and Austin wasn't sure whether or not the big man was satisfied with his answer or just distracted. "Talk of doin' away with this depot. Economizin'."

"Oh?"

"A-yuh. But they'll forget it 'fore they do it. It's a forgettin' kind of town. Nobody much in it anymore. Specially in the wintah. In the wintah people go deep south, to Massachusetts. Don't suppose I'll sell many tickets today. Only reason I came in was to see if you got here."

"Place any bets?"

"Last bet I made was that McGovern would carry South Dakota." Jack was up and looking through the window again, his coffee cup so lost in his huge hand that all Austin could see of it was steam. "Why'd ya want to get to Belden?"

"Friend of mine left me a house."

"In Belden? He ain't no friend."

"Maybe you knew him. Maynard Whittier."

"A-yuh. Maynard."

"Maynard Whittier." Austin wasn't sure that Jack remembered him at all, since he was so unaffected by the news.

"I remember him. Ain't seen him around in some time. Probably close to two years."

"He's dead."

"Figured that by the way ya told me."

"You didn't know about it?"

"Nope."

"Nobody told you?"

"Nobody can tell me if nobody knows."

Austin felt increasingly annoyed at the big man's indifference. "He was killed in action."

A glimmer of recollection registered on Jack's face. "That's right. He was in the Army."

"That's right."

"Killed in action, ya say?"

"Yeah. I say."

"Whereabouts?"

"Bermuda. He was killed by a tourist. Run over on the beach by a paddleboat."

Jack didn't laugh. He seemed to understand the emotion and the sarcasm behind Austin's remark. "You mean Vietnam."

"Yeah. I knew it was *some* vacation spot."

"Left ya his house, ya say."

"Yeah. I say." Austin was bristling.

"Ain't much of a house."

"He was my friend. That makes it a *great* house." And now Austin was spoiling, moments away from throwing something at the big clod. Anything. A plate, the coffeepot, the whole table. He stood up, threateningly, his chair scraping the floor sharply as it was sent to pushing backward. "Listen—the hell with you!"

"Easy, son."

"And I'm not your son, you ignorant sonofabitch!"

Jack was admirably composed, his voice never rising. "Folks die."

"That a fact?"

"A-yuh. After a while ya get to understand that."

"He was twenty-three years old!"

"Guess he *was* about twenty-three." Jack was clearing the table, and Austin couldn't fail to see the big gnarled hands, like the surface roots of an oak.

"He was *exactly* twenty-three!"

Jack piled the plates and stuff into the sink and turned the water on, his back to Austin. It was a big back, as broad in the beam as the *Mayflower*. "Goin' to have to get used to folks up here appearin' callous, Austin. Don't really mean to be. Just they don't know how to express their sympathy like city people, so they let it be ya own business."

"Maybe they just don't *have* any feelings." Austin's fists were clenched. They were rawhide and purpling, but the pair of them could fit into just one of the big man's palms.

"Actually, I remember Maynard very well. Nice boy. Always had a smile. Funny little smile. Not like you. You don't smile at all."

"When there's something that's funny, I'll smile."

"Kept pretty much to himself. I picked him up and drove him to the train the day he reported to the Army. He was actin' pretty strange. Didn't particularly like goin'—but he went."

"He shouldn't of."

"Well, he had to."

"Well, he shouldn't of." Austin's fists were clenching, flexing.

Jack knew it but wasn't quite ready for a showdown. "I think it'd be a good idea if ya just let go of those fists, son, 'cause I don't think they really belong to you." He wiped his hands on something that once was a towel, and he glanced up at the wall clock. "After the snow-pusher gets here, I'll take ya up to Maynard's house. Ain't that far." He looked at Austin and smiled. "That okay with you?"

Austin felt suddenly stupid and his fists dissolved. "Listen,

I'm sorry."

"No need to be. I understand."

"I've been travelin' a long time and I'm still a little shook up, and…well, I'm sorry."

"I am, too, son. About Maynard. Truly." Jack sat down at his desk and sharpened a pencil that was already so small that only its eraser seemed to emerge from the sharpener. Then he checked some ledgers, made some notes, and generally ignored Austin, who didn't know what to do with himself beyond wandering around the room and studying schedules and pretending that they were very significant to him and to the world.

After circling the room four times and running out of feigned interest he felt his feet begin to chill on the bare wooden floor, and so he removed his socks from the stovepipe and slipped them on. They were cuddly and warm and his feet were grateful, though his boots were another story. Warped by the heat, they tended to point their tips toward the ceiling without having consulted on the matter with Austin. But even more bothersome, and burdensome, was that they seemed to have shrunk three sizes. It was hell getting them on and worse getting them off. After a second try, when his tortured toes still tried to curl under and hide beneath the balls of his feet, Austin found out why. Jack had stuffed wads of newspaper into the boots' tips in hopes of helping them dry back to their natural shape. It was a grand gesture but a failing one, and, with Jack not looking, Austin pulled the paper out. Then, *with* Jack looking, Austin pretended to be reading that paper just as if he were on a bus with *The Cincinnati Enquirer.* Moments later his feet went better into his boots and no one was the wiser—except Jack, who, looking away, smiled and said nothing.

The telephone rang, coming as so fierce an interruption to the quietude that Austin straightened where he sat, even his toes stretching to their full once-upon-a-time length.

"Life is just one damned thing after another," said Jack, not looking up from his work. "That was said by either Mark Twain or Richard Nixon."

"Aren't you going to answer it?"

"Not until five rings." It rang the required five times and Jack answered. "Belden Depot, Stationmaster Jack Meeker speakin'. Your nickel...Oh, hello, Guerney." He covered the mouthpiece and winked at Austin. "It's Guerney."

"Ahhhh," said Austin, as if he understood.

"I don't know how to answer that, Guerney.

"Well, the boy came in half dead, and, because you and me is such good friends, and because you had such a heavy bet goin', I figured I'd let him die and then drag him back out and drop him a few yards up the tracks.

"Well, then I figured I'd tell Nawm he died before ever reachin' the depot, and you'd win ya bet. How much did ya bet, Guerney?

"That much?"

Austin felt the depot house begin to shudder as a distant thunder began to mount, the floorboards trembling underfoot as if in fear. If Jack felt and heard it, he didn't let on. He just kept right on talking to Guerney, passing the time of day.

"Well, anyway, Guerney, there I am, standin' ovah this fella and damned if there ain *anothah* fella out there, runnin' and a-staggerin' up the tracks. No one told me there'd be two fellas, Guerney.

"A-yuh. Two.

"I shot him.

"I say, 'I shot him.'

"Well, it looked to me like he was gonna make it, so, to protect ya bet, I shot him 'fore he evah reached the door.

"A-yuh. Went down like a bucket o' pits.

"Pits."

The noise grew louder, far off but closing perilously. The chairs complained, and the windows rattled, and the stove door flew open in awe, a lump of coal shooting out like a pulled tooth. And still Jack kept on, chatting folksily with Guerney.

"Did it for you, Guerney—so's ya could win ya bet.

"Ain't gonna be no autopsy, Guerney. Why should there be?

"Really?

"Hmmmm…

"Well, if ya think *that's* a problem, wait'll I tell ya about the *third* fella."

The noise was ear-splitting, the depot house seeming to fly apart like a circus house. And Austin hit the floor as if under enemy bombardment, assuming the fetal position with both hands covering his head.

"That'll be the snow-pusher, Guerney. Got to hang up now. Congratulations on winnin' all that money.

"The thutty-five cents, Guerney. What ya got to do now is invest it wisely. I hear Coca-Cola's a good thing."

Jack hung up and Austin got to his feet sheepishly, smiling at Jack as if to say, "Shucks, I knew it was the snow-pusher all along."

"Fall down, did ya, Austin?"

"Yeah. Slightly."

The lumbering snow-pusher came on, shoving a mountain of snow ahead of it that seemed to Austin to be an Alp. Everything shook and ratcheted, the stove door repeatedly slamming open and closed like a harpy speaking its mind, the floor bending, the door straining against its bolt as if trying to withstand the onslaught of whatever beast it was outside.

Jack was standing alongside his rolltop desk, assuring that faithful antique that there was nothing to fear. And even as he steadied the desk his head was grazed by a swinging light bulb. And the coffeepot swan-dived to the floor, spilling its contents as though shot in the stomach. And things dropped from shelves, and the stovepipe chattered.

Through the window Austin could see the smoke exploding straight up as the ancient engine grumbled past, much of the snow it pushed spilling sideways onto the station platform, practically to windowsill height. The engine came to a halt some twenty yards farther up the platform, though its boiler kept cooking, declaring that it had just so much time to tarry, there being other places it had to go, other track to clear, other buildings to intimidate.

"Come on, Austin—let's see what we got."

Austin again wrapped his blanket around his middle, like an Indian, and followed Jack. The big man pulled the door open and immediately sidestepped, like a matador, allowing the snow to tidal-wave into the room. He got none of it. Austin got all of it, up to his knees and over his boot rims.

Jack explained it as best he could, fighting off an incipient smile. "Up here, Austin, sometimes ya have to let the snow in afore you can get out."

"I'll try to remember."

Austin followed Jack out onto the sun-garbed platform, literally shivering in his boots and looking like a frozen Navajo. He was confronted by a huge deposit of snow but was surprised at how warm the unimpeded sun made everything feel. It was actually warmer on the platform than it had been inside the depot.

At the far end of the platform a man, larger even than Jack Meeker, climbed down from the engine cabin. He landed hip-deep in the snow, and the snow gave way. On one shoulder he balanced a huge mailbag, on the other shoulder Austin's duffle bag, neither burden seeming to hamper him as he giant-stepped his way to where Austin and Jack were standing.

"Mawnin', Jack," he called out, his voice a bellow that shook snow dust from nearby firs.

"Mawnin', Martin," Jack answered.

"See ya had some snow."

"A-yuh. Last night. A bit."

"I think this'll be all of it."

"Can't tell. Always a little more comin'."

"One way or anothah."

"A-yuh."

Austin listened to the witty exchange and almost gagged while wondering why it was always thought that America's biggest men came from its Pacific Northwest. For right there, in Maine, he was looking at two behemoths whose size and strength had to surpass that of Samson, Goliath, Atlas and the Pittsburgh Steeler defensive line.

Martin was soon standing alongside them, both bags still on his shoulders like twin oaks. He gave Austin the casual once-over. "Ain't goin' to sell many of those blankets up here, Chief. Folks got their own." He nudged Austin's duffle bag with his ear. "This yours?"

"Yes, sir. Thank you, sir—"

Martin flicked the duffle bag at Austin as if it were a bag of feathers, and Austin, unprepared, caught it amidships, staggering backward a fair distance before falling on his rear, in the snow, and rather unceremoniously.

"Good catch, Chief," said Martin as he entered the depot house carrying only the mailbag. "Got two months' mail here, Jack. Expectin' anythin' urgent?"

"Just my *Playboy* calendar."

"Wait'll ya see Miss January."

"Burt Reynolds?"

"Athah Godfrey."

Jack followed Martin in, paying no attention to Austin, who was pinned down in the snow by his own duffle bag, an ignominious position for a combat veteran.

He pushed the bag off and stood, shaking off the snow like a wet terrier, his temper growing like a Doberman. He put the duffle bag on his own shoulder and reentered the depot house, trying to summon up some small amount of lost dignity. Also he was mad as hell at being made sport of.

He let the bag drop with a loud thump, deliberately. As expected, it got everybody's attention. Martin, who had been standing at the stove rubbing his hamhock hands before it, looked over at Austin as if deciding whether or not to eat him right then and there or wait until he got a little bigger. "Drop somethin' there, Chief?"

"You're some kind of funny lumberjack, ain't ya," said Austin, giving no true thought to the possible consequences of such a lunatic question.

Martin was unruffled. "Funny? Lost a dollah bet on ya, Chief. Figured y'd be dead." He helped himself to some coffee, what was left of it in the tipped pot.

Austin, ridiculous in his blanket, continued tempting fate. "Well, you figured wrong, you tall turd."

Jack gulped, unsure of what Martin's reaction might be to that. But Martin reacted rather objectively.

"Ain't so tall. Got a brothah what's tallah."

"Is he turdier?"

"Can't say as he is. Fair to say we're equally turdy. Just what do ya mean by 'turd'?"

"Cow flop."

"What I thought. No mattah." Martin sipped and switched the subject. "What do ya think it's worth, my returnin' ya bag?"

"What?"

"Ya bag. Must be worth *somethin'!*"

"A dollar." Austin's attitude was distinctively take-it-or-leave-it.

"A dollah?" Martin registered anguished surprise. "Hell, if I was an official railroad porter, ya'd nevah get me to carry that bag all this way for a *dollah.*"

Austin was crafty. "Are you an official railroad porter?"

"Nope. Can't say as I am."

"Then all you get is a dollar." Austin dug into his pocket and found his money. He hoped he had a single in there, because he was pretty sure he'd be getting no change if he were to hand Martin anything larger. He found a single and slapped it onto the table. "One dollar. For services rendered."

"Obliged." Martin took the dollar and, in the same motion, handed it to Jack. "Give this to Nawm, will ya? Tell him I'm paid." He finished up his coffee and took his cue from the clock. "Got to be goin'. Twenty mile of track got to be busted out 'fore I can give old Annabel a rest. Hear that MacCauley Notch is downright impassable." He was at the door, smiling at Austin. "See ya, Chief. And watch where ya step. Might meet a turd what's a little smarter'n you are."

In moments he was gone, the depot house still trembling in his wake, old Annabel bumping and lumping her way farther north.

Jack was picking up around the room, picking up and

straightening out, resettling what the snow-pusher had knocked askew. He spoke flatly. "Shouldn't of given him the dollah, Austin."

"No?"

"No. Goin' to ruin it for everyone else leaves a duffle bag on the tracks. Goin' to set a bad precedent."

"What *should* I have given him?"

"Nothin'."

"Nothing?"

"Should've just said, 'obliged'—like he did. Would've been enough."

"Well, he *took* the dollar."

"'Cause ya *give* it to him. Never would've *asked* for it."

"Sounded to *me* like he was asking for it."

"Nope. Martin'd never be that vulgah. He just asked ya what ya thought it was *worth*. *You* come up with the figure—and the dollah."

Austin was annoyed with the whole thing. "Maybe I'm just offending people because I turned up alive."

"*Was* pretty thoughtless of ya. Nobody up heah likes to lose a bet."

"Yeah. I'm gettin' that message."

"After the train comes in, we'll go up to ya house."

Austin was surprised. "You mean that same train'll be *back?*"

"Track's busted out. Why not?"

"But...they let me walk all this way—"

"They didn't *let* ya. They just didn't *stop* ya."

Austin was fuming. "They said they'd be backin' up, all the way to Millinocket."

"Which they did—to let the snow-pusher on. Then they all had a night's sleep and got back onto the track."

"Jesus Christ, I don't believe it. I could've *died* out there!"

"A-yuh. That's what they were bettin' on."

Austin inhaled and exhaled deeply, to defuse himself. "People really have a lot to do up here to occupy themselves, don't they?"

"A-yuh. Whole area can get pretty racy on occasion."

"Look, I've got my duffle. Why do I have to wait around?"

"Because, Austin, everyone who had a bet on ya is goin' to be on that train."

"What the hell do *I* care?"

"Well, there'll have to be a habeus corpus afore any money can change hands. Seems to me ya owe that much to the people what bet on ya."

"I don't owe anything to anybody in this whole world."

"All the more reason." He sat down and it was apparent to Austin that, like it or not, he'd be waiting for the train from Millinocket. "Should be here in an hour or so. Care to wager on just when it'll come in, Austin?"

Austin sat down. "Yeah. Thutty-five cents."

"Too steep. No bet."

4

Jack Meeker proved to be right about the train, the clattering thing rolling up in just under an hour, a half-dozen mackinawed men soon clomping about in the old depot house, breathing steam and sipping coffee out of blue-and-white speckled cups—and looking at Austin as if he were Dr. Livingstone.

Some money changed hands, all of it good-naturedly. And some sideways questions were asked of Austin, about his health, his war experiences, and his home town, Cincinnati making about as much sense to those men as Shangri-la. But, for the most part, it was a rather congenial respite for them all, even for Austin, Guerney being the one exception—that dour man sulking in a corner, playing at being catastrophically undone by his thutty-five-cent loss, mostly because it was expected of him, he being the town "cheapo."

Norm appeared to be the greatest beneficiary of the betting and said as much to Austin. "Didn't do too bad. Comes to eleven dollahs, thutty-five cents." He riffled the singles and jangled the change.

"I guess Guerney paid," said Austin.

"A-yuh. Through the nose. But he wouldn't pay for those *othah* two fellas. I don't remember any othah two fellas, do you?"

"Jack shot 'em."

Norm never batted an eye. "Well, then, Guerney's right in not payin', as that'd be against the rules." Norm studied Austin for a moment and then spoke quite innocently." I don't see my lantern anywhere. Wouldn't happen to know where it is, would ya?"

"I guess it's lost."

"Lantern cost me five and a half dollahs."

"I thought you made me a present of it."

"I saw it more as a loan."

"You made eleven thirty-five on the whole deal, right?"

"A-yuh."

"I'd say the five and a half was an investment, to help you win."

"That what you'd say?"

"I'd also say, though I'm no expert, that you can deduct it from your income tax."

Norm nodded, beginning to see the wisdom of Austin's thinking. Then he brought up a new and imposing problem. "Chocolate bar cost me twenty cents."

"Tough shit."

"A-yuh."

Norm smiled and strode away. And Jack Meeker, who had overheard it all, also smiled. And Austin smiled at Jack, who winked in return, as if to say, "Ya learnin', Austin. Ya learnin'."

An hour or so later, the mackinawed men were back aboard their "little train that could," heading into further spine-tingling adventures with a whistle and a toot, while Austin sat alongside Jack in the feistily churning open-topped jeep that had a snowplow slung horizontally across its front, like an elephant carrying a log.

The sun was sharp, the landscape a crisp mixture of blue sky, low snowy hills and ice-crowned trees as the jeep pressed along a road that didn't happen until the snowplow carved it out.

They drove a fair amount of time with neither of them talking, giving Austin a chance to take in the countryside with nothing in his head but a clean blackboard. There was no wind to speak of and no airstream created by the slowly grinding jeep. It was quiet. Oddly quiet. Awesomely so, the air dry and crackling, the crystalline embossed horizon catching the sun and flashbulbing it back.

Austin knew that he was in the White Mountains and was staggered at how those mountains rose almost perpendicularly from ground level. Somewhere, way up there, he could see how the trees backed off, nothing showing but eroded topsoil that had been clawed out by ice-age glaciers—one peak in particular climbing so abruptly from the relatively flat snow that it seemed to be still on the move, still rising, extending well beyond the point where the tree growth stopped, to a spot somewhere in the blue mist where it topped off into a group of summits like a crowd of giants.

"Mount Katahdin," said Jack. "Indian dialect. Means greatest mountain. Goes well over five thousand feet."

Austin nodded and kept staring at the mountain. He had never seen one that tall and that straight up.

"Don't feel like talkin', Austin?"

"Maynard used to tell me that Maine people didn't *like* to talk."

"Oh, we talk. We just like to make sure there's somethin' to talk *about.* My fathah used to say that state-o'-Mainers knew not to say *anythin'* unless it improved the silence."

"Your father say that?" Austin was being patronizing. He knew it, wished he wasn't, but couldn't help it. He had lost so much self-esteem in so short a time in that frozen state that any little victory he could get, even a petty one, seemed worth it.

"A-yuh." Jack was content to talk no further.

"What'd he say about this cold weather?"

"Said it sometimes gets so cold, the words freeze soon as they leave ya mouth. Have to wait till spring to find out what ya were talkin' about all wintah."

Austin liked that one and he relaxed, even smiled.

"Careful there, Austin. Don't want to go crackin' that serious face with a smile."

"That was funny. What you just said was funny."

"Truth is, no one says much of anythin' about the weathah, 'ceptin' fools and strangers, or both."

Austin let that zinger go by. He had earned it.

The jeep was groaning. If there was a heart under its hood it was quite likely under attack. Jack pulled a lever, and the plow raised a few inches, the jeep sighing with relief. "Have to let it win a few every now and then, otherwise it gets to complainin'. Only thing worse than a complainin' jeep is a dead one."

Austin looked over the jeep's hood at the straight-ahead. There seemed to be nothing out there other than an aimless unraveling of huddled mounds and rises and dips as in a frozen ocean. "How much farther is the house?"

"Soon as we run out of telephone poles and electric wires it'll show itself."

"It's cold."

"My fathah used to say we only had two seasons. Nine months of wintah and three months of damned poor sleddin'."

"Your father say that too?"

"Actually, 'twer my grandfathah."

"Whole family was pretty big on that folksy…stuff." Austin had wanted to say "crap," but had censored himself.

"A-yuh. We been called droll."

The word escaped Austin. He hadn't intended that it be heard. "Sheeeet."

"No. Droll. But only if we feel folks are interested in hearin' what we have to talk about."

"And how often is that?"

"'Bout every othah week."

"Regular?"

"Well…we have been known to skip a week from time to time."

Austin knew not to mess with the man any further. He had obviously been funnin' people for years and was not of a mind to suddenly start treating Austin any differently.

The jeep hit a hidden furrow and quivered bumpily, causing Austin to grab his duffle bag to keep it from flying over the side. It also caused him to bite his tongue, which he very quickly hung out of his mouth like a necktie so that it could lap up some of the pain-killing cold air. "Na mu of a roe, is it?"

"How's that, Austin?"

Austin drew his tongue back in. "Not much of a road, is it?"

"All the road we got. Belongs to the Great Northern Paper Company. They let people use it free of charge so we don't send 'em too many letters of complaint."

"And Maynard grew *potatoes* in this?"

"Nothin' grows around here. Frost in every month and snow sometimes in July and August. No—Maynard picked in Aroostook County. Near Canada. That'd be about sixty miles north of heah."

"How could *anything* be north of here?"

"Can be done. It's an area 'bout as big as Massachusetts. Fine, fertile potato land. Somethin' happens with the wind and rivers to make the soil rich. In 1925 over three thousand potato farmers paid off their mortgages with what they grew in that one year."

"Your father tell you that?"

"A-yuh. He was one of 'em. Maynard, I think, worked around the Aroostook River. Did pretty well. Farmers up there send potatoes as far south as Florida and west as Ohio."

"You sound like you're tryin' to sell me real estate."

"None left to buy, 'ceptin' if ya go due west of here. Lots of real estate there, but it's all wilderness. Go in there and ya goin' into the last unexplored area of the United States."

"Come on—people go in there."

"A-yuh. But they don't always come *out.* Nothin' grows in there but trees, and they're so hard to get out it just ain't worth the goin' in."

"There have to be *some* people."

"Oh, ya might find *some* life in there. Caretakers. Hermits. Hunters. Indians. People escaped from institutions. Bears. Couple birds. Three maybe."

"Indians?"

"Not the kind ya thinkin' of. Not with feathahs. *Furs.*"

"And nobody else goes in there?"

"Canoe trippers. Summah months they swarm like black flies, up to the Allagash River region. Campsites stretch all the way into New Brunswick. Lose a few of 'em to the rivers every now and then—but they keep comin'."

"You mean...they drown?"

"Well, they don't come *up.*"

HERMAN RAUCHER

Austin let the subject drop and the jeep plow on, a wind swirling up, prompting him to lower himself deeper into his parka. "Hey, Jack, where does this road end?"

"Never really ends. Splits off and runs south to Elephant Mountain and north to Allagash country."

"Listen, not to be disrespectful, but if I'm goin' to live up here I'm goin' to have to get a few straight answers. I mean, no more of this quaintsy-folksy stuff."

"Ya nevah said anythin' about *livin'* up here, Austin."

Austin thought on that. Jack was right. He had never said it because it had never occurred to him—until just then, the wind seeming to whip the idea into his head. And he felt his fingers twitching, in his gloves, in his pockets, and a sweat building under his clothing; and a twinge of fear rollicking through his stomach. "Well—it's a possibility. For a while. Couple days, I don't know. There's nothing pressing in my life, calling me back. I mean, I didn't exactly leave my heart in Cincinnati."

"Road'll run ya up to Ripagenus Dam, which is about five miles west of Baxter State Park. Ya house'll be a left turn from here, northern shore of Nahmiakanta Lake."

"Jesus Christ..." Austin sank even deeper into his parka, his upper lip hanging over his collar.

"Indian names, Austin. 'Most everythin' up here has an Indian name. 'Course, later, when the English came, they spent a lot of time namin' things, too. Lakes, mountains, ponds. In the wintah it was about all any of 'em had to do—namin' things. French did it some, too. 'Bout the only names we *don't* have up here is Chinese and Russian, and maybe a little bit of Hawaiian. And a smatterin' of Hebrew."

"Any other houses around?"

"Might be a couple. Early townsfolk built homes close together for mutual aid. But, where *you* are, houses'll be furthah apart. Wouldn't go lookin' for none if I were you. And, if ya *were* to find any, ya wouldn't want to count on anyone bein' in 'em. From what I remembah, Maynard liked it that way. Liked to be by himself in the wintah. Hibernated. Bearlike in that respect, Maynard."

Jack turned the jeep, against its will, to the left, where it groped and pawed crankily before sniffing its way onto an unseen road, after which it moved along more obediently, though oil fumes sifted up from between its floor struts as if to deliberately assault its riders' noses. It was not a vehicle that Austin particularly trusted. Rather, it was more akin to an attack dog—loyal for as long as you kept it in line; demonic should you turn your back on it or forget to give it water. Certainly it was not something anyone would care to casually cross with a Chevrolet Impala.

Jack called out invisible sites like a tour guide. Austin couldn't see them, because there was nothing to see, but Jack called them out all the same. "Chesuncook Pond. Pym Pond. Buck Pond. Bean Pond." At Bean Pond the ride got a little better, but not by much.

"Excuse me for asking, but are we still on the road?"

"More or less. We just picked up the old Appalachian Trail, Austin."

"Yeah—I didn't think it was the *new* one."

"Runs from Mount Katahdin to Mount Springer—in Georgia. 'Bout two thousand miles. Lean-to shelters all along the way, 'bout one day's hiking time apart. 'Course, that's in the summah. Wintah might take ya longer."

Metal markers periodically bore out what Jack had said. APPALACHIAN TRAIL—MAINE TO GEORGIA. And large wooden signs indicated the distances in miles from place to place. But *all* signs, metal and wooden, quickly disappeared when the trail swung obliquely to the right—the jeep, rather arbitrarily, juggling on more or less straight ahead.

A few miles of that and the route came close to being totally unnavigable, the big man raising his plow, stopping, and easing the jeep into neutral. And he sat there, bulked behind the wheel, his narrowed eyes solemnly appraising the bleak landscape before him. The snow blanket had turned more foreboding, less of a fluffy white, more of a hoar-frost gray. And Austin began to wonder anew just what in God's name he was doing in the middle of that snowy nowhere with a man who could easily be the biggest put-on artist in all of New England.

"Can I ask you a question?"

"Ya just did."

"Do you know where we are?"

Jack closed one eye, cocked the other, and continued to survey the horizon. "Think so."

"I mean—have you ever *seen* Maynard's house?"

"A-yuh. Couple times."

Looking where Jack was looking, Austin could see nothing unusual, other than that the area was suddenly without such sky-blemishing contrivances as telephone poles and electric wires. "We've run out of telephone poles."

"A-yuh."

"So where's the house?"

"It'll be ahead."

"I swear I don't see anything."

"It'll be snow-covered." Jack cut the engine, and the jeep shifted into quiet.

"Do *you* see it?"

"Nope, but if I were a house, that's where I'd be." He reached behind their seats and produced two pairs of snow-shoes. "Familiar with these, Austin?"

"They're snowshoes."

"Good. Thought ya might say they were tennis racquets."

"No. They're snowshoes."

"Fine. I like the way ya stick to ya guns. Now, ya slip 'em on, Austin, and when ya walk ya bend ya knees up like ya climbin' stairs. Elsewise ya ain't likely to get very far exceptin' down."

Austin slung his legs over the side and slipped into the snowshoes.

"Pull 'em on tight, Austin, or they escape. They'll do that if ya give 'em a chance. Knew of *one* pair walked all the way down to Miami. Settled down and raised a whole family of surfboards."

Austin allowed the story to go by unchallenged, and soon both men were in the snow, trudging along in a direction that Jack had chosen seemingly at whim. "How far is it?"

"Oh—mile or so."

It was the "or so" that bothered Austin. Jack was so diligently approximate about time and distance that the "or so" could well turn out to be five hundred miles and three years. Nevertheless they walked on; Jack first and then Austin, imitating the big man's style. And he sensed that he'd be walking in that manner for quite some time, knees pumping like a slow-motion fullback. He sensed, too, that if and when he ever got back to Cincinnati, he'd continue to walk in that fashion—which would be all right going up a flight of stairs, but going down could kill him.

There were no other snowshoe prints, only a few bird scratches and some sleepy pine cones. The snow lay deep, muffling whatever sounds the wide forest had to offer, and all Austin could hear was his own breathing, the mist of his breath shooting out a foot ahead of him before fishhooking up and disappearing in the sky. Then the snow, which had until then spread itself generously over placid rolling hills, suddenly flattened.

"Walkin' on a pond, Austin. 'Bout two foot of ice under ya. Wouldn't try it in the summah."

They crossed the pond, and the hills reasserted themselves, spruces and firs more evident because they were taller and fuller than other trees in the immediate area. They soon walked through a brooding section that housed no trees but one—Austin worrying about that one because it was so unlike the others he had seen thus far.

It was gnarled and twisted and barren. It sported no foliage, not a sprig of green or a somnolent bud waiting for April. Nor was there snow on any of its branches. It was just stuck there, apparently lifeless. And even in that sunlit afternoon where the evergreens shot mammoth black shadows across the snow, this tree cast no shadow at all.

Austin thought to ask about it, but since it was the first time during the frigid trek that Jack was not spouting some precious, folksy observation, he decided against risking the questions and receiving in return a four-hour-twenty-three-minute dissertation on nothing in particular.

He followed the waffled prints of Jack's snowshoes, the air clean and beautiful and worth the breathing—the kind of air that city people heard about only in commercials for Idaho and Montana. Eight years of cigarette smoking had left a residue of carbon on his lungs that he could suddenly feel falling away, all those blackened stalactites dropping off like rotten plaster. He drank so hugely of the air, such long and penetrating drafts of it, that he could feel himself filling like a balloon. And had his clothing not been so heavy, and his feet not so mired in the snow, he'd have surely caught the north wind like a Canada goose homeward bound.

The mythical trail soon lost itself in a clutch of thick trees— first-growth trees, tall and ramrod straight, clustered so side-by-side that they almost completely blotted out all traces of what Austin knew to be a most vivid day.

"Stay behind me, Austin. Don't want to step in a bear trap ya first day out."

Austin complied, following Jack between the big trees, the sun unable to send down more than a dribble of itself to usher the way. And to Austin it was as if he were walking through a tunnel, under a canopy, while carrying an umbrella.

The trees thinned out, stepping aside as they might for royalty, the land beginning to flow gently upward. And there, perhaps a hundred yards ahead, built against and tucked within the snow drape of a slowly rising hill—a house.

"Welcome home, Austin."

The house crouched low and gray and brown like a cat, its tail pressed against the cushiony hill, its mind semi-shut in a winter nap. And it was as covered with snow as was everything else on that pristine day, a three-foot layer of it lolling on its roof. And because its windows were shuttered its eyes were unnoticing of visitors, though it surely must have sensed their presence, cats and houses having that power.

"Welcome home, Austin," were the words—but was it Jack Meeker who had said them, or the house itself, appearing so suddenly out of the tree-caused twilight, so evocative of Maynard in that sweet and gentle breeze?

No matter. Whatever the explanation, weariness or wistfulness, all that lay before Austin's gaze was so invitingly familiar, so dizzily *déjà vu* that, though logic could dispute it, he immediately knew two warming and irrefutable truths: He was home. And he had been there before.

5

Jack Meeker paused to light his pipe, and pretty puffs of mapled smoke picked their way up through the resisting trees. For a moment Austin saw the big man as a combination Marco Polo and Father Christmas, for he had found the house. Across that endless white desert he had found a route. The voyage from Vietnam to Lake Nahmiakanta was over and Maynard's gift was complete.

No crowds, no ticker tape. No Indians with maize and pumpkin and good wishes for the first winter, none of that. But then, none of that was ever required. All that was required was standing before him, singular and stalwart, framed by evergreens and set in crystal—a place out of the way, to be alone in. In all his twenty-three years he had never known such a haven, let alone suspected that it might indeed exist, for someone like himself, a loner and a nonplanner, a man with no concept of tomorrow and no predilection for backward glances. Bless you, Maynard. You will always be my friend. And bless this house, long may it thumb its nose at blizzards.

He studied the house more closely. Whatever he had expected it to be, what appeared before him appeared to be better. It was a low-slung thing, cedar-shingled and loosely built, seemingly haphazard yet somehow indestructible. A long, tapering roof, sweeping down almost to the snow—facing north, the better to deflect the wind, causing that invisible beast to spend its strength riding the roof, arriving in the trees beyond with nothing to show for all its muscle but an echoing whistle.

The house had two stories, though the second story could hardly be considered much more than a squinched attic, two grimy windows peering out of it like the milk-glass lenses of a blind man's spectacles. A low fence of wired-together light boards stood some two feet apart from the house's foundation. It reached sill high, the berm between fence and house being filled with natural insulation, hay and grass and dry leaves, things that nature grew in summer and cast aside in autumn—dead things, or dying, that, properly used, might benefit those who chose to stay on in the house to the displeasure of winter.

"Buttoned up for the wintah," said Jack, admiration in every word.

"I don't have a key." It had never occurred to Austin until then that he might need a key.

"No mattah. As I recall, it was never locked."

"How old is it?"

"What ya lookin' at—oh, a hundred years." Jack nodded his head at other structures in the area, small ramshackle buildings that Austin had failed to notice right off. "That'll be ya woodshed, Austin. And that'll be ya icehouse over there. And over there, ya backhouse."

"Backhouse?"

"Outhouse, backhouse—don't mattah what ya call it long as ya keep it out and back."

Austin looked at the compact little hut, no bigger than a phone booth—and damned if it didn't have a crescent moon carved into its door. It appeared to be some thirty to forty yards from the main house. "Pretty far away," he volunteered.

"In January it's far away. In August it's never far enough. Aristocracy up here used to have *two* backhouses. One for summah and one for wintah. Finicky about where ya set, Austin?"

"Not if I can get there in time. I take it there's no toilet in the house."

"Maybe for decoration. Make a nice planter. Best to stomp out a path to ya backhouse *before* nature calls."

"It'll be the first thing I do."

"Ready to go in?"

"Why shouldn't I be?"

"Well, ya look kind of…uncertain."

"I'm not uncertain."

"Then let's go."

They walked the remaining distance to the house, Austin's heart kettledrumming so hard that he could feel it in his temples. It was one step up to the shallow porch, after which both men kicked off their snowshoes.

The roughhewn door hung a little crooked but with manifest character. There was no lock or latch for a lock—just a leather handle worn and frayed to an almost unnatural degree, as if a lion had used it for a teething ring. The door was set flatly in ice, only the leather handle protruding into the third dimension.

Jack grasped the handle and pushed gently at the door. It did not give. "Can't push too hard. Wouldn't be respectful." And he stepped away from it, examining it as if he were a safecracker sizing up the situation.

Austin didn't understand what Jack was waiting for. "Well, how do we get in?"

"Oh, we'll get in. Trick is to be invited."

"I don't have any invitation."

"Patience, boy." Jack thumped his gloved fist, rather delicately for him, all about the door's frame—gentle raps, like Michelangelo working in ice. And again he stepped away, waiting.

"Is someone supposed to answer? I don't think they heard you." Austin moved for the door, about to pound at it harder than Jack had thumped.

But Jack restrained him. "I said patience, Austin." A few seconds later, on its own, the door sighed and small bits of ice let go and crackled out. Jack tapped at the doorframe again, but still it did not give. "She's thinkin' it ovah."

He stepped back again, relighting his pipe and looking away, apparently not caring whether or not they gained access to the house.

"Hey—I'm freezing, okay?"

There then came a loud crack, and larger sections of ice dropped away from the door to crash onto the porch, freeing the door from its frozen state—and it swung open on its old hinges, as if the house were inhaling it, creaking and bitching like phony sound effects.

"She's willin'," Jack said, stepping aside for Austin. "After you, son. Your house."

Austin nodded, pausing for a moment to firm himself up for the task. Then he strode into the house, a wind coming immediately with him, almost pushing him, causing things inside to rattle—metal things, wooden things—conjuring up an image in Austin's head of a skeleton jigging on an elastic string. He couldn't see, his eyes yet to accommodate to the darkness, but he could hear a loud clumping behind him, almost ferocious, and he wheeled around.

"Good floor. Strong. Oak. Original floor, Austin." It was Jack, testing the floor, flexing his knees and stamping his feet on it, scaring the hell out of Austin.

"Jesus Christ! Did you have to do that?"

"Do what?"

"Nothing." Austin's vision was slowly returning. If his heart would come down to where it belonged, he would be all right.

"Been in here before but never took notice." Jack tested the floor again, more earnestly, his full weight. And there was a scurrying of small noises underneath them, a scratching and a scraping that Austin was not prepared for, the vibration tickling right up through his boot soles.

"What the hell is *that?*" He asked Jack.

"Oh—rabbits. Weren't expectin' visitahs. They'll be in ya cellah."

Austin began to see things. Still, the only light in the room was coming from behind Jack. It was a pale light, rebounding dully off the snow, making the far wall appear as though a sickly spotlight were playing on it. The rest of the room devoted itself to shadows.

"I'll go out and open the shuttahs, Austin. Spread some light on the situation."

Jack went out, leaving Austin alone in the room, quietly overwhelmed. One by one the shutters outside fanned open, noisily but without incident. And as each shutter was pressed back against the outside shingles, each window was emancipated, and shafts of sunlight came crisscrossing in from diverse angles, from the left and from the right, from the fore and the aft, from under the door itself and through cracks in it.

And in that conspiracy of light, Austin found himself standing in the dead middle of it all, caught as in a laser crossfire, and he saw himself on a crucifix, pinioned, pain in his palms and in his insteps. It didn't last long, neither the image nor the pain, an unclockable moment at best, a blip, and it was over, the room soon as bright inside as was the outside. And what had been at first a brooding and foreboding structure was turned happily around into a cordial house, cheerful and fit, and ready for occupancy.

Austin stood stock still as light and life filled the room. The first thing he took notice of was the big Boston rocker, the kind of chair John F. Kennedy used to like, only older and cruder, with flaking paint and uneven runners, and glued-on-again struts that had been whittled down and wedged into weary seat holes ten times too often.

There were other chairs, clunky and handmade. And a poker-scarred table, and a copper-fitted dry sink. And a long-handled pump; pewter pots and pans; utensils, bowls, pitchers and mugs.

Shelves and cupboards were crammed cranky with powdered milk, canned meats, vegetables, juices, flour, shortening, dry cereals—you name it, Austin had it. Jars, cans, bottles and boxes enough to start a supermarket and two delicatessens.

It was a spacious room, a combination kitchen/living room, dominated by a rough-rock walk-in fireplace with hanging copper kettles blackened by years of open-hearth cooking. And beside it a firescreen, a poker, tongs, bucket, broom, a dutiful load of cordwood and a proper pile of kindling. And a black bearskin rug sprawled in front of it all, snoozing in eternity.

Kerosene lamps, boxes of candles, matches, soap, colorful candies in glass jars. Rifles standing vertically against a barnwood wall—a .30-.06, a .32 Special Winchester, a twelve-gauge shotgun and, on a peg of its own, a .44 Smith & Wesson revolver. And boxes of ammunition of various calibers. Enough ammunition to stand off Cornwallis, Napoleon, Kaiser Wilhelm, Hirohito, Ho Chi Minh and John Dillinger.

Austin looked into the room beyond, the only other room in the house. It too was a combination room—bedroom/storeroom. The bed looked to be carved from one enormous chunk of anthracite, and to have been assembled either inside the room or before the house was built. It could never have gotten past the door. A colorful quilt of lovingly stitched cotton squares lay sprawled over a lumpy mattress; and odd-shaped pillows, stuffed with pine needles still fragrant, huddled together on top of it all. And, from under the bed, another black bearskin rug peered out for a peek at its new master.

Other chairs, a handcrafted standing closet, a pine bureau with trinkets on a doily, an oblong mirror in an oak frame. And on the walls, things on pegs—parkas, boots, gloves, snowshoes, caps, hats, sneakers, mocassins, fishing rods, tackle and baskets. Knives, saws, chisels, icepicks and hammers and additional items not immediately identifiable by Austin.

And on all the wall that was left: books. Shelves upon shelves of books. Books packed so solid that they could serve as sandbags if the dam broke and the river overflowed.

A barrel-shaped Franklin stove squatted in the middle of the room like an oversized black iron Buddha, its smoke pipe curving acutely so that it ran across the wall just above the bed before turning dead square *into* the wall, its nether end emerging somewhere outside the house. A dozen dry logs, cut to fit the stove's mouth, stood ready, a box of twigs and assorted kindling flanking it.

"Looks ready for ya to move in." Jack was standing beside him. "Tried that bed?"

"No. Not yet."

Jack eased himself elephantinely onto the bed, taking special care to keep his big boots away from the pretty quilt. The bed creaked and sagged but held, though the sound it made was of a hundred hawsers straining. "She's a rope-spring, Austin. Might want to put a little oil on it, or wax."

"Check."

Jack bounced lightly and the mattress rustled like a wind on the move. "Corn-husk mattress. Noisy if ya a light sleepah. Mice like it. So ya might want to check it." He completed his small trampoline act and landed, feet thumping, onto the floor, like a circus performer. "Well, holds Goliath. Should have no trouble with David."

"That an old bed?"

"'Bout as old as the house."

"Wow."

"Probably slept a whole family. 'Course, people were smaller then." He was examining some of Maynard's books. "Lots of readin' mattah. Old days, folks'd have but two books. the *Bible* and *Pilgrim's Progress*. 'Course, we've branched out since then. Now we have *Farmer's Almanac* and *Everythin' Ya Ever Wanted to Know about Sex*... Helps a man know the best time for plantin'."

Austin found himself laughing aloud and he wondered, quickly, if Bob Hope hadn't blown it by not having Jack Meeker on the bill for all those Vietnam holiday shows.

Jack moved along, his eyes searching the floor, until he gently kicked aside a small scatter rug that had masked a black iron ring set flush in the floorboards. "This'll be ya root cellah, Austin."

He bent, reached down, and pulled at the ring. A two-foot-by-two-foot trap door yawned up and open. He found a kerosene lamp, but the wick was dry as bone. He found a can of kerosene and refilled the lamp, explaining to Austin, "No electricity, Austin. You have stepped back into the last century."

Austin knelt and peered down into the blackness of the cellar. "Looks that way."

Jack lit the wick, and the lamp sprang to life. Holding it, he all the same dropped down into the hole with an ease and grace that belied his bulk. Busy shadows soon played up on Austin's face, Jack's voice accompanying them. "This'll interest ya, Austin."

"You want me to come down?"

"Up to you."

Austin lowered himself through the opening and trustingly dropped down alongside Jack in the cellar. It was creepy-damp yet smelled earth-washed, a little bit of good to go with the bad. It also afforded very little headroom, perhaps six feet at the most.

"Not much room for tall haircuts, Austin. Studs and nails'll bite ya if ya let 'em."

"I'll be careful. Smells...cold."

Jack was kneeling, listening. "Hear that? That's runnin' watah."

"I hear it." It was water, all right trickling steadily and benignly, bringing images of paper boats to Austin's mind.

"Familya with a cistern?"

"No, sir." Austin was beginning to think that he knew nothing about anything and that Jack Meeker was some kind of woodland guru who knew all about everything.

"It's simple enough." Jack was standing again, but not all the way, beams that were really tree trunks offering him an unfriendly lack of clearance. "This here is a barrel. These tin pipes, see 'em? They're the downspouts from ya roof. Rain comes down and into the barrel. Pump in ya dry sink draws it up and ya have it—watah."

"I see."

"In the summah."

"Oh?"

"In the wintah ya draw ya watah from this underground stream. Never freezes, 'cause it never stops runnin'. Runs right through ya barrel and goes on its merry way. But it always leaves ya with a barrel full of pure spring watah."

"Great."

"All ya need is a trout in the barrel."

"A trout?"

"A-yuh. Eats insects. Keeps ya watah pure. 'Course, that's in the summah."

"It's winter."

"Hard to find a trout in the wintah, Austin."

"I'm sure."

"Have to saw in the pond."

Austin found himself becoming newly impatient with the big man's meandering explanations. "Yeah. Okay."

"Have to do it sooner or latah. Come summah ya'll be wantin' ice. Only time to get ice is in the wintah."

"Yeah, well, that makes sense."

"Bound to be some spoilage to ya food down heah. Maynard left close to two years ago. Means a summah got sandwiched between two wintahs with no one around to look after things."

"I guess so."

"Then there's the animals. Moles. Rabbits. Mice. They'll have helped themselves to some of ya stock. Squirrels, raccoons, they always find a way in."

"All right. Okay."

"And whatevah ice Maynard stored in the icehouse, that's got to have all gone last summah. Melted, I imagine."

"Right. Right."

"And ya'll be *needin'* ice *next* summah."

"Ice. Right."

"Only it don't grow on trees."

"Right."

"Have to use a groovah and a saw."

"Groover and a saw, right."

"Probably find them in the icehouse."

"Of course. The icehouse. Right. Correct."

"Gettin' a little testy there, Austin. That'll be the wrong attitude for a man left out heah to his own devices. Be needin' patience."

"I'm sorry." And he was.

Jack was playing the lantern light on a dozen or so bushel baskets. "Maynard left ya lots of edibles. Apples might be sorry, though. Beets, parsnips, potatoes—they look okay to middlin'."

"Ah, potatoes. I *knew* I'd see potatoes *one* day."

Jack was nudging little pellets with his boot tip. "Ye never free of company, Austin. Have to ride herd or ya food'll be gone before ya inventory it. And ya'll end up eatin' animal droppin's."

Jack and his lantern were soon up and in the house again, Austin clambering after, pulling himself up without the practiced ease of a big man.

"Firewood'll last ya three, four days. Probably more out at the woodshed. But ya got no telephone and no neighbahs if ya took sick or have an accident—"

"I'll be okay."

"—or die."

Austin forced a grin. "Why should I die?"

"People die."

"*I* never did."

"Maynard died."

"People were shootin' at him."

Jack sat down, rather deliberatedly and cryptically. He was going to make a point. He crossed one leg over the other and pretzeled his arms. "Very old house, Austin. Old houses have stories."

"Oh Christ, you're goin' to tell me the place is haunted."

"Back a ways we passed a witch's tree. Ya may have taken notice." He paused, puffing his pipe, allowing it all to register on Austin. "A witch's tree is where a witch was hanged. That bothah ya, Austin?"

"When did it happen?"

"Long time ago."

"Then it don't bother me."

"Top part of this house is about a hundred years old. But the foundation's oldah. Much oldah. Maybe by two hundred fifty years. Original top burnt down, somewhere along the way. Rest of it, the foundation? That didn't burn completely. Timbers in the cellah, I checked 'em. Ain't even charred."

Whatever Jack was getting at, Austin was going to ride it out. "Good."

"Used to be, they'd burn down a witch's house all the way—to purify the area."

"Seems reasonable."

"If the house didn't burn completely, it was allowed as to how the witch might still have possession—from the othah side."

"I don't believe in witches."

Jack slapped his big hands against his thighs and pushed himself to a standing position. "Well, that's good, Austin. That's good."

"Do *you*?"

"What?"

"Believe in witches."

"Would it mattah?"

"It might."

"Well, people up here are inclined to be kind of religious. Believe there's good, believe there's evil. Believe in God…" He allowed the sentence to hang there, suspended in pipe smoke. "Believe in witches."

"Do *you* believe in witches?" Austin asked the question more emphatically, very Perry Mason, feeling as though he could just as easily be asking, "Do you believe in the Great Pumpkin, Peter Rabbit, Pinocchio?" The whole subject seemed that frivolous.

"I don't live here, Austin. So it don't mattah how *I* answer that question. What mattahs is *how you* answer it."

Austin smiled triumphantly. "I think you're avoiding the question."

Jack lowered his voice and became very softly direct. "I believe in witches—to some degree. Only I *don't* think they can occupy people as much as they can manipulate 'em."

"What's the difference?"

"Well, I think a witch has to have a home base it don't move too far out of."

"Like a house."

"A-yuh. House would be fine."

"Like *this* house."

Jack took his sweet time, trying to appear casual but, more importantly, wanting Austin to hear and absorb and understand every word. "A witch can occupy a house and do things to ya if ya cross its threshold. It can be layin' in wait for ya, baitin' a trap. Because it has a sense of orderliness—things happenin' on specific dates, by the numbahs, accordin' to schedule—a witch can confuse ya by rearrangin' time and space so's ya almost don't notice. A witch can make ya wish ya nevah come near it."

"Okay."

"If it has a place and a purpose, a witch can be a very terrible thing."

"You actually want me to believe that stuff, don't you?"

"Nope. But it might not be a bad idea if you was to *respect* it."

"Okay. I'll respect it. But I don't want to hear any *more* of it. Bad enough I'm going to be out here all alone, I don't need all that cutesy folklore to worry about."

Jack broke into a grin, and for a flashing moment Austin wondered if the big man hadn't been pulling his leg all along, as he had done to Guerney on the phone. "Well, then, Austin, seein' as how secure ya are in body and mind, I guess I'll be leavin'." He walked to the door, shaking the house and talking to Austin while facing away. "Tell ya what we can do. Once a week, if ya can find ya way back to the road—there's a postbox. Ya may have noticed."

"I didn't."

"Don't mean it's not there. Right on the road. So, anythin' ya may need or want, or want to tell me, ya just leave a note. I'm up and back that road pretty often, since I'm also the postman around here. Actually, I'm *postmastah*. Town of Belden voted me that title because it was both an honor and vacant. Anyway—if ya finished laughin', or chucklin', or whatever it is ya doin' there, in ya sleeve—"

"I'm not chucklin'."

"—I'm sure there's some pencil and paper somewhere in here, because Maynard's got the place stocked like a general store. So, once again, anythin' ya care to relate to me, ya just let me know via that postbox. That is, if ya not chucklin'."

"I'm sorry."

"No mattah. If I don't hear from ya from time to time, some little note or scratchin', I'll figure there's a chance somethin' might be wrong and I'll come lookin' for ya."

Austin could only shake his head in bemusement. "I come ten thousand miles, and I get ghost stories for my trouble."

"I didn't say anythin' about ghosts."

"Boy, you're beautiful. You really are."

Jack was moving toward the door again, looking out the window, trying hard to be nonchalant. "I'll look forward to hearin' from ya, from time to time."

He galomped out of the house, pulling the door closed in his wake, sunlight dancing in and out with the opening and closing of the door. Austin heard him on the porch donning his snowshoes, then crunching over the snow that distance back to the jeep—after which he heard nothing. Nothing at all.

And he stood there in the smack-middle frozen silence and chuckled anew, cranking out all the chuckles he could, and even more after that, because it was all the sound there was in his new house, and, were it to cease or leave, there'd be nothing for his ears to perk up to beyond the wind picking its way down the chimney—and the mice picking their way up.

His laughter grew small and unconvincing, so he dispensed with it, realizing all too soon that he was very much on his own in that wind-hewn wilderness, and that there was no ski patrol to defrost him if an avalanche fell on his house, and no Red Cross to serve him doughnuts if animals ate his food.

In Vietnam he had managed nicely. With the exception of Maynard he had played it pretty much high lonesome—no one to lean on and no one to lean on him. Still, there had always been interested bystanders in the wings, to assist if there was trouble, professionals at the stick and at the ready. There had always been a place to sack out where "friendlies" made the meals, and stood the watch, and told the jokes. And, if there *were* any ghosts or witches, they never badgered Austin Fletcher, because he was only a transient, someone passing through, a wandering minstrel singing "God Bless America." Whatever he was doing, for Country and for self, he would do and move on. And every village, every hillock, every bamboo hut and every rice paddie was but a temporary address, a way station with a number classification and a funny name, populated by thin people with spent faces and vacant eyes. And he, Austin Fletcher, was simply putting one foot in front of the other, making his way from one such place to the next and as quickly as he could, for to remain in any one given spot for too long a time was to draw killing fire from the invisibles.

He had been a floater and a waster, a time-marker and a corner-cutter. He had lived his entire life as if poised on a diving board, yet all he'd ever done was tense his toes and arch his insteps—he had never really jumped in, not into anything. Ever. Not of his own free will. Not even in Nam.

But this time he *had* jumped in, and off the deep end. And this Maine, this house by this unpronounceable lake, this dead-cold stop, this was it, for today and tomorrow. And it might well be it for a helluva lot longer.

The house and all about it smelled of a cunning impermanence. Stocked with all he'd need for a year at the least, it had nothing with which to record time. Not a clock had he seen inside. Not an hourglass or a sundial or a metronome. Nothing to measure the spilling of minutes or the flicking away of life. And he felt as if he'd been sucked in and ambushed. By a piece of paper. By a will, if you will, scrawled out by someone who, a few months back, he didn't even know to speak to.

The house was frigid and growing more so, the cold laying heavy hands on his shoulders, breathing ice on the back of his neck and frost on the flexes of his face. He would have to build a fire. Thoughtfully he played his fingers over the stubble on his face. He couldn't feel the whiskers, because his fingers were too numb. But he could hear them, snapping rigidly back to verticalness each time they were whisked. If nothing else, he needed a shave.

But it wouldn't be easy. The water in his overturned helmet was swimming with mosquitoes, and the blade in his razor, its cutting edge worn down into little more than a rumor, had long ago enjoyed its last hurrah.

Other men were spread out in the heat, reading, smoking, shaving, sweating. And Maynard sat by, cleaning his rifle, sliding the wire brushrod up and back through the barrel's bore, his pale eyes barely taking notice, his hollow cheeks wreathed with that never-flagging smile. "...nearer to Canada than to anywhere else. Big trees. Spruce. Fir. All sorts of animal life. In my house, I tell ya, I'm never alone. There's a mink slips in, steals things soon as I go out. And a chipmunk's been workin' on my bedpost, carvin' it into somethin' I don't know what. And squirrels all over the place like they're runnin' a relay race. Deer are plentiful but awfully skittish. Crow'll shake some snow off a tree and a deer'll run for five miles. 'Course, when they're hungry, they'll take risks. Starvation'll make a wild animal tame."

"And no neighbors?" asked Austin, getting nowhere with his shaving but doing it anyway, inertia and boredom asserting themselves over logic and awareness.

"Don't want any neighbors."

"But isn't it spooky?"

"Spooky? It's beautiful. There's life all around. Oh, sometimes a loon'll scare ya with its cryin', and an owl with its questioning but it's not spooky. There's legends, of course, but ya ought not place much stock in 'em."

"Like what?"

"Ya don't really want to hear, Austin."

"I do. I swear."

"Well, for example, right near my place there's a Devil's Dancin' Rock, and, a couple times, when the light's not too good..." Maynard was enjoying himself, knowing full well that he was titillating Austin.

"What?"

"Well, ya see, Austin, the Devil's Dancin' Rock is a kind of a wide, flat stone. Old settlers used to say that in a dim light, like at dusk, or in the full of the moon, if ya looked sharp, ya might just see Old Scratch himself, doin' a jig on it."

"Old Scratch?"

"The Devil, Austin."

"Did you *ever* see him?"

"I think half of the seein' is in the believin'."

"Okay, then, do you *believe*?"

"Well, there are the Minnawickies."

"The what?"

"Minnawickies."

"Come on, Maynard…"

"Where to?"

"What the hell are Minnawickies?"

"No one really knows."

"Oh, swell."

"Because ya can't really catch 'em. What we do know is, they're small. Stand four, maybe four and a half feet tall. They've got kind of big heads and very big eyes. And they're shy, very shy. And quick. Gone about as soon as ya see 'em. They'll drop in on a hunter, let's say unannounced? And if they're in a good mood, they might just cook him a dinner and leave it over his fire; or hang a couple fresh-caught fish for him, on a stick? Or leave their names spelled out in the dirt or the snow."

"Nice of 'em," said Austin, pretending to give no credence to anything that Maynard was saying—but hooked all the same.

"They have this giggle. Ya can hear it, 'specially at night when sound travels best. Like kids laughin', or a turkey gobblin'." Looking skyward and cupping his mouth, Maynard demonstrated the sound of a Minnawickie, and it came out as described: a chortle and a gobble, a blending of mischief and mystery, sounding, all at once, present and amusing and far-off and chilling. The other soldiers, too tired to comment on Maynard's apparent lunacy, paid him no never mind, so he did it again.

"What if they're in a bad mood?" asked Austin.

"Oh, then they might just upset all ya things; toss ya gear down a gulley, hide ya blanket in a cave. I guess a Minnawickie's some kind of an Indian. They wear colorful costumes and do a crazy kind of dancin'—which is why, when they come across a Devil's Dancin' Rock, they just go bananas. If they like ya they're no problem. But they can be pests. I heard of an incident where—"

The sound was of a whining and a whooshing. Incoming mail. Someone yelled, *"Mortars!"* and everyone hit the ditch. Austin could hear the monotonous whump-whump—closer each time. And he threw himself through the air like the others…

• • •

...hitting the floor prone, in the prescribed manner, his right hand groping for the M-16 rifle that wasn't there, his eyes staring at the closed door swinging open. The sunlight barreled in and Austin knew that he was as hopelessly lit up as New Year's Eve, in full view of whatever it was that was standing in the doorway.

"Left ya duffle bag again, Austin," came the twang. It was Jack Meeker, backlit and imposing, tossing the duffle bag into the room, unnerving the wallpieces and retesting the floorboards.

Austin snapped himself up like a yo-yo, tucking his knees to his chest and getting to his feet while very much aware of the cold sweat swimming in the hollow of his back.

"Catch ya takin' a nap, Austin?"

"Yeah, I was fast asleep."

"Bed might be softah."

"Think so?"

"A-yuh. Ya seem to keep leavin' ya belongings. Don't ya want 'em?"

"Naaah. Nothing in there but my toothbrush."

"Mighty big toothbrush."

"Sixty-eight pounds."

"Wouldn't happen to have a transistah radio in ya duffle, would ya?"

"Not that I know of."

"Too bad. Radio station in Millinocket. Keep ya abreast of things. Farm prices, temperature, ball scores."

"Why don't you just leave the daily paper in the postbox?"

"Can't do that."

"No?"

"No."

"Why not?"

"It's a weekly." Jack looked at the big fireplace. "Might considah buildin' yaself a fire. That is, if ya stayin'. Ya stayin', Austin?"

"I'm stayin'."

"And if ya flue ain't boarded up. Some people do that. Chimney steals the heat. In the summah, hornets make ya sorry. Some people like to go with just the Franklin stove. Does the job pretty good. Checked ya flue, Austin?"

"I was napping. I'll get around to it."

"Ya know *how* to build a fire, don't ya?"

"I think so."

"My guess would be that Maynard boarded up the flue, especially with him goin' off to war like he was." He walked over to the fireplace and stuck his head up the flue. His voice came booming back. "Bricked up. Maynard probably got all the heat he needed out of his Franklin. Economical." He emerged brushing loose soot from his jacket. Then he pulled off his right glove and extended that bare hand toward Austin. It came out like a pizza shovel, and Austin dropped his hand into it and watched it disappear. "If ya want, Austin, ya can forget this whole adventure and I'll take ya back."

"I'm stayin'."

"Luck to ya, then." He released Austin's hand and nodded. Then he walked out through the still-open doorway, and never looked back.

Austin stood on his doorstep and watched Jack Meeker slosh back to the jeep where the big man kicked off his snowshoes, hoisted himself up, lodged his bulk behind the wheel and turned the ignition key. The jeep protested and kicked, refusing to go, and Austin felt a momentary warmth at the thought that Jack might just have to stay, at least for the first night. And wouldn't that be the best of all possible worlds, in that it would allow Austin to honor his pledge to Maynard while providing himself with the companionship and security of what had to be the greatest hunter-trapper-hiker-talker in all of Maine.

That idle hope was shortly blown away by the belching exhaust of the jeep, which had apparently decided against crossing its owner. Jack stuck a big paw on the air, a gesture of goodbye which Austin returned. Then the jeep did an about-face and, eating up its own tire tracks, rambled off, soon to become a black blob on distant snow. And very soon after that—nothing at all.

6

He was alone. Not just alone but all the way alone. There was not
one small, friendly sound to offer even the meekest argument against
that conclusion, or any way in which a fire might spring up in the
old stove, of its own accord, as if by magic. Austin Fletcher would
have to supply the labor, pile the logs, stuff the kindling, strike the
match—all of which he did, happy to hear the sounds he made in
the accomplishing of those chores. For it meant that someone was
on the premises, a noisemaker, a presence, alive, alive-o.

In a short time the fire was going, orange light twittering
through the cracks of the cast-iron stove; wood aged and dry, ready
and willing, was spitting and snapping raucously. The stovepipes
lining the wall grew warm to the touch and then hot. Old beams,
floors and ceiling, creaked and sighed and stretched as the cold
room grew increasingly more hospitable and embracing. And Austin
experienced a deep gut satisfaction at having personally bestowed
upon the old house a new reason for being—a new tenant, a new
lord of the manor. He had been the passing prince and, having
bussed the sleeping beauty, had restored her to her former self. All
hail, let there be joy in the tiny kingdom. Let the bells ring—anything
to break the oppressive silence.

The heat soon burgeoned to such a degree that he was able to
remove his parka—and happy he was to shed that heavy skin, for it
had restricted his movements and bound up his spirits for too many
days in too many diverse places. He lounged there, in the old rocker,
without a clear thought in his head, and it was enough to not have
to think, or be, or answer to, or question—though he *would* have
appreciated a cigarette. Even a stale one. Or one of those so low

in flavor that shredded sofa smoked better. But none was around, not in that house. That Maynard, what a long and cough-free life he would have lived had he not been killed.

He had no idea how long he sat there in his self-induced state of suspended animation, a leg slung over each of the rocker's armrests. Nor would he have budged from that chair had his stomach not reminded him, with gurgles and yowls, that it too had a small fire going that needed feeding.

The canned goods were as stacked together as building blocks, their colorful labels facing out as would have been the case had they been displayed in the A&P or stocked by the Swiss Family Robinson in anticipation of their legendary shipwreck and subsequent maroonment.

In honor of New England, he selected a can of baked beans, prying it from its clam-tight place with diligence and vindictives. He opened it, set it on the stove top, and allowed it to simmer right in the can—until the bubbling sound of it and the molasses-sweet smell of it overpowered his senses. Then he plunged into it with a wooden spoon and ate it all like a hungry terrier, surprised at the slurping noises that came out of him, glad that his mother was in Ohio.

He followed the honored beans with a can of mashed pumpkin originally intended to be a pie filling but with really very little to say on the matter. And all of it he washed down with a quart-size can of Florida grapefruit juice, deliciously citric, just the right thing to cut the sweet gook of the beans and the pumpkin.

To further establish his mastery over menu, he opened and dispensed with a jar of kosher dill pickles, putting them away as might a sword-swallower, one after another, without pause for applause. There followed a short but furious acidic belly dance inside that a normal man's digestive juices would have been hard pressed to upstage. It didn't last long, just long enough to inspire wonder—churning, cavorting, straining and then subsiding. An older man, or a lesser man, could not have survived such an affrontery to his metabolism.

There were some four dozen cans of ground coffee from which Austin could choose. He selected one from Colombia because he had heard that it was grown on the side of some kind of special mountain where wind and rain combined to give it exceptional qualities that coffee grown in valleys and Ecuador could not equal. The pot perked happily and Austin soon had a mug of the stuff in his hand, a dash of dried milk and a lump of sugar rounding it out to bare palatability.

Thus armed and newly invigorated, he wandered about the big room with a greater sense of propriety than he had earlier evidenced. And he began to notice things, things he had missed at first glance. Things on the walls. That pine-framed photograph, for example— very Mathew Brady. A faded tintype, very period.

It was of a mustachioed man in his mid-twenties, posing stiffly, his eyes staring into Austin's from some seventy-five years ago. He was dressed in some kind of uniform. Perhaps he was a sailor. He might even have been a postman, an ancient predecessor of Jack Meeker. Whatever he was, he was nothing if not impressive. And there was an inscription on the photograph: "Dear Sara, until I return. Love, Jason."

Return from where? Austin thought. Certainly it would seem to rule out the man's having been a postman. Then again, maybe not. A good postal route, those days, might just well have kept a man on the road so long that his wife would indeed need a photograph of him to remember him by.

Austin looked more pertinently into the man's eyes as if expecting him to say something. And he wondered, Jason who? Sarah who? Who are the two of you who knew this house how many years ago?

A surge of melancholy swept over him, for, whoever the man and woman were, they were no more, their bones moldering under some granite headstone that idle travelers made rubbings of. "Here lies Sarah Somebody." "Here lies Jason Whoever." They had lived, and possibly died, it would seem, in this very house. Lived and died, dead and gone, their story—whatever it was—forgotten, if indeed it had ever been told at all. "Dear Sarah" and "Love, Jason"—two lives played out before Austin Fletcher had ever happened. Ebb and flow. Sarah and Jason. Dust unto dust—and all that.

Austin tapped the frame with his fingers, as much to reassure himself that the photo was there as to reassure Jason that someone was seeing him again, posed in perpetuity.

He then experienced a flood of emotions all at once, some of them contradictory, others murky, all of them hard to line up for analysis. He felt a security in that he was suddenly a part of a continuing scheme of things that had been set into motion years before—a man, a woman, a house, and now himself. That was good. He felt an awareness of mortality, his own in particular. Jason had been alive when that picture was taken, alive when he inscribed it. Sarah had been alive to receive it. And Austin had been alive when he discovered it. *Was* alive. *Is* alive.

The tenses jittered erratically, time and grammar crossing swords in his mind. He had never been good at utilizing either and so felt incapable of separating the confusions they were causing.

He felt ruffled at having looked at the face of dead Jason. He felt cheated at finding no photo of Sarah at all. He felt purposeful in that he knew it was his place to keep the fire lit, the hearth of Jason and Sarah, the stove of Maynard Whittier. He felt distraction as to why they were all bunching up in his mind, melding into one being, clawing at his singularity, insisting that he allow them to be he, and he to be they. He felt resignation at no longer having free and clear choices—his last choice leaving with Jack Meeker in the obstreperous jeep. He felt hemmed in, honored, burdened, exhilarated, and—to hell with grammar—he felt more present-active than at any other time in his life.

He saw something on the far wall. How could he have not seen it before—it was so large. He walk toward it, his stride long and assertive, shaking the floor, for it was now *his* house and the little animals beneath the floor had better start getting used to the gait of their new giant.

It was flat and smooth and hung perpendicularly. It was perhaps an inch thick, eighteen inches across, and some five feet in length. Nailed to the wall, it first looked to be a small door. But as he drew closer it more nearly resembled a warrior's shield, some kind of ornate design brocaded upon it. It proved to be neither. It was a plank of white pine, honied yellow by time, upon which some words had been carved with meticulous thought. The words were small and finely strung, completely legible once Austin's eyes adjusted to their minuteness, even the i's being dotted.

Starting at the very top, the words ran from left to right in four carefully etched lines, the cutting instrument apparently having been a small knife, maneuverable and sharp.

> Jason Booth Adamson, despite rumors and dire predictions, rebuilt this house, 1876–1877. He lived in it with his wife, Sarah Margaret, and one son, Thomas Caleb. A daughter, Katherine Marie, died February 21, 1882, aged three, of the winter. He wishes a good life to all others who may inhabit this house, successors and purchasers, and he leaves room on this wood for them to add their words to the history of this house.

A deeply etched horizontal line was laid onto the wood just below the inscribed words, the line running from one side of the plank to the other, marking a period to the thoughts of Jason Booth Adamson. Another set of words began directly beneath, carved by a lighter hand, a shallower cut.

> Jason Booth Adamson, husband and provider, passed September 22, 1889, the last warm day of that year. He was 34 years in this world and I do not forget him.
> —Sarah Margaret Adamson

Another horizontal line and the next set of words appeared. These were carved with less care, almost in haste—reflecting an angrier mood.

> Sarah Margaret Adamson passed July 15, 1894, aged 38. Thomas Caleb Adamson, son and heir, leaves this house

with no thought of returning.

A horizontal line sealed off the above words as if put to the wood by an ax. And beneath that line—more words. And Austin felt as though he had come upon some sort of Rosetta Stone, a key to the emerging hieroglyphics of a house that suddenly seemed to have more to say than just wood, nails and mortar.

William Evers Houlton and Anna Jane Houlton occupied this house unhappily, 1897–1898.

Another horizontal cut and Austin wondered what had happened in the years between 1894 and 1897. Had the house been unoccupied for three years following Thomas Caleb Adamson's departure? Certainly it was clear that that man had left because the house held too much personal unhappiness for him, his parents and his infant sister all having died there. But why had William and Anna Houlton stayed on but one year? And why should *they* have been unhappy? All houses witness death, if for no other reason than that houses live longer than people. Why should the Adamson griefs have rubbed off on the Houltons?

The knife-whittled words continued, the next legend set down by an unsteady hand, a hand either infirm or frightened. And Austin had to bend slightly to read it, for he was then reading halfway down the pine plank's depth.

Little or nothing will grow here. The witch's tree casts no shadow. A. G. Roberts, June 1906. One season is enough.

1906? What about the eight years between? And how was it that A. G. Roberts gave it but one season before leaving? As to the witch's tree, Jack Meeker had apparently not been making it up to "fun" Austin, for there it was, referred to in 1906, by a man who had no trouble accepting its existence and that it cast no shadow. It had cast no shadow for Austin either.

Another horizontal line, a deep one, so deep that it looked to have been inflicted upon the wood by the slashing stroke of an infuriated hatchet. Beneath it, the tale continued.

> Thomas Caleb Adamson exercised legal claim on this house, December 12, 1909. He lived in it with his wife, Elizabeth Deere Adamson, until her death, March 8, 1910. This house is not fit. It never was. Nor will it burn. To hell with it.

Fifteen years prior, Thomas Caleb Adamson had left with "no thought of returning." But he did return, to try again, to his father's house, bringing with him a wife who died in less than three months. Had he really tried to burn the house down? If so, why wouldn't a wooden house burn? It was more and more like the unraveling of a Gothic tale, and Austin's heart raced in anticipation of the next chapter.

> John and Martin Rivers, trappers by trade, stayed two nights here, January 23rd and January 24th, 1919. We did not sleep.

The developing picture was coming in sharp and clear—and it was not a pleasant one. True, it was fair to assume that everyone who had come upon the house, whether by accident or by design, had come upon its dark history as recorded on the wooden plank. And true, the power of suggestion in so solitary a house in so remote a region could easily have frightened them, or at the very least caused them to be apprehensive. But these were hardy New Englanders, self-reliant and rugged, descendants of tough early-immigrant stock. Why, then, should they reveal such susceptibility—and put their names to it?

The chilly conclusion, the only conclusion that Austin could arrive at, was that something in and about that house was not right. Over the years, what had once been a happy and hope-filled home had become instead a grim mausoleum, an icy vault in which were stored the bad dreams and fragmented fears of various people—a solitary structure, secretive and suspicious, with gaps in its history so wide that, with very little information, one could populate it with creatures bizarre and tales macabre, and intermittent years of unrelenting terror.

Austin knew that he was doing a ghost-story number on himself but was unable to check the flow of it. He read on.

> Seth Hamble tried this house two months in 1923. All that they say may well be true.

What might well be true? Austin felt the disquiet crawling in his every cell, growing and splitting off and breeding new and more virulent disquiet. Who was Seth Hamble? Had he been there alone? Why was he as unspecific as all the others about the things that had frightened him? Why no *examples* of "All that they say may well be true."? Who were *they?*

> John Lee Babcock, November 12, 1948. Phooey!

Good for you, John Lee Babcock. "Phooey" is right. Phooey on the whole thing. Phooey, too, on the twenty-five years between you and Seth Hamble. But—how could the house have stood unattended for that long? How could any house have thumbed its nose at erosion and storm and snow—and animals and vandals— and not have a beam fall, or a floorboard crack, or the roof leak, or the whole thing burn down?

The question answered itself right off. It could. This house could. This house could stand a thousand years unattended because, for some unworldly reason, not only could it do without humans— it *thrived* without humans.

And it hit him. Christ! And he slapped his forehead as the realization took sudden hold. It was all a joke. A beautiful, elaborate, well-conceived practical joke. Some weisenheimer, alone and in the area, fresh from tromping ye olde Appalachian Trail, had crafted the whole thing in just one night before the fire, a can of beer in one hand, a penknife in the other. "April Fool, traveler—joke's on you. Try some *real* American Graffiti."

A *better* variation on the practical-joke theme was that there were more than just one person involved—there were many, as many as those names appeared on the plank, each one adding his own little fillip to the continuing leg-pulling. That would certainly explain why the carved words varied in character and depth from person to person. It was a collective practical joke, like a chain letter. And those people did not even have to know one another to pull it off. Nor were they required to use their real names. They made up names. All the names and events alluded to on the old plank were fictitious. Ha-ha. How dopey of Austin to not have seen through it right off. Ho-ho.

He read on, smiling, for he had cracked the code, figured out the caper. These Maine cats, as symbolized by Jack Meeker— they all sure did have a finely honed sense of humor, a-yuh and yessirree bob.

All smug self-satisfaction with his newfound intelligence exploded and dispersed when he came upon the next and final set of words.

> Maynard Whittier took occupancy of this house on October 7, 1968. He left to serve with the U.S. Army, January 14, 1971...

Scratch one happy rationalization. And fasten the seatbelts of your mind, because here comes bad news. Maynard was no practical joke and no practical joker. Maynard was *real*—*had* been real. Austin was struggling to string it together into some kind of sensible image when his eye went to the last line that Maynard had carved into the wood with such precision and finality.

> I fear that I may not return.

A spasm took hold in Austin's stomach as big and as grabby as an undulating catcher's mitt. He tried to intellectualize Maynard's clairvoyance. After all, any man leaving for war might well experience such a foreboding. It had occurred to Austin himself that *he* might not come back. Statistically, one in twenty men was either killed or wounded in combat. Was it not perfectly reasonable, then, that the same thought might also have occurred to Maynard? Especially after having lived in that house, looking at that pine board every day, influenced by the desolate mood of it, picking up the dark vibrations of it—it was natural, almost proper, that Maynard set down so dire a closing statement.

Beneath that last inscribed thought was the usual horizontal cut. And beneath that—nothing. No room for any further carved words. No room for Austin to add *his* thoughts if and when, like all those before him, he might choose to carve them onto the plank. And it rankled him that he was being excluded. And he wondered if that exclusion was by happenstance or design.

He straightened up, stepped back from the board and tried to rethink the whole thing. A conclusion was floating around somewhere, an explanation. He would find it—and yet, it seemed to be defying him.

He sat on the rocker. People on rockers always thought more clearly. He sat on the rocker and thought. Since its construction, God knows how many years ago, the house had been empty more years than it had been lived in, its occupants frightened off with an almost predictable regularity. Added to that was something Jack Meeker had said—about the foundation being older than the house itself, perhaps by two hundred years. Also: "Used to be, they'd burn down a witch's house all the way—to purify the area…If the house didn't burn completely, it was allowed as to how the witch might still have possession—from the othah side."

Swell house, Austin thought. Nice place. Cozy. Charming. And now it was his. Austin Fletcher's. And who the hell was Austin Fletcher? How many people were there who could attest to whether or not *he* was real or imagined—fact or fiction? Who could tell, in this house, which end was up, or what witch was which? Or which witch was who? And—the one overriding question of them all, the question that could never be answered by anyone in *this* world— what happened in this house three hundred years ago?

Again Austin felt the cold sweat, clammy, crawling. He reached for his parka and slipped into it, all the while aware that, though it still carried on in the stove, the fire was no longer warming him. He tossed in more logs, leaving the stove door ajar so that he could hold his hands closer to the warm flames.

He was tired. Easy enough to understand when considering that he really hadn't slept since leaving Vietnam, not deeply, not without interruption. Yet sleep and he had parted company long before that, patrols and skirmishes preventing the pair of them from hooking up for longer than three or four hours at a time. So lack of sleep was not the cause of his fatigue.

Nor could he readily attribute his weariness to the house and its misshapen history, for he had never been one to place much store in haunted houses and the like—not yet, at any rate. So the house wasn't it, either.

Nor was he willing to concede that Maynard had been so dominant a force in their brief relationship that just being in what had once been Maynard's house could assert that dominance anew. Actually, if the truth were known, Maynard had been a nondominating companion, Sphinxlike and cryptic, seeming to know a great deal about much, yet actually displaying precious little knowledge about anything—beyond his house and the general area in which it stood.

His mind was convoluting, searching for a bit of applicable wisdom through which he might be able to explain away the nagging uneasiness. But none was forthcoming. Worse, his fingers felt suddenly on fire, and he recoiled from the stove, angrily kicking the stove door closed, causing the ashes inside to shift grumpily, like a big animal that had been dislodged and that you would hear from shortly. So he latched the stove door. Anything inside would thus stay inside.

The room was once again warm. The threat, if that was the word, had passed. The house was just another compilation of timber standing mindlessly in the middle of just another Maine winter. And the once-ominous pine board was but a chunk of smooth wood, carved with the overdramatic ramblings of people either frightened or playful and now dead.

But the beans—ah, the beans. And the pickles—oh, the pickles. And the grapefruit juice, and the coffee, and the Dr. Jekyllish formulation of all that Austin had so cavalierly tossed into his maw left no doubt in his head that nature was not only calling—she was screaming bloody murder.

He made for the door and, opening it, squinted out toward the backhouse. It was still there, a silent sentinel to man's desire to cloak his natural acts with secrecy. And it wasn't all that far—though it might just as well have been a mile, for there was no path to it. Only untouched snow. Drifts of it. Three to five feet high in places. It was a job for snowshoes.

He ran to the wall where Maynard's snowshoes hung. He grabbed them, hurried back to the door, slipped into them, and took off, waist-high across the snow. Next trip to the backhouse he'd have to remember to not cut it so close. Certain things, like good wine, should not be hurried. Good wine and dashes to the backhouse...

He used his entrenching tool laconically, picking at the earth and shoveling it aside almost sleepily, because he was in no great need to utilize the latrine ditch immediately upon completing it. Alongside him, Maynard was in a similar non-hurry, though other men had already assumed the position—looking more like khaki hens over nests than heroes over trenches.

"Well, I tell ya, Austin, in the summah it's no particular problem. But in the wintah? In Maine? There's a bowel-movement equation, goes somethin' like this: the depth of the snow multiplied by the distance to the backhouse divided by the urgency to go equals the allotted time to get there."

"I understand."

"And that is divided by two if ya run into a bear."

He thrashed on to the backhouse, feeling as though he were flying across the snow at a pace that would have matched that of Little Eva skipping over the ice floes, whereas, in actuality, thoroughly impeded by the huge snowdrifts he had to flail through, he was covering the distance about as quickly as a tortoise on flypaper.

By and by reaching the backhouse, he grew understandably ill at the tableau before him. Snow, a six-foot-high pile of it, was leaning against the old door like a drunken polar bear. It would be a battle against the clock. The door or his bowels—something had to give.

No Alpine rescue team ever worked with greater fervor. Throwing, kicking, shoveling with his hands for minutes that played as hours, he eventually cleared the door, only to see leaning innocently against it, standing there like the Planters Peanut Man as if to say, "Hi, what kept you?"—a shovel.

There was no time to reflect on how much easier it all might have been had the shovel taken the trouble to reveal itself sooner. And there was no energy available for cursing or crying or sweating and saying "Whew." The door stood before him and the door had to be opened. It was as simple as that.

He found the rusted handle and pulled on it, but, as seemed to be the case with all the doors in Maine, it resisted, not caring to discuss the matter any further. He picked up the shovel and slammed it smack against the unyielding door—but it stood its ground like Leonidas at the Pass.

He stepped back to reassess the task, time running out in his innards. Then, stepping back some five feet farther so as to afford himself the required distance, he launched himself into a running block that would have delighted Vince Lombardi. Head down, torso extended horizontal with the snow, his shoulder slammed against the door with a dashing determination, ripping that weatherbeaten old thing from its hinges, causing it to fly apart into the three single boards it had once been. The castle thus breached, Austin tumbled inside.

But the battle was not yet over, for everything beyond where the backhouse door once stood was overlaid with a vinelike vegetation as impenetrable as a steel jungle. And somewhere buried within all the tangle was the object of Austin's charge—a one-holer, loyal to civilization, and waiting to be freed.

He fought the cabled Medusa, again with his bare hands,

his stomach trumpeting the attack, and he prevailed. For it soon revealed itself, with a bucket of ashes and a scoop at its side—a grateful one-holer, looking up at him like a black moon. No Holy Grail was ever more adored or more quickly utilized.

The seat was cold. But temperature and wind velocity and cloud formations and bird calls were not the issue. The issue was time, and Austin had come in under the wire. That knowledge warmed the seat, and he sat there where very probably Jason Booth Adamson himself once sat, and he felt at one with nature.

A thick Sears, Roebuck catalogue dangled beside his head like a hung man, making half-turns right and then left at the will of the wind.

Closer examination of the catalogue revealed it to be the 1970 edition, fairly recent, current and provocative reading—though, for Austin, it began on page 353, the preceding 352 pages having evidently been pressed into service for the good of mankind at an earlier time and, presumably, not all at once.

The doorless backhouse commanded a fine panoramic view of his land, evening beginning to glint on a hilltop, conferring a dab of mauve to the canvas, a touch of gloam to the frame. And in that gradual waning, trees were browner and grayer, bushes and pines greener, irrepressible winter blooms pinker—the entire day, so harsh white and ice blue theretofore, was suddenly sprung with color.

The two front windows of his house caught the low sun and played it back at him as twin crimson carpets that unfurled to a stop only inches short of his boot tips. And a gentle splash of white-speckled beige was moving about near his porch, *on* his porch, and then off, like a big caramel sundae sprinkled with mini-marshmallows. A deer.

Curious perhaps at the smoke coming from the chimney—and hungry, judging from the way its ribs protruded from its thin flanks—the deer was considering the door to the house, which Austin, in understandable haste, had left open.

It sniffed at the snow on the porch, burying its muzzle in it. It placed a foreleg again on the porch—only to withdraw it. It was painfully tentative, instinctively afraid to go farther. But it was also close to starvation, and, drawn on by the lingering fragrances of Austin's adventurous dinner, it was prepared to take the risk.

"Hello, Bambi," Austin called out from where he sat—softly, for he didn't wish to alarm the pretty thing. The deer stiffened at Austin's voice and froze, as in a calendar picture. But it did not bound off as it always does in woodland tales, for it was too exhausted to run, too hungry to take cover. Instead, it turned its head and looked back at Austin, its ears bristling, its nostrils flaring in hopes of picking up and identifying Austin's scent.

"Nobody's home, Bambi."

Confused, probably closer to death than Austin had at first realized, the deer moved inexplicably toward him on wobbly legs, and Austin was glad it was a deer and not a lion. A lion and he'd have stood up, pulled up his trousers and jumped for cover—into the only place in the backhouse that afforded cover. So he was certainly glad it was a deer.

All the same, it was moving toward him and looming larger— and no longer did it look so delightfully Walt Disneyish. Austin tried to wave it off. "Hey! That's close enough, will ya! Beat it!"

But the deer kept coming, its nose vacuuming the snow, its spindly legs quavering. Austin reached for the door, to pull it closed. But the door wasn't there anymore and he began to feel rather ridiculous, sitting there as he was, half expecting a crowd of people he knew to appear and fall over hysterical at his situation. Aunts, uncles, coaches, ministers, girl friends, all splitting their collective guts at his humiliation. He windmilled his arms. "Shoo! Beat it! Fuck off!"

But the deer continued to advance, never pausing, never quickening or slackening its pace. And Austin became fascinated, wondering just how close the animal would come before thinking better of it and bouncing off in terror.

The answer was—all the way. And soon the deer's sweet face was protruding into the backhouse where Austin sat like Lincoln on on his monument. Its nostrils were semaphoring, its huge sable eyes filling with awe at seeing, up close, the King of the Woods, Austin Fletcher—also known as the Dean of the Latrine.

Austin's mind slot-machined frantically, spinning wildly in hopes of coming up with something winningly amusing, some point of view that might make his situation either humorous or acceptable. He wasn't frightened, but neither did he have a plan of action. And he certainly did not feel compelled to reach out and offer an upturned palm of peace to the hungry animal. So he tried to strike a bargain. "Listen, the house is open. Go on in and help yourself. Tell 'em Austin sent you."

The deer deliberated, hardly moving and barely breathing. The voice of man seemed to hold no fear for it, and so it sashayed right up to where Austin sat, until the pair of them were literally nose to nose, Austin able to feel the animal's hot breath and wet fur on his bare knees. Man and beast, partners in No Man's Land, they continued to eye each other, the deer looking even less delicate than ever. And less cute. And less loving. It looked pretty damned large and menacing, and its nose hairs, so gossamer in children's books, looked more like steel brushes. It began to probe its rough nozzle into Austin's crotch, furrowing for a meal, any kind of meal—even that odd carrot.

Austin slammed his legs together, smashing his knees rather painfully while still trying to speak to the deer as he thought Albert Schweitzer might have. "That'll be enough of that, sir."

The deer kept probing and Austin grew more concerned. He had no weapon other than the scoop in the bucket of ashes. Yet how many times in how many movies had he seen a man armed with far less turn defeat into stunning victory? But in a backhouse? On a crapper? Not once. Not Cagney or Bogart, and certainly not George Brent, had ever come up against so challenging a situation. There was no precedent for Austin's doing anything beyond saying, "Don't do that. That's not nice. Shame on you. Tsk-tsk."

The deer looked up at Austin and then backed off slightly, its rump very much outside the backhouse, its unblinking eyes fixing on Austin's as it wondered just what lunatic ravings the creature had lapsed into.

Seeing the effect that mellifluous human speech was beginning to have on the animal, Austin continued to talk, for he certainly did not want to risk panicking the deer by making any move that it might interpret as a provocative act. And he certainly did not have the heart to either toss ashes at the starving creature or bonk it on the snout with the scoop. "That's a good fella. That's a nice Bambi. Just you keep on backing out—nice and easy. Now, as I told you, I'm a little busy at the moment, but the house is open and…"

Obediently, the deer backed off farther and, turning, made straightaway for the house, bounding up and onto the porch, and from there going right in.

My God! thought Austin. I can talk to the animals! I'm— Dr. Doolittle!

From within the house there shortly came a collection of noises that fell hard on Austin's ear. The deer was knocking things about, helpless things like cans and jars and dishes.

"You sonofabitch deer!" Austin bellowed, tearing off catalogue pages 353 through 359 and applying them to the task they were there to perform. "Get the hell out of my house!"

The deer emerged, a gnawed-open box of crackers in its muzzle, contents flying. And again it looked across the snow at Austin, as if surprised that the fellow had lost his cool and turned so suddenly hostile.

Austin was indeed hostile, as who wouldn't be when a guest oversteps himself. And he stood pulling up his trousers and buckling his buckle—at which point the deer acted as if it had been shot. It leaped into the air and did a right-angle turn before coming down. And when it did come down it was in full flight, the cracker box still clamped in its jaws as it disappeared over the nearest hill.

And Austin knew why. Sitting there as he had been, dramatically lit and framed picturesquely in his doorless backhouse, he had appeared to the fuzzy-thinking animal as something it had never before seen—and something it need not fear, since its computer had no print-out on it. But once he stood up, on two legs, he was man.

Man, the hated biped. Man, the cruel predator. And the computer flashed its word and the deer disintegrated in the sunset.

The contest thus concluded, Austin was once again King of the Hill. He just didn't much care for the hill he was king of, and so he finished up and headed home, taking a proper amount of time in which to stomp out a flatter, firmer path—so that his next trip to the backhouse might not again end up as a flaming five-alarmer, and there'd be no wicked old deer to run off with his favorite crackers.

7

Austin reentered his house numbly, pulling the door closed and bolting it in the momentary fear that the deer might return with hungry reinforcements, some with huge antlers, others with sharp teeth, all with a predilection for odd carrots.

The fire in his stove was still doing nip-ups, the house managing to keep warm despite his having left the door open. He hung up his snowshoes with affection. They were his friends and he patted them as such, wanting them to know, tactilely, his everlasting gratitude. At his first opportunity he would wax them, or oil them, or twang them, or whatever had to be done to snowshoes to keep them in tiptop happiness.

He took stock of his situation. It wasn't bad. He had arrived. He had taken possession. He had lit a fire and had eaten. He had made friends with his backhouse and had had a chat with one of the neighbors. He had followed his nose all the way from Vietnam and had made it to this pinpoint on a map that there probably weren't ten copies of in the entire archipelago. It was okay. All was well. Good show.

And so, feeling good, he sang:

> "I left my ass—in Cincinnati,
> Beneath a blue, enchanting sky.
> And I'll return to you, Cincinnati—
> When my ass learns how to fly."

His had never been a good voice. In high school he had been labeled a listener and told to merely stand there and mouth the words. But this was his own house and if he wanted to sing he'd sing. And if he wanted to sing a second chorus he would, and did. And if he wasn't any good, there was nobody around to say so.

The angle of the sun was lowering, the once intense rays weakening and filtering through the windows in beams practically parallel to the floor. It would soon be dark. He looked over the room. He had enough lanterns. He had enough firewood. He had all that he needed—except one thing. A bath. He needed a bath. He was beginning to smell like a hyena pelt and he needed a bath.

Toward that end he selected the largest vessel he could find, a huge oaken tub hugged together by rusting iron bands. It was three feet in diameter and equally as high, the inside bottom of it coated with a half-inch of mossy slime. But bathers couldn't be choosers. Besides slime was better than splinters any old day. Plus—and very important—if Maynard hadn't wanted it that way he'd have done something about it, like scrape it clean, or disinfect it, or apply Vigaro for a richer, fuller growth, or switch to Astro-Turf like your more affluent football teams.

He was finding it mitigating and assuaging to explain away every unattractive and malfunctioning item in the house as being that way by Maynard's design. It was comforting to play such a game, like relying on a higher power for both love and guidance, or possessing an efficacious religion to fall back on whenever the going got rough. The extension of such thinking, of course, was to make a golden idol in Maynard's likeness and worship it, and offer sacrifices to it— part of his larder, small animals, chickens if they'd ever show up. He thought on the matter no further than that—first, because there was no gold on the premises; second, because it was easier to remain a nonpracticing Presbyterian; and third, because he needed that bath and right away.

The pump goosenecking over the dry sink was well greased and, with just a little gentle coaxing, brought the water up from the cellar cistern as advertised. He filled two metal pitchers and a copper kettle and set them on the stove to boil. It was a time-consuming affair and he began to understand why the old pioneers had fixed on one bath a week as being proper enough hygiene. Two baths and there'd be no time for planting. Three and they'd have to *adopt* their children.

The old tub was soon full enough for human immersion, and he stepped into it, a bar of pine tar soap in one hand, a worn scrub brush in the other. All he needed was his plastic duck.

It was a fine bath, setting Austin again to singing.

"Shenandoah, I hear you calling
Across the wide Missouri..."

The plaintive lyric brought tears to his eyes, though it could have been his voice. The soap lathered and slathered, the warm water had magical soothing powers, the scrub brush had gotten his blood to running, the steam was happily rising, the windows were fogging, his skin was tingling—and someone was watching.

It wasn't really a someone. It was more of a something. He could sense it, feel it. He had learned to do that in Nam. If something was around that wasn't supposed to be around, he was the first man to know it.

The water in his tub turned almost immediately cold. Whatever it was it was impossible to discern in the fading light, for, even though he had thought to do it, he had neglected to light one of his lanterns.

His eyes eventually picked out the "thing," and he saw that it had form, hovering as it was in a corner where the two walls met to fuse darkness and darkness into greater darkness. Its bulk, though unmoving, was coiled, its eyes shining—more light in them than in anything else in the room. Judging from the distance he estimated the corner to be from his tub, the thing's eyes were not more than an inch apart. And they were like lumps of oily coal, dead but glistening. Shark's eyes, reptilian. A snake! And Austin let out a cry and stood up in his tub, the suds flying every which way, his toes struggling to maintain their grip on the tub's greasy bottom lest he topple over the side like a man overboard.

The snake was caused to move at all this, and it wasn't a snake at all, because snakes didn't have bushy tails. It was a beaver. Or a mink. Or an otter. Or a raccoon. Actually, it was a squirrel, and it perched there, looking at Austin as if he were mad, splashing around in a bucket, foaming like a rabid ape, yowling like a cornered stag.

The squirrel was not alone in this opinion, for it had two companions, the three of them soon bounding about up there in the nooks and niches, watching Austin do his imitation of the Statue of Liberty, soap in one hand, brush raised high in the other.

"Jesus Christ!" he cried out, as much in relief as in surprise, for squirrels were cute little things not known to harm humans. And far better it was to be in the company of three small squirrels than in the range of one long snake.

Austin submerged again calmly into his tub, where the water was once again warm and from where he could see that his three little squirrels had obviously been exercising squatters' rights over his foodstuffs for quite some time. They were that round and decadently lumpy. The only squirrels in Maine with the gout.

Playing Dr. Doolittle again, a role he was beginning to feel more and more born to, he addressed his subjects with grace and assurance. "Hi, gang—I'm your new landlord. You guys from around here?"

The squirrels placed their heads together, the better to discuss the matter. They were quite animated in their fits and starts and adorable spasms, so quaintly winning in their scramblings that it was impossible for Austin to look upon them as being bona-fide members of the rodent family. They gabbed and chattered, wrung their little claws, scratched their heads, and sat on their haunches like furry andirons. They reminded Austin of three green second lieutenants he had once seen trying to make a combat decision.

Soon enough the ranking squirrel dropped to the floor and herky-jerked across for a closer look at the lathered Gulliver in their midst. It advanced in movements so spurty as to appear that its shadow was running a split second off the pace. It looked up at Austin, its nose atwitter, its tail patting the air behind it like a train signal. And it remained that way, just looking at Austin, as the deer had done earlier, and Austin began to wonder if both animals weren't trying to figure out whether or not he was Maynard Whittier come back to the Old Homestead. Certainly it was possible that Maynard had domesticated them, had possibly allowed them full run of the house. Ah, but they had not been included in the will, and, should the issue ever go to court, Austin would win, paws down.

Austin and the squirrel remained that way for some moments, wiggling noses at three paces, with Austin the first to break eye contact when it crossed his mind that he might have inadvertently joined the little fellow in some kind of cabalistic mating dance—and if there was one thing he did not want to contend with while nude in a tub of water, it was a horny squirrel.

He looked up to where the other two squirrels were squatting—only they weren't there anymore. Perhaps they had had the decency to leave the lovers. How civilized.

One thing, though, was for sure: the bath water was turning chilly, this time for real, the lather caking and the moss beneath his ass evidencing unmistakable signs of sea life. So, reaching for his towel, he stood again in his tub, the ribbony soapsuds sluicing off him as if he were a melting Good Humor. And seeing Austin in so preposterous a posture, the heartbroken squirrel scampered off, disappearing into a corner—and the love affair was over.

Lighting a lantern, Austin knew that he would one day have to ask himself if his naked body was truly frightening or merely absurd. Whichever it was, various animals indigenous to the area were fleeing at the sight of it. He toweled off briskly because the room wasn't really warm. It was warm only by comparison with how cold it had been.

He pulled some clean clothing from his duffle bag, wondering what he was supposed to do with his soiled clothing. The answer was simple and forthcoming. He'd wash it in the very same tub in which he had just washed himself. Waste not, want not. And so he tossed it all into the greasy water, to soak. In the morning he would give it artificial resuscitation, no starch.

Looking like a Roman senator in his towel, he unpacked, stacking his clean G.I. clothing onto shelves already neat with Maynard's carefully stored civvies. And he realized how good it was that he and Maynard had been just about the same size in just about everything. For not only had he brought with him precious little clothing of his own, but none of it was really suitable for that Northeastern winter he had waltzed into so cavalierly.

He glanced up at the bowed ceiling, wondering how many squirrels were up there in that space between the ceiling and the roof. He'd have to look into it, of course, but not tonight. Any attempt at disenfranchising his tiny tenants would have to wait until morning. And even as he slid into a pair of his G.I. scivvies, he could hear the little beasties up there, scampering about, spreading the word that a new master was on the premises and that, on first appraisal, he appeared to be acceptable.

He banked his fire rather well, for he had had some experience with barracks fireman duty during basic training and had acquired a passable professionalism. He checked his windows, making very certain that they were secure, just in case a wind came up, or a burglar, or anything capable of skinnying itself through some chink in his wooden armor. Not that anything out there anxious enough to get in was likely to be dissuaded by a window. Still, for it to gain entrance, a window would have to be broken and he would hear the glass shatter—and, whatever it was that was coming in, it would have just one quick look at Austin Fletcher going out.

His tiredness was more akin to exhaustion as he made his way to his giant bed, leaving one lantern lit as a beacon against all things that might go bump in the night. He pulled the gaily-colored patchwork quilt back and sandwiched himself between it and the sheets, not concerning himself with whether or not the sheets were clean (which they were) or cold (which they were).

He lay on his back, arms folded behind his head, and he stared at the ceiling which was alive with the rustle of squirrels. There was no way in the world he'd be able to fall asleep that night, what with nosy deer and noisy squirrels abounding, and ghosts and witches and visions of backhouses exploding in his head. But in minutes he was asleep. Soundly. Deeply.

The night was hushed and obscure, nothing between moon and sun but a forlorn hooting owl surveying the predawn from a pine tree already dripping with dew. *"Hoo hoo hoo, hoorer-hoo."* It was all the song he knew.

But it was not the owl that woke Austin. And it was not the kerosene lamp flickering and then dying, plunging the room into abject darkness save for the few glitters of moonfire that rebounded off the snow-laden hills. And it was not the wind picking up and pressing its way through the uncaulked splits of the solemn old house. It was the Boston rocker, camped in the parallel blackness of the other room, creaking. A steady and repeated creaking—as if someone were in it.

Austin stirred, the sound beginning to sift into his head. His left arm, the dreamer, pulled the quilt over his chin so that he might slide deeper beneath its mantle and coax more sleep from the night. But his right arm, the guardian, pushed the quilt away, a rush of cold sweeping over him, causing him to sit quickly upright in his bed, his unready eyes striving to pick out the noise, to track it to its source.

The creaking was persistent, nothing to compete with it but the owl and the wind which was pushing at the morning fog and licking down the chimney. Another noise, distant and erratic, insinuated its presence. Dogs, barking. Or so he thought. Two of them.

Not asleep and not awake, his dilated eyes fixed on the other room, Austin eased himself from his bed, his toes momentarily ensnared in the bearskin rug on the floor. Two steps toward the creaking—and it stopped. And all was silent, even the dogs—or whatever they were. Probably foxes, barking fitfully at the moon. And he stood in the hanging silence, unsure of anything he'd been hearing and very little of what he'd been thinking. The cold draped itself around him and he fled from it, returning to the warmth of his bed like a prodigal pea to its pod.

In seconds he was back to sleep, while outside, the owl and the wind—the two constants of the night's music—played on into the night's remainder.

8

The early sun speared through eastern windows, and Austin awoke. Above him the squirrels, up and active, padded about beyond the ceiling. Busy, busy, busy. Shake, rattle and roll.

The room was bright and cheery, the banked fire having survived the night though the kerosene lamp had not. He'd have to check the wick. He'd have to check *all* the wicks of *all* his lamps. Months of non-use had very likely dried the lot of them to a brittle unusability.

Outside in the good day, beyond windowpanes white-furred with a half inch of frost, some discordant Canada jays were giving a pair of foraging partridges what-for. And sparrows, some sharp-tailed and some white-throated, seemed especially diminutive alongside the grackles and grosbeaks so inclined to corpulence. Chimney smoke had attracted the birdlife, and Austin knew they'd be hanging around from then on, voicing their appetites, awaiting their handouts.

The night wind, now stilled, had laid patterns on the snow, covering slightly Austin's snowshoe prints of the day before, though tracks of rabbits and foxes and mice were morning-fresh, powdery indications of the quiet hubbub that had taken place during his slumber.

Stepping into his living room, he looked over at the Boston rocker and remembered, fleetingly, how it had intruded on him during the night. Had it really rocked? And did it really creak? He walked over to it and nudged it into action. It rocked, but it didn't creak—and he smiled, accepting the hypothesis that it had done neither except in the limbo of his susceptible mind.

He shrugged it all off, for there was work to be done, things to be set into motion if he was to survive in the good old glacier-scarred "Pine Tree State." State flower: white pine cone and tassel. State bird: the chickadee. He had looked all that up before starting on his journey. It was all the knowledge he had accrued on Maine but had seemed enough at the time.

He poked the fire in his stove, and new flames kicked up. Then he fed the iron beast another log, as reward for having done its night work so well.

He donned some of Maynard's clothing, which fit well if not perfectly. And, to put on Maynard's insulated boots, he sat unthinkingly on Maynard's Boston rocker. It creaked. It did not escape Austin that, with no one in it, the rocker had *not* creaked. To test this point, he stood up and agitated the rocker—and it did not creak.

"Someone has been sitting in *my* chair," he quipped. A dozen or so unseen little denizens set to running every which way at the sound of his voice. And he stepped away from the rocker, not frightened, for he was certain that it was a dream that had conjured the rocking and the creaking. Still, he had a new respect for the chair, and he chose to not reflect on the incident further.

His laundry needed attending. It had soaked all night in the soapy tub, and picking up pieces of it, scivvies and socks, was like hauling oiled frogs from a gooky-bottomed creek. He dragged the oaken tub out onto the porch, tilted and dumped it, and hung the khaki pelts over the tailing. He went back into the house and pushed at the fire again, until his stove gave off a ruddy and hospitable glow—for Maynard had once told him that "a good fire makes a proper housekeeper for when ya goin' out." And Maynard ought to know.

His woodshed was nothing more than an asbestos-covered platform supported by poles. The poles were of differing heights, giving the shed a lean-to construction, thus minimizing the obvious peril that tons of snow would present to any flat-topped edifice. Heavy tarpaulins hung down on all four sides to ward off winter drifts and summer squalls. It was, all in all, a rather serviceable affair if not something worthy of *The Architectural Digest.*

Neat piles of wood cut into stove lengths lay awaiting their fate, while nearby a sturdy chopping block and a variety of bladed instruments were readily available for duty. Axes, saws, files, knives, hatchets, plus tools old and new. And cans of rusted nails. And coils of wire. And a confused bag of screws, nuts, bolts, tacks, glass and jars. It could all have been construed as junk were it not for Maynard's having stacked, hung and labeled everything with consummate affection and care.

With hammer and nails, and hinges and screws, Austin repaired his backhouse door. Yes, Maynard might have done the job better and neater, but Austin was not a complete nincompoop in such endeavors, and he viewed his accomplishment with the same glow of satisfaction that an ancient Venetian artisan would have basked in upon rendering an urn, or a fountain, or a glass chandelier. Also— he was hungry.

Back at his house he selected from his larder a saner meal than his helter-skelter dinner had proven to be. Powdered eggs, crackers and coffee. It went down easy and caused no furor.

He shoveled a path to his icehouse, a much more substantial building than his woodshed. It was stone on the outside and brick on the inside, six inches of air probably in between for maximum insulation. The door was also doubled and took no small effort to dislodge from its sluggishness. Inside, heavy burlap lay on thick butcher-block wood as sterile sheets would lie on an operating table. And everywhere sawdust. No ice, but Austin hadn't expected any. There were, however, implements with which he might avail himself of ice. Picks, tongs, groovers, saws and a pung. The latter being a long, low-slung sleigh with two sets of steel runners, the front set being on a pivot so that a sharp turn could be more easily executed. It was perfect for hauling, and that was what Austin had in mind for it.

From where he stood on the frozen pond, the forest was more luxuriant than ever, blue-tipped trees spilling down rugged crests to flood the rich valleys. Junipers and spruces everywhere, many of them bravely shouldering their way through minute crevices to come up gasping for sun. All the land encircling him, lake-studded and rock-fringed, was ablaze with a sharp light that summer could never match. And above his head a formation of honking geese sailed by, their wings pounding loudly, like a ship's canvas in a gale.

It was stupefying to witness, the shine and the glass of it, the primeval pull of it, and he let loose a shout, adding his own noise to that of the geese and the quail and the sparrows and the hawks. "Yaaaaa-hooooo!" he cried, feeling brother to the wind and cousin to the sky. "Yaaaaa-hooooo!"—and his voice bounced all over that wooded wilderness of loons and trout and beaver and fox, and never in his life did he feel more at the core of things and more hopeful for the world.

With groover and saw he carved from the lake top three blocks of ice, each measuring two cubic feet. As hard as the carving had been, the loading was even harder, for the ice blocks tended to slide off the pung's lacquered surface. Of course, he should have brought with him some of those burlap blankets he had seen hanging in the icehouse, but he hadn't, and there was no sense in crying over spilt ice. In any event, to avoid the constant on-again, off-again of it all, he packed the ice blocks with snow, on all sides and in between. And it worked, as mortar with bricks, and he headed back to his icehouse where he would hoard his big diamonds until he and the summer would chip away at them with ice pick and heat.

Something faint caught his ear. A new sound and not a forest sound. It came again, at random, without pattern as with a butterfly trail—the laughter of children or the call of some bird. In, out gone.

It came again and again, intermittently, Austin unable to set his ear so that he might anticipate and thus identify it. He could not define whether it was real or imagined, animal or human, bird or breeze. It simply played the wind and floated off. Now you hear it. Now you don't.

His ice blocks eventually wrapped in burlap and vouchsafed, his icehouse door pressed firmly shut, he next set to the task of digging a series of crisscrossing paths in the snow that would link the house, the icehouse, the backhouse and the woodshed. The completion of it took longer than he had reckoned on, but when the trench-digging was done he took pride and assurance in the knowledge that he had quick and easy access between his four buildings—come what may, eat as he would.

The only thing really wrong that he had done that morning was to leave his wet clothes to dry on the porch railing. For they had not so much dried as they had frozen stiff, and he collected them from their perches as if they were linoleum samples. Inside his house he spread and bent the board-stiff clothes over his stovepipes, where they steamed and sizzled and smoked like fish, and generally sagged themselves back to life. He was learning. He knew it. Everyday he was learning.

Wearing snowshoes, he walked out to where there were no paths at all. He was just reconnoitering, checking out his land, of which there were eleven acres though most of them would have to wait till spring. And as he sloshed he heard it again—high-pitched and funny. And there was no mistaking what it was. It was the wind-carried giggles of children, and it was all about him, like the delicate thrustings of an expert duelist. It was in front of him and then behind him, blocking his path, spurring him on.

He kept walking, not wanting to appear unsettled by the taunting laughter or frightened by whoever or whatever was creating it. He passed a large flat rock, about the size of an oval tabletop. Clear of snow and highly polished, it picked up the sunlight in gauzy patches, giving the appearance of a large jewel set in white gold. And all about the immediate area were signs that someone or something had been there since the snow last fell.

There were footprints merged with one another so tightly that the snow looked to have been stamped down almost into a carpet. The footprints had been made by small feet. Two pairs of them. One small, the other smaller.

He examined the rock more closely, removing a glove and running his fingers over the glazed surface. He could almost see his face in it, distorted to be sure, but mirrored there just the same.

And as he peered into his own eyes in the mirroring rock it came again, the laughter, almost as though it was his own reflection that was causing it. And it was closer by than before. Much closer. And he looked up quickly to see—

Two heads, multicolored and large-eyed, popping up over a snowy crest, prismed within a hovering cloud of their own breath. But they were gone almost as soon as he saw them, only the vapor of them remaining, and only for seconds.

Unable to figure it, and uncertain as to whether or not he was being "funned" or "taunted," he moved on across the snow. In short time he came again upon his witch's tree, more spookily provocative than the first time he had encountered it. No foliage, no snow on its charred branches, its gnarled roots holding to the ground tenaciously, as if to defy anything to cause it to relinquish its grip.

He looked to see if it cast a shadow. But as he did, the sun ducked into a gray overcast, and nothing had a shadow, not even himself. There was, however, a strangeness at the base of the tree that he had not noticed before. A yellow fluid bubbling, almost imperceptibly. And he wouldn't have noticed it even then had he not been aware of the terrible odor it emitted, an odor so foul and offensive that he almost toppled.

And then the laughter came again, as if in conspiracy with the sun's capriciousness, and he was beginning to fail to see the possible humor of it all.

He walked on, with a snowshoe rabbit hopping across his path, kicking up a skitter of snow before losing itself in a series of cleverly executed right-angle leaps. Up ahead was his postbox, camped on a thick stump and sticking out of the snow like a small covered bridge. The name on the box read "Maynard Whittier," and just beyond it Austin could see the tire tracks of what had to be Jack Meeker's jeep, dawdling over what had to be the road back to Belden.

He smiled, because it meant that civilization was not all that far away. It was the first time in his life that he had ever attached such happy significance to tire tracks. They were as twin arteries, available to him for sustenance, support and good fellowship. As such, they were a welcome sight, as welcome to him as the note within the postbox, pinned to the bulky package.

> Some sausage, ham, bacon and other meats. Also some cigarettes, hope they're your brand. Pencil and paper, too. Write what other things you might be needing. Guerney's betting a dollar and a quarter you're out of there inside of two weeks. No takers. Best to you.
>
> JACK MEEKER

Austin reached inside and found the promised pencil and paper. And he wrote a note that he would leave for Jack.

> Could use some detergent and margarine. Please keep a tally of what you're laying out. Are there any books on Minnawickies? I think I may have a nest of them. Thank you.
>
> AUSTIN FLETCHER

Placing note, pencil and paper back in his postbox, Austin turned again for his house. He passed the witch's tree and the sun went in and he walked a little faster. He walked another fifty yards, turned to look, and the tree was bending in a wind—though there was no wind where he was standing, and no sound of wind anywhere.

Walking more quickly, if that were possible, he passed the Devil's Dancing Rock—for that's what it was and he had might as well face it. And there was something new about it. In the snow, some words had been fingered. And before the words, and after—a star. And between the words, a slash. Like so:

ARA/FROOM

The sun was swarming all over the day when he reached his house. He clomped up the porch and in, carrying Jack Meeker's care package while balancing some additional food for thought.

9

Austin sat looking at his fire, the air in his house dry and motionless though the outside wind shook his interior beams and caused his stovepipes to sway like suspension bridges. The sun had left town at 4 P.M., not unusual for a Maine winter, when the days were often like long twilights and the nights dictated that all activity end by five.

He had stored his new meats, smoked four of his new cigarettes, had cleaned his guns, waxed his snowshoes, fed his fire and swept his floors. His house was providing him with the solitude he wanted, but the price he was paying for it was being calculated in boredom. He had been there but one day and the old urge to cut and run was rising in his blood. Emotion said, "Go." Logic countered with "Go where?" Pragmatism summed it all up with "Give it a shot. What do you have to lose?"

Maynard's books appeared as though they might offer some diversion. By lantern light they looked most inviting, like invaluable archives—the wisdom of great men, the knowledge of the ages. Ideas, opinions, visions, summations, the collected spawnings of the human mind. In short—nothing that he really cared to read.

The essays of Mencken, plays by Wilder and Morley, Gide and Camus, all of them packed solid like irregular bricks in a patchwork wall. Thackeray, Fielding, Stendahl—had Maynard actually read them? Gorky, Tolstoy, Joyce, Auden—touching shoulders in an array of intellect that had to flatter the old house. And a section on humor. Thurber, Perelman, Bill Mauldin, H. Allen Smith. And the complete works of Henry David Thoreau.

This last volume lay on a lectern, apparently having received much attention from Maynard. Austin opened it and found, just inside the front cover, a handwritten note:

> Maynard Whittier—1969. I come from little and figure
> to amount to less. But rather than disappear and leave no
> mark, I have tried to make myself a part of this house as
> others have done before me. Most of what I believe can
> be found here, in Thoreau, a man who knew there was
> more to living alone with nature than in the company of
> a near-sighted civilization. My own notes, for whatever
> they're worth, are in the smoke closet. I'm not sure they'll
> ever serve any great purpose, but they do pertain to this
> house and this area, and they now belong to whoever
> comes across them.

Austin stepped back from the lectern and wondered aloud.
"That's swell, Maynard, but where the hell's the smoke closet? *Better*
question might be, what the hell *is* a smoke closet?"

He was aware that he was talking to himself. He had done it
a few times that day and it concerned him, because he normally
adhered to the school of thought that believed that people who
talked to themselves were wacko. But with no one around to pass
such judgment on him, and with very few sounds abounding that
might serve to keep his eardrums in shape, and with the lingering
suspicion that if he didn't talk aloud he might just lose his power of
speech altogether, he had taken to talking to himself. Also, it made
him feel less alone, the sound of his own voice in an otherwise
soundless void coming as undeniable proof that he was there. It
was a self-deception, of course, and he knew it, but he needed that
crutch, at least in the beginning. When the time came that he could
throw it away and walk without it, he would do so.

It was late. So he banked his fire, said good night to himself,
and slid—a bit uneasily—into his second night's sleep in the first
house he'd ever owned.

It was a good night's sleep, deep and uninterrupted. Ten full
hours of it. And he awoke rejuvenated, his eyes and ears reporting
that morning had sprung with a clangor, another sortie of geese

pelting the sky with their wings, creasing the day with their honking. His squirrels were busy above, and some mice were roller-skating below. It was, all of it, such a sudden whir of noise that he was caused to leap from his bed and question where he was for a good five seconds.

Later, a mug of coffee in his hand, he gave serious effort to finding his smoke closet. "Smoke closet, smoke closet. Where would I be if I were a smoke closet?"

To the stove: "Are you a smoke closet, sir?"

To the cellar: "Hey—you happen to see a smoke closet around here?"

To the flue: "I'm looking for my smoke closet. If you happen to see it, let me know. Big reward."

But as he was sticking his head up the flue, he noticed how the chimney continued straight on through the low ceiling. It would emerge on the roof, to be sure, but to get there it would have to pass through the squinchy little attic he had seen on his first appraisal of the house. And, wedged into the ceiling, just to the left of where the chimney went through, he saw a wooden square about the same dimensions as those of his cellar's trapdoor.

He pulled up a chair, climbed upon it, pressed at the square, lifted it, balanced it on all ten fingers, raised it higher and flicked it aside. The attic was open to him.

He hauled himself up into the cramped crawl space, and 322 startled squirrels made for their emergency exits. "Douse the butts, fellas—fire inspector."

Two grease-caked windows, though facing south in the early day, provided him with enough light to see what he was doing. On all fours he poked about, keeping his head down because too many sharp beam studs were there to rake his scalp if he made one false move.

The chimney indeed went up and through. But enough of it, about three feet of it, was very much in the attic. And set into one of the brick-faced sides was a small iron door hung on batten hinges. "Smoke closet. Sonofabitch. How do you do?"

He lifted the latch and slowly, respectfully, coaxed the iron door open. "Come out, come out, wherever you are."

Nothing came out and so he peered in. It was much too dark for him to see what, if anything, was inside, so he reached in with his right arm. "Just call me Lefty."

A mouse catapulted out and took off, which could only mean that the smoke closet was not quite airtight, and that anything in it, papers or such, might well be little more than a pile of ashes.

Austin groped within and came up with something that had bulk. He drew it out. It was a looseleaf notebook, eight and a half by eleven inches, and some three inches thick. He bellied over to the windows and lay the book down and open. There were many pages, all of them in a clear script that Austin recognized as Maynard's handwriting. Maynard had utilized the book's inside front cover as an index page, and Austin's eye traveled it from top to bottom:

1. Uninhabitable areas
2. Great Northern Paper Company
3. Mount Katahdin
4. Baxter State National Park
5. Millinocket
6. Belden
7. The seasons of Maine
8. Summer equipment
9. Winter equipment
10. People of the area
11. Animals and wildlife
12. Firewood and materials
13. Tools, utensils & supplies
14. Natural forest woodpiles
15. Early thaw
16. Old stone walls
17. Foot stoves and bed warmers
18. Thieving animals
19. Burning trash & compost pile

20. Birdlife and bird calls
21. Indigenous Indians and campsites
22. Thoreau
23. Rivers, ponds & lakes
24. Bears
25. Minnawickies
26. Devil's Dancing Rock
27. Buttoning up for winter

Item 25 drew him back. "Minnawickies! You *know* it!" But almost as soon as his index finger struck that number on the page, he heard the laughter again. Outside somewhere. Drifting up at him like noisy smoke.

Peering through one of the grimy windows, he saw them, whizzing through his snow trenches—two small hurrying figures. Scampering and laughing and tumbling and chasing each other as in a fun house.

Austin rapped at the window. "Hey! Hey!"

The creatures seemed not to hear. Decked out in the gayest of colors, they moved swiftly, up and back, ricocheting off snow walls, surprised when they slammed into each other, bouncing away in opposite directions, laughing with each and every erratic step.

The sunlight splashing on the snow, combined with the smeary windowpane he was squinting through, made it impossible for Austin to evaluate the trespassers' true dimensions. He rapped again at the window, harder. And shouted again, louder. "Hey!"

The little figures froze—but only for a moment. Then they ran off, climbing out of the trenches, one going one way, the other another, all of the action viewed by Austin as if through greasy contact lenses. "Hey! Wait a minute! Hey!"

But they were not waiting, they were leaving, and Austin decided to give pursuit. He crawled back to the opening in the attic floor, dropped through, missed the chair, fell, cursed, picked himself up, and raced out of the house. Too late, too late. They were going, going, gone.

He stood there, hoping for a clue, a hint, another laugh, anything that he might pursue, for he was sure he could catch them, the little one at least. But, stymied as he was, he simply turned to walk back to his house—and they popped up anew, Jack-in-the-Box and Will-o'-the-Wisp, appearing and disappearing in one sweeping motion, poking up again, elsewhere, over another mound, multicolored and big-eyed, red and yellow and laughing.

He made another move at them, and they were gone. He gave chase but felt foolish, skidding and sliding more than he was running, coming close to nothing more than a blur of color or an image without substance—the kind a camera snaps when it has no film, allowing light through its lens but recording no picture. His Minnawickies were as visual echoes, and he knew that even if he were lucky enough to snare one, it would be but a reverberation of the slippery original.

There were only two of them, but they moved so mercurially that they could just as easily have been ten. On two occasions snowballs flew at him, but he was unable to fix on the direction. And always the odd laughter, coming from every which way, goading and gobbly, firing like Chinese firecrackers, exploding like sparklers.

It was apparent that he had involved himself in an impossible task, that the hunter was the hunted and the arrow the target. It was apparent, too, that he was out in the cold without parka or gloves or boots. He turned again for the house, the cackling laughter of his tormenters still playing in his ears. And he smiled, for whatever else they might be, his Minnawickies were not terrifying. They had done no damage, stolen no goods, smothered no fire. Perhaps the little finks had taken a liking to him—and wouldn't that be fine?

Nearing his house, he saw it again, in the snow, and not all that far from his porch:

ARA/FROOM

He reasoned that those were very likely their names, or some kind of Indian message like "Go with God" or "Three, mebbe four horses go by not too long ago."

He glanced back at the horizon and there they were, two bobbing bits of color, waving to him. He waved back and went into his house, feeling good. They had made him feel good and, in so doing, had more than made up for those grim provocateurs, the witch's tree and the Devil's Dancing Rock.

10

After a dinner constructed around some more of the meats that Jack Meeker's generosity had provided, Austin sat before his stove and checked out the Minnawickie section in Maynard's book. And it was as Maynard had told him in Nam, no surprises. The Minnawickies were small, elusive, playful and difficult to get a glimpse of, let alone catch. They were also reputed to be able to read the future. Most probably they were a branch of the Penobscot tribe, a common Algonquin stock that had all but vanished because of interbreeding with other Indian tribes of the area. What was not all that clear was whether or not the Minnawickies were real or legend. Maynard himself seemed to leave that open to interpretation, apparently possessing his own small streak of Minnawickie whimsy.

> Things are attributed to Minnawickies which contradict logic. Unless you see them for yourself, you are not likely to believe they exist at all. They don't reveal themselves to everyone, which is why people scoff. It is an individual matter, each of us to his own experiences and opinions…

"Thanks a lot, Maynard. You sure do have it nailed down." Austin poured himself another mug of cocoa and turned to Maynard's section on Thoreau, item 22.

> Thoreau sought to prove that man could escape a stifling civilization by embracing nature. Like Thoreau, I have all my winters and most of my summers free for clear study…and believe that "to maintain one's self in the wild is not a hardship but a joy…"

There was a knock on the door, and, startled, Austin tilted his cocoa mug, the contents spilling hot upon his thigh. He did not move beyond that, his eyes fastened on the door—which he had neglected to bolt. Outside, a fox barked and a raccoon whinnered, and over it all lay the spooky song of the hooting owl—all the sounds arriving at once, as if orchestrated by some grand design to heighten the moment.

Trained to react quickly to the untoward, Austin laid the book aside and reached for the .44 Smith and Wesson. The knocking came again, coinciding with Austin's realization that the .44 was not loaded. Calmly he reached for the ammo box—but too late. The door was opening, snow and wind the first things to leap into the house and rush for the corners.

And in the dim light, framed within the doorway, stood a man, dripping with raunchy furs all the way to his snowshoes. His fur hat appeared to be either molting or melting, coming down around both his ears and flowing into a wraparound muffler that had once been a fox. His gloves looked to be bear paws; a leather bag, bulging with whatever, was slung over one shoulder; and he was holding a rifle.

Gray-bearded and wizened, the man looked to be part Indian, part derelict and part mad, his eyes so dilated that the pupils appeared to be black. Austin judged his age to be somewhere between thirty-five and a hundred and fifty.

Seeing the .44 pointed at him, the man scratched his beard grubbily and placed his rifle against the wall, an indication that he intended no malice. Turning his back to Austin, he kicked off his snowshoes and tossed them out onto the porch. Closing the door, he turned again to face his host. Standing there, he said nothing.

"You're on," said Austin, still holding the .44.

The man removed his gloves, dug into his shirtfront and pulled out a chain that hung around his neck. It had a medallion on it which he held out for Austin to see, as if he were the F.B.I. and the medallion his proof of it. His voice matched his countenance, stolid and furry—John Wayne with a glean of Louis Armstrong. "Name's Benson."

Austin could see "M. Benson" engraved on the medallion. "That's a beginning," he said, keeping the .44 trained on Benson's belly.

"Be needin' foodstuffs," Benson said, stuffing the chain back into his shirtfront.

"Help yourself."

"I'm not fixin' on payin'."

"No charge."

"Obliged." Benson helped himself, casually plucking items from the shelves as if he were in the A&P and his pouch was his shopping cart.

"You seem to know where things are around here."

"Been here before."

"Really?"

"A-yuh."

"This house has been empty for some time."

"Has it?" Benson was dispassionate. Nothing would ever ruffle that man's furs.

"You just come by and help yourself?"

"A-yuh. Like *you're* doin'."

"I own this house."

"Good house. Sits good against the wintah."

"Think so?"

"A-yuh. Like a ship turned to the wind. It'll keep its balance." He opened a can of apple juice and drank it in two gulps.

Austin laid his .44 aside. "You're welcome to stay the night."

"Can't do that."

"Hey, it's the middle of the night out there."

"A-yuh."

"Well, where you goin'?"

"Trailin' a bear."

"A bear?"

"A-yuh. He's out there somewhere."

"You trail a bear at night?"

"No choice."

"Why?"

"Might've hit 'im."

Austin understood the significance of Benson's statement. Nearsighted as it was, a running bear could sprint for more than a hundred yards. And a wounded bear, pained and infuriated, could be an incalculable danger to anything it scented or sighted. "Should I be worried?"

"If I hit him, yes."

"If not?"

"Maybe."

"How'll I know if you hit him?"

"Be blood in the snow. Ya'll see it in the mawnin'."

"What about tonight?"

"Best ya close ya shutters. Bears don't understand windahs." And with that low-key directive, Benson reset his hat, put on his gloves, picked up his rifle, and stepped again into the night, pulling the door closed behind him and, like a good hunter, making no sound.

Austin considered things, but not for too long. Putting on boots and parka, he went outside and shuttered all his windows. He would have strung electrified barbed wire had he had it. He would even have dug a moat around the entire house.

Back inside, he had to think. Benson was gone. Almost as soon as he'd arrived he left. And Austin had to wonder if the old geezer had been there at all. The apple-juice can—that would be evidence. Austin searched for it but couldn't find it. Of course, Benson could have simply stuffed the empty into that copious leather bag of his where it would never be seen again. As to the other supplies the man had taken, Austin couldn't tell about those either. He had tons of stores and no inventory, no way in which to check, nothing signed for in triplicate, no supply sergeant to ride herd.

He let the matter go. He simply bolted the door, promising himself to do that every night from then on.

It was quiet again, and again he curled up with Maynard's book, first loading his shotgun and placing it within quick reach. It was comforting to read Maynard's words, written in Maynard's own hand. It was like having Maynard with him, as a guide and a buffer. He could almost hear Maynard's voice as he read, Maynard's accent and unmannered delivery, Maynard's presence.

"I have a lot of company in my house even though I don't always see 'em or hear 'em. Weasels squeeze through my stone walls lookin' for mice but takin' whatever they can find. And once I caught a beaver at my water barrel, that rascal lookin' to build himself a summah home at my expense. Family of rabbits I know are always into my beets and parsnips, and moles and shrews'll eat a man out of house and home without his ever knowin'.

Outside the night's another affair, not so humorous. I'm not fooled by the silence of the night. Wild animals never really rest. They're predatory by nature and, when food is scarce, it's not a good idea for a man to go strollin' or lookin' at the stars—'specially after eatin' and puttin' the smell of good cookin' on the wind. I think men are afraid of the dark for good reason..."

Austin shut the book and put it aside. "Thanks a lot, Maynard. You get me up here and then try to scare the crap outa me." He banked his fire. "Bears. Damned bears are supposed to hibernate, aren't they? In the winter? What the hell did I read all those *National Geographics* for if bears don't hibernate? Sheeeet." He loaded *all* his guns. "Next thing comes through that door is goin' to get it—all barrels. You just tell 'em that, Maynard. You just pass the word. Pow-bam! Everythin' I got."

He was half fooling, of course, smiling even as he raged. It was fun to let off steam, and see the humor while comprehending the danger. And yet, if he *was* half fooling, it followed, then, that he was also half serious. Actually, if he were to truly allot the percentages, he was one-third fooling and two-thirds serious.

There was something about his house, something in it and something outside it, in the walls and in the night, something that was beginning to get to him. But whatever it was, he wanted it to know that he would not be run off, that he was digging in his heels, positioning his weapons and making his stand. Bears, witches, Minnawickies and the lot—fuck 'em all. The next thing through his door, or down his chimney, or up from his cellar, be it animal, mineral, vegetable, plastic or nylon, was going to get it. Pow-bam! Everything he had.

It was a bad night for him, sleep coming only in short rations, fatigue pursuing him like an ever-gaining specter. He thought he had left all that behind in Nam, but apparently he hadn't. Being in Nam had given him a knee-jerk reaction to things off kilter. And his knee was jerking.

11

In the morning, of course, what with the birds chirping and the little animals whisking about, things looked decidedly brighter. And with the day perky and the sky a shade of blue rarely seen except on kids' wallpaper, Austin stepped out onto his porch, stretching and yawning, and balancing his coffee mug in the crisp cold.

He unshuttered his windows, which lit up his house, and, in pajamas, boots and parka, he moved onto the path that would lead him to his backhouse, for he had some business there.

Twenty yards along the path and he saw it. In the snow. Spatters of it and blotches of it. A pint of it, a quart of it. Blood. As red as a valentine heart. So fresh that it was still melting its way into the snow. He did not have a moment's thinking time beyond that—for the huge shadow was blotting out all the pretty daylight. And the heat of the bear, and the guttural roar of it, and the fishy breath of it were upon him, as if the shadow had a weight that equaled its width.

Austin ran, making for the only refuge the horizon afforded him—the backhouse. And the bear pursued, making the path a little wider than it had been before. And Austin knew that, had he dug the trench properly, two feet wide instead of one, the race would have been over before it had started.

As it was, the issue was still in doubt, the man having to run almost crabwise through the narrow ditch, while the bear had to contend with the divots and slides its lumbering body was creating.

It was a clumsy race, perhaps even laughable to an observer. But if the bear was running for his breakfast, the man was running for his life. And what with fear being a stronger propellant than appetite, Austin got to the backhouse first.

In one motion he pulled the door open, raced inside and pulled the door shut. And he stood there, his back against the door, waiting for the crush that had to come. He didn't have to wait long—perhaps three horrific, silence-filled seconds—and the bear arrived, roaring and steaming, slamming against the backhouse door as if he didn't see it there. And the door flew from its hinges, this time in one piece because, when Austin had rebuilt it, he had reinforced it with horizontals and nailed on diagonals for good measure.

It all collapsed on him, making for a strange sandwich—Austin on the bottom, his head ridiculously close to the one-holer; then the unfettered door, lying across his back like a floor; and then the bear, bellowing and bleeding and slathering in frustration.

The torn-off door was all that kept the bear from getting at Austin, while the backhouse walls had all they could do to not fly out centrifugally like an exploding artichoke.

Austin knew that the jig was about up, the full weight of the thrashing bear pressing him flatter and more insistently to the hard ground, his ribs beginning to bend the wrong way, his lungs unable to draw in new air. In a last effort to live, he tucked his knees to his chin and put his back to the task of catapulting the bear from the door. It didn't work, not that he thought it would. But at least he had tried.

He collapsed under it all, like a grape under a truck wheel, his body fluids pushing out of every orifice, his breathing coming harder and more frantically, like an accordion under a rock slide—a helluva way to die.

It was one shot, that's all, piercing the sounds of his own gurgled breathing—and he felt the bear go slack and become immediate dead weight.

"Ya all right?" It was Benson's voice, flat and disinterested.

"Jesus Christ…" Austin turned sideways, freeing his diaphragm enough to pull in air for speech. "Yes."

"Take but a coupla minutes."

Austin couldn't answer, choosing to conserve what breath he had for breathing. But he thought to himself, "My father always said

I'd end up in the shit house."

Benson worked quickly, for he had no way of knowing the extent of Austin's injuries—time, therefore, being an element not to be squandered. With an ax or a sledge, Austin couldn't determine which, the hunter knocked down one of the backhouse's side walls. Then, using part of that wall as a lever, and because he was both strong and intent, he lifted the bear-laden door from Austin's back, just enough so that Austin could roll out from under.

It was the sweetest breath of air that he ever drew; sweeter even than the breath he took after staying underwater fifteen seconds longer than Tom McGee, winning both the seventy-five-cent bet and the admiration of half of Cincinnati. Sweeter, too, than coming up and out of that long French kiss with Amelia Battersby, America's sweetheart, Ohio branch.

He looked up at the fur-strewn Benson, that man appearing as hirsute as the bear he had just dispatched, and just as loquacious.

"I'll assume ya all right unless ya tell me otherwise."

Austin was surprised at how quickly and how well he was able to speak. "I'm all right, you stupid sonofabitch bastard."

"Good."

"Isn't a hunter supposed to make *sure* an animal is dead?"

"A-yuh."

"—and not let it walk around all...pissed-off?"

"A-yuh."

"Well?"

"I made sure."

"Yeah. This *morning.* I'm talking about last *night.*"

"I'm talkin' about this *mawnin'.*"

Later, as Benson squatted alongside the bear, skinning it most dispassionately, Austin was once again repairing his backhouse, hammering it all together while grumbling unhappily. "A man's got to find better things to do with his time than to keep knockin' the door off his shit house."

"Man should know if he's afoot or ahorseback."

"And what is *that* cutesy-folksy saying supposed to mean?"

"Means maybe ya don't belong out here." Benson's hands were blood-drenched, the bear suddenly looking like a sorrowful thing, deserving of a better fate.

"I'll tell you something. I don't belong *anywhere*. People been tellin' me that my whole life. My mother told me. My father told me. My school told me. The entire U.S. Army and all of Vietnam told me. So I don't *need you* to tell me."

"I'm the only one around."

"You want to tell me something? Tell me something original, like I'm a prince among men, or a credit to my race. But don't tell me I don't belong. It's this *place* don't belong. *Maine* don't belong. Why don't you secede it from the Union? We'll let ya."

Benson, unimpressed, let it all sail by. "Bearskin's mine. But I'll leave ya most of the meat, if ya like."

"No, I don't like. Take it with you. You killed it, you eat it. Make yourself a hero sandwich." Distracted by his own wit, Austin hammered his finger. "Goddammit!" And he hurled the hammer over a hill. "I don't need this!"

"Hurt ya fingah?"

"No. What makes you say *that?*"

"Ya yelled."

"I yelled because I *love* it. I do it all the time. Every chance I get I hit my finger with a hammer."

"Ya got nine more chances."

"Jesus…"

"If it bleeds it'll clot real fast. Cold'll do that."

"It's not bleeding. I hate to disappoint you, but it's not bleeding. It's mashed flat, but it's not bleeding."

"Best ya burn the carcass if ya not goin' to eat it. Unless ya care to freeze it."

"I don't care to freeze the carcass. I'm freezing my *own* carcass—I don't have to freeze a bear's."

"Then ya best burn it. Leave it out here it'll attract all sorts of things. Timber wolves been seen here on occasion."

"If I see a wolf, I'll build my house of brick. And he can huff and puff…" Austin smiled at his upcoming bon mot. "Jesus Christ, I'll have built myself a brick shit house." He shouted it to the countryside. "A brick shit house!" The words echoed three times over the hills and Austin added to them. *"There's* something to laugh at, you Minnawickies!"

"Havin trouble with Minnawickies?"

"Me? Naaaaah."

"I think ya havin' trouble with Minnawickies."

"Wrong. I don't *believe* in Minnawickies."

"Then why ya callin' to 'em?"

"To hand you a laugh."

"I ain't laughin'."

"Do you *ever* laugh?"

"Nope."

"Then what's your point?"

"Don't have any. What's yours?"

Austin said it quietly, defeatedly. "Nobody seems to know."

After awhile, the backhouse in one piece again if leaning slightly toward England, Austin headed home, sarcastic in his farewell to Benson. "A-yuh. Ump. Grump. I don't know how you people understand one another. Everythin's a goddamn abbreviation, or a gurgle, or a burp."

Benson didn't look up. "Want me to burn the bear?"

"I wouldn't care if you *waltzed* with it."

"Little late for that."

"It's not even noon."

"Closer to one."

"Benson?"

"A-yuh?"

"Goodbye." Austin returned to his house, mumbling and grumbling.

Benson skinned the bear, rolled and bound the hide and slung it over his shoulder, stuck some choice slices of meat into his leather bag and stayed on long enough to burn the rest of it. Then he stepped into the woods, looking like a bear himself.

Watching from his porch, Austin had to admit to a certain admiration for the man, surviving out there on his own, unflustered by danger, just taking each day as it came, each meal, each breath. The only thing that Austin could do that Benson could do was grow a beard. He started immediately. It wasn't nearly enough, but it was a beginning.

12

The next few days trundled by unremarkably. He read a great deal, Thoreau and Whittier (Maynard, not John Greenleaf). Some snow fell, halfheartedly. The deer came by again. At least it looked like the same one, and Austin gave it another packet of crackers—from a distance. Geese continued to honk overhead, convincing Austin that they were either stupid or lost, because weren't they supposed to have migrated south by now?

He saw a bobcat when he was cutting more ice from the lake, and the damned thing scared him to jumping. But he also scared the bobcat, so it was a tie, each of them walking away from the other with one eye looking back. Partridge came out in the morning and took off as soon as the smoke shimmered more heavily from his stovepipe's chimney. And curious woodchucks looked him over at his shed, fascinated by his wood-chopping technique. The whole forest was radiantly alive wherever he looked, earth and sky, valley and hill, all of it abounding with activity that he was more and more able to define and enjoy.

And on a sudden warm day, the land caressed by a breeze curling out of the south, his roof began to drip and steam in an unwinterly sunshine. Trees made cracking noises. Hidden rivers bobbed out for a look see. Green grass popped up. And the ice in his gutters melted and ran. All of it was over in a day, ending with another wind, a colder one, blowing out of Canada as it was supposed to do, freezing fresh mud and refreezing old snow—winter reasserting itself, summer's one day being nothing but a lucky punch that the old man had quickly recovered from. All of it was thoroughly described in item 15 of Maynard's book as "early thaw."

It was time for a trek to the postbox, to see what he could see. Perhaps there'd be something there from Jack Meeker, or a family of field mice happy in their new quonset hut. As to any letters, he wasn't expecting any. First, because no one knew where he was. And second, because he never got any mail, not even in Cincinnati, the only thing he ever received there being his draft notice—and that hardly qualified as friendly correspondence.

There was indeed another package from Jack Meeker, the attached note reading:

> Margarine you asked for, and laundry detergent. Plus some other things you might be needing. Also, couple magazines donated by Alan Walter, dentist in Millinocket. Been in his waiting room for awhile but not so's you'd notice. No books on Minnawickies, but worst they'll do is burn down your backhouse. Try not to rile them. They don't bribe and they don't scare. Best to you.
>
> JACK MEEKER

Austin examined his treasure trove and left his own note for Jack Meeker.

> Thank you for the supplies and the 1953 *Life* Magazines. I could use some powdered milk and coffee. Please keep a record of what I owe you.
>
> Thank you,
>
> AUSTIN FLETCHER
>
> P.S. I don't need any help from Minnawickies in destroying my backhouse, as I have been doing it myself.

He placed his note in the postbox and started back for his house. Walking, sloshing, mushing—he was much better on snowshoes than he ever thought he'd be. Actually, he was much more at home in his new environment than he had ever dreamed he'd be. Even his beard made him look indigenous. And, not to be dismissed lightly, no new scares had occurred. No chairs, bears or Minnawickies to rattle his imagination or camp in his unconscious.

All of that quickly changed when he saw, in the snow, not five feet from his house:

ARA/FROOM

It didn't unsettle him, for the truth was, he had missed his little confrontations with his Minnawickies and was delighted to discover that they had not grown bored with him.

He called out to the echoing mountains, "Hello, Minnawickies! Where've you been? Why don't you come up and see me sometime?" There was no answer, of course, but Austin was certain that they were out there and that they'd heard him.

Later, at his woodshed, while chopping at a length of stubborn oak, he was struck squarely in the back with a snowball. He smiled, for he had been half expecting it and rather looking forward to it. But he didn't react to it. He didn't miss a stroke. He was too crafty for that.

Another snowball came. And another. Both of them splatting softly against the back of his neck, much of them trickling icily past his collar and into his shirt. And still he did not turn, for he was getting a fix on just where the salvoes were being launched from and had to play possum a little while longer, damn the torpedoes.

He absorbed three more hits before dropping his ax and tearing off swiftly in the direction of the enemy's emplacements, running a quick and straight course down the trench a dozen strides, then vaulting up and over the side, where he caught the pair of them so frozen in surprise that they had no chance to execute their usual laughing withdrawal.

They yowled and scratched and clawed, one of them breaking away. But Austin had the other, a furry thing no more than four feet tall and with an outsized head. It squealed and squirmed as Austin pinned it to the snow and sat on it, straddling its chest, holding down its arms. Its face was red, with a green nose, large yellow eyes and a wide blue mouth.

The second Minnawickie regrouped and attacked, flying from out of nowhere to land roughly on Austin, squarely between the shoulders. Larger than its companion, it knocked Austin flat into another sandwich—a Minnawickie sandwich, one above him, one below.

They were slippery and they were sly, but did not pack all that much weight that they could prevail over Austin. They were combative and determined, but Austin was more of both, so that, after much blurring of color and flying of snow, and screeching and eeling and punching and pulling, Austin had them both, a knee on each of their chests, a strong hand on each of their outside shoulders.

He looked down into their furry faces and they weren't faces at all. They were woolen ski masks with deliberately exaggerated features and comically pointed tops. And they were not Indians. They were kids. Two small kids, and it didn't take Austin all that long to figure it out. "Looks like I've got me a couple of desperate Minnawickies."

Sitting astride them, he pulled the tight ski mask from the face of the smaller one, causing its eyes to go Oriental and its hair to stand on end as if in fear. It was a boy—perhaps eleven years old. Upon being unmasked, it immediately proceeded to spit a mouthful of snow into Austin's face. Austin retaliated by rubbing snow all over the youngster's face. "Tit for tat, Charlie."

Austin then turned his attention to the larger Minnawickie, pulling off its mask, and it was a girl—some sixteen years of age and starkly pretty, with pale-rose skin and rich black hair, and velvet-lashed eyes the color of shined pewter. She too had her cheeks puffed with snow and was ready to fire, but Austin discouraged her. "I wouldn't."

Thinking better of it, she swallowed the snow, her face falling back into its natural set, the finely etched chin and the well-defined lips looking briefly to be more the features of a woman than a child.

Austin was struck foolish by her beauty and felt momentarily lascivious at being on top of her, for hers was a woman's body as well as a child's, and he was a man as well as a victor. None of it was made easier for him by the unblinking grey eyes looking up at him, seeming to tell him tales of another time and place, yet telling him nothing.

"Now, then," he said, "which of you is Ara and which of you is Froom?"

"I'm Ara," said the girl, a distinct touch of Maine to her clear voice, her eyes never leaving Austin's.

Austin turned to the boy. "And you're—"

The boy spat new snow into Austin's face, evidently having kept enough of it in reserve for just such a sneak attack.

"He's Froom," said Ara.

Austin rubbed snow into Froom's face all over again, more than enough to make the point that he was not to be trifled with. "Okay? Now—I'll let you both up, okay? But only if you promise not to run away. Okay? Do I have your word?"

Ara and Froom both nodded yes, and Austin let them up, Froom immediately scrambling to his feet and taking off to a safe distance, from where he razzed Austin and resumed throwing snowballs.

Ara felt compelled to explain to Austin. "A Minnawickie never keeps his word."

"You kept yours."

"I'm a lousy Minnawickie." She didn't smile, though she had the tools for it, a fine mouth, and teeth to shame the snow. Nor would she often smile or confess to being funny, or allow as to how humor had any place in her arsenal. She would, instead, hide behind her eyes, as if knowing that they were power enough to dominate any conversation.

Austin held her arm dopily. "Well, you're my prisoner."

"Don't care."

"And tell Nutsy to cut it out with the snowballs or I'll have to torture you."

She called to Froom. "Nutsy, cut it out with the snowballs or he'll have to torture me!"

Froom stopped launching snowballs but continued to jump about and generally reveal his displeasure via indistinguishable epithets.

Austin tried to smile at Ara, but it came out goony and he knew it and felt stupid. "Come back to my house and I'll make us some cocoa. If you're afraid—" he let go of her arm— "you can go."

"I'm not afraid."

"My name is Austin."

"I know."

"You do?"

"A-yuh. Read all ya mail."

"I don't get any mail."

"Ya get packages."

He smiled and took her hand again, and, gloved as it was, a sweet electricity passed from her hand to his. "Tell Nutsy he can have some cocoa, too."

"Nutsy! Ya can have some cocoa, too!"

By way of answering, Froom hopped, cursed, razzed and spit.

"Says he don't want any." She smiled, a sneaky one, working only the left side of her face, closing her left eye to a wink, creating left-sided dimples and left-sided friendship—the right side of her face remaining stern and unmalleable. Again the quick contradiction. Half woman, half child, half funning, half judging.

"Is that Minnawickie he's talking?"

"Nope. That's profanity."

They walked back to his house. He held her hand and she let him. And he tingled at the strange excitement of her. She was his first friend in his new environment, his first visitor come-a-calling. And his house, warm and embracing, seemed pleased to receive her.

She removed her bulky jacket and shook her black hair, and she was pretty in that fledgling teenage way. In her blue sweater she was lean, her breasts barely assertive. And in her Levis she was endearing, her legs stretching north to that immaculate face and south to a pair of boots that, though clunky, seemed winged.

She smoothed her long hair, both hands working left and then right to part it perfectly in the middle. And it flowed past her shoulders, picking up along the way all the light that the humble house could muster.

He was an oaf when he fed the fire, tripping twice on a floor that he should have known better. And in pretending that it hadn't happened he caused it to happen again. Lout, clod and bumpkin—

he had become all three at once.

"Ya boots too big," she said, sitting Indian style on the floor in a corner, her legs crossed, her hands playing her hair as if it were a lyre. "Or else ya just clumsy."

He smiled at her, but she didn't smile back. She just sat there, casually pretty, haughtily unaware of her effect on him, and he was passingly reminded of all those Ohio high-school girls who used to taunt him similarly with their cruel disinterest. What a fool he was, he thought. For here was a girl and a pretty one, all to himself, and he could do nothing more than trip and fumble and smile like a buffoon. Had he been alone too long? Where was his poise? Whatever would become of him? Questions better unasked—the answers so heartlessly obvious.

He prepared the cocoa, setting the kettle to boil on his stove. And he lowered his voice when speaking, hoping to somehow reestablish his worldliness. "Get comfortable. Take your boots off."

"Ain't stayin' that long."

And all the air went out of his balloon. Through the window he could see Froom, on a mound, jumping about and carrying on, stomping angrily, shaking his fist at the house.

"He's Froomin," she said.

"Pardon?"

"That's what he's doin'. Froomin'."

"Is there such a word?"

"A-yuh. Since he started."

"Is he your brother?"

"That's what I'm told."

He poured a mug of cocoa for each of them. "Here you go."

"Obliged."

"Careful. It's hot."

"It's not."

He was losing ground terribly fast, the earth sliding out from under him. But he was still trying. "You live around here?"

"A-yuh."

"Reason I ask—I haven't seen any houses."

"Live up near the dam. My father's with the Great Northern."

"Oh. I guess just about everybody is."

"Not everybody."

"Who's not?"

"Those that ain't."

"Hmmmm. Isn't the dam pretty far from here?"

"Dam far," she said, almost smiling. "That's a joke."

"I know."

"We do it by sled."

"Dogsled?"

"Regular sled, dummy."

"Oh."

"Me and Froom, we haul it up a hill, then coast down. Cuts the time." She sipped at her cocoa, her eyes looking over the rim of the mug into his, knocking him silly.

"Do you...a...go to school?"

"Who wants to know?"

"I guess *I* do."

"I go."

"High school?"

"A-yuh."

"What year are you in?"

"Junior."

"What's your favorite subject?"

"Don't know."

"And how long've you been a Minnawickie?"

"Couple years. Wintahs, mostly. Summahs there's more to do."

"And 'Ara'—that's not your real name, is it?"

"Nope."

"Will you tell me your real name?"

"Who wants to know?"

"*I* do."

"Can't tell ya my real name."

"Why?"

"Can only tell ya my Minnawickie name. Promised Froom."

"I told you *my* name."

"Didn't ask ya to."

"What's the big deal of not tellin' me your name?"

"What's the big deal of ya havin' to *know?*"

"A-yuh. Ump. Grump. Even the kids talk that way."

"A-yuh. Ump. Grump."

He was running out of chitchat and finishing well out of the money in his banter with the gray-eyed girl. "Isn't there *anything* you'd like to ask me?"

"Nope. Ump. Grump."

"Did you know Maynard?"

"A-yuh. A little."

"What does that mean—'a little'?"

"Means not a lot." She was standing and slipping into her jacket. "Have to go. Have to be back before dark. My father's a bad man to rile."

"Will you come by again?"

She thought about it for a moment, looking at him sidewise, just the flicker of a smile feathering across her face. "Might."

"Well, if you do, you can come right up to the house. You don't have to seek out and destroy."

"Minnawickies prefer sneakin' up. Otherwise makes no sense in bein' a Minnawickie."

He accepted her logic. "Whatever turns you on."

"What?"

"Whatever *pleases* you."

She was at the door. "I'll be goin' now."

"Well, I hope you'll come by again."

"*Said* I would."

"No. You said you *might.*"

"Meant I would." About to go, she turned to him, the words coming most importantly. "Have to tell ya."

"What?"

"Cocoa's too sweet."

"I'll work on it."

"Best ya do. Teeth'll fall out."

"A-yuh."

"Whatever turns ya on."

And she left, airily, Austin beginning to sense the strange nonform of her. Blunt, offbeat, funny and guileless, she was childlike yet staggeringly seductive, driving through his defenses so quickly and effortlessly that he had to wonder whatever became of the grizzled combat veteran he had been when last he looked.

Rejoining her brother, she turned and waved, whereas Froom thumbed his nose and kicked snow. Austin watched from his porch as the pair of them hauled their sled to the top of the nearest hill. They climbed on and disappeared down the far slope, mufflers flying like the flags of a sinking ship.

"Outa sight," he muttered to himself. "A-yuh. Ump. Grump."

13

Some days passed and she had yet to return, though he never once doubted that she would. In the void between, he was sinking his roots more emphatically into his new habitat. Things that had at first startled him no longer did, for they came with a predictability that he was fast becoming accustomed to. The squirrels in his attic, the partridge in the snow, the deer on his porch, all of them doing things almost by the clock. During the day he cut and stacked wood, caulked holes, oiled hinges and learned to read the snow prints that his animals left nightly—checking them against the prints Maynard had so painstakingly drawn in his book, happily learning that his land hosted red fox, raccoons, bobcats and porcupines, as well as such exotic creatures as the Canadian white-footed mouse, the Labrador jumping mouse, the almost extinct coyote and, he had to face it, the black bear, which, more than all the others, had to be respected and/ or avoided.

Following Maynard's written instructions, he burned his trash early, well before the peace-shattering morning wind would arrive to breathe up mischief. And, even though it was winter, Maynard's notes advised him that it was not a bad idea to feed the compost heap with pea pods, potato parings, corn husks and even cigarette butts.

At bedtime, again following the book, he fed his stove dry pine for kindling, adding to it some chunkwood—oak or elm, choked with unsplittable knots. By morning his room would be summer warm, glowing coals snoozing at the stove's bottom, the whole affair so incendiary that just putting an armful of any wood on top of them would give him a fire that was quick, prudent and toasty.

He learned to identify his trees: maples laced with squirrel scratchings, birches scarred with the deeper cuts of raccoons. Itinerant woodpeckers had worked on all of them, cherry and hickory in particular. And reconnoitering beavers had nibbled away at fallen beech limbs, marking them for future use as a dam or a cabin or a toothpick.

In his postbox he found, on two consecutive days, some most welcome packages from Jack Meeker, the accompanying notes being both amusing and reassuring.

As to his nights, he apportioned the time they afforded him to short trips through Maynard's notes and magnificent hikes through Thoreau's pages, the latter writing that "for more than five years I have maintained myself thus, solely by the labor of my hands, and I found, that by working about six weeks in a year, I could meet all the expenses of living. The whole of my winters, as well as most of my summers, I had free and clear for study."

Austin was beginning to understand Maynard's fascination with Thoreau. There was an eternality to that man's writings, a oneness with nature that stunned time and laid low mortality. Austin could slide very easily into such a life style, for it seemed to bestow upon man, any man, a singular satisfaction in being any man.

On a particularly bright day, the sun so blinding that he could not go out into the reflecting snow without his dark glasses, he decided to try his luck at fishing. He cleared a spot on the pond, cut a hole in the ice, and pulled up a log to sit on. Then he dropped his line and waited with the serene patience of an old fisherman.

It was two hours later, with nary a minnow nudging his line and the cold creeping into every one of his knuckles and joints, that he decided that he didn't like fish all that much. He stood up slowly, fearing that any too-sudden move might snap his frozen spine like a twig—and he saw it, a burst of color on the top of a hill, a sled with two vivid passengers, snowplowing deliberately down the steep decline so as not to build up too much steam and go flying out of control.

The sled shushed to a stop some thirty yards from him, Ara stepping off lightly, Froom rolling off exaggeratedly, as though shot or skewered. But where Froom recovered enough from his invisible wounds to stay with the sled as a guard, Ara came directly to where Austin was standing trying to coax his spine back to life by pressing his fists into his kidneys while bending his body backward into a banana.

Again, the girl was so pretty that he feared he would be unable to speak. The fact that she wasn't smiling didn't help matters. It intimidated him, making him feel stupid and uncertain. There was no way in which he could voice a greeting, and so he just waved, a frozen paw in an uncrackable glove. And even in that he was clumsy, the motion causing him to slip slightly on the ice, though he didn't think she saw.

She brushed past him and he could feel the heat of her right through his clothing. She peered down into the fishing hole, her thick lashes looking as though they could reach into the water as deeply as his line, if they wished, and catch all the fish they wanted, if they chose.

"Trouble is, when ya cut a hole like that, draws muskrats."

"Oh?"

"They see what ya doin' and take all the fish the light attracts."

"But I've seen Eskimos fish like this."

"You an Eskimo?"

"Close to it."

"What ya have to do is let the muskrats take their share."

"Swell. I've been here over two hours."

"Muskrats been here all wintah."

"Jesus. Is everybody in Maine a philosopher?"

"Only hunters and fishermen. And everyone's either a hunter or a fisherman."

"Is that a joke?"

"Nope."

"Come on. I've been working on my cocoa. It's not as sweet anymore."

"Have to get back."

"But you just got here."

"Nope. Been here all my life." She turned, walked back to Froom, and the pair of them were soon out of sight on the back slope of a hill.

Austin felt immediately denied. He had waited for her, for a year it seemed—and she was gone, over the hill with her brother. It was very unfulfilling. But, over the three days that followed, with pride and logic as his companions, he saw his disappointment turn into mere annoyance. Who the hell was she anyway but a snippy little girl who, if you took her out of Maine, wouldn't know Kentucky from Dubuque or Stan Laurel from Oliver Twist?

All of that self-hypnosis melted into farina when, on his fourth day without the sight of her, her sled finally flowed over the hill and into his heart. Froom stayed with the sled, against his nasty will, but Ara allowed as to how she did indeed have time for a mug of cocoa—and she went with Austin, to his house, where he conjured up a pitcher of the stuff and waited for her opinion.

For the longest time she said nothing, just sat there crosslegged, rolling the cocoa around in her mouth as if she were in Paris and all of France hung on her evaluation of that year's wine.

"Well?" he ventured. "How is it?"

"Not sure."

"Come on, it's been over five minutes."

"Don't want to come to a conclusion too soon. Wouldn't be fair."

"It loses its flavor as it cools."

"Who says?"

"You get one more sip. That's all. That's as far as I go." She took the one sip, contemplated it in a most superior manner, and said, "Passable."

"Still not right?"

"Not *hot*."

"Oh, for—" He took the mug from her. "Well, what'd you expect? I'll put it back on."

"Best ya do."

He smiled without her seeing. He was being bested, but he

rather liked it. The girl was formidable. She had style. It was fun. He poured her cocoa back into the kettle because there wasn't enough left to pour her a fresh mug. And he turned to her, mucho adult. "So—you're in high school."

"Barely."

"Not long to go?"

"Grades keep up as they do, not long at all."

"Having trouble in school?"

"No trouble *in* school. Trouble *gettin'* there."

"Is it that far?"

"Nope. I plain don't like it."

"You mean you don't go because you don't *like* it?"

"I mean, I go a *little* because I don't like it *much*."

"Ara—you're funny."

"Think so?"

"Funny or weird, yes."

"I don't think it's funny or weird to not like school."

"Rather do something else?"

"Rather do *anythin'* else. Cocoa's boilin'."

"Jesus Christ!" The cocoa was boiling and bubbling and spilling over. He had to use a glove to remove the kettle from the stove.

Ara was superior. "Now it'll be too hot. Make it too hot, kills the flavah."

He set the kettle on the floor, where it calmed noticeably, though brown streams ran down its sides and caked upon fusing with the cold floorboards. He was not thrilled and became short with her. "Does *anybody* make cocoa the way you like it?"

"Nope."

"Marvelous." He was cleaning up, on his hands and knees like a charwoman.

"But that's because I really don't *like* cocoa."

"Jesus Christ."

"Hardly ever drink it."

"Thanks a lot."

"Don't drink it at *all*."

"I'm hip."

"Cocoa was *your* idea, not mine. I'd just as soon have tea."

"Well, I don't have any tea, so there you go."

"Minnawickies prefer tea. Didn't ya know that?"

"No. I'm new around here." He had cleaned up as best he could, though he suspected there'd be a burn mark in the floor where he'd set the kettle down.

"Minnawickies prefer tea. Penobscots like coffee. Passamaquoddies prefer cocoa. Wabanaki like milk. Abanaki'll drink anythin'."

"I'll try to remember."

"Best ya do."

It suddenly occurred to him to ask. "You're not a *real* Indian, are you?"

"I'm a Minnawickie."

"Isn't a Minnawickie an Indian?"

"A Minnawickie's a Minnawickie."

"Ara—"

"Ya asked and I answered. Best I could."

"Let me put it this way: Can you stay a Minnawickie all your life?"

"Don't know. Haven't really tried."

"Can I assume you're not interested in this cocoa?"

"Any left?"

"A little."

"I'm not interested."

"I wish you'd of told me. Could've saved me a lot of trouble."

"Ya never asked."

"You know something? You could drive somebody crazy."

"I been told."

"Well, you're being told again."

"Nothin' new."

"It's new to *me*."

"Minnawickies know the future."

"Pardon?"

"Minnawickies can foretell."

"You mean predict the future."

"That's what I just said, dummy."

"*Can you?*"

"*Older* Minnawickies. I can only sense it."

"Do you want me to believe that?"

"Don't care."

"Then why'd you mention it?"

"Thought it might interest ya." She shrugged, what the hell. If he didn't care, she didn't care.

The whole conversation had taken a strange turn, and even though she seemed ready to drop it he felt compelled to pursue it, especially since she was the one who had digressed in the first place. "It does interest me."

"Well…" She was sulking.

"Did you know this was once a witch's house?"

"I been told."

"Did you know that's a witch's tree out there—and a Devil's Dancing Rock?"

"It's what they say."

"Who?"

"People. Folks."

"Do you think there's a witch in this house?"

"No way of knowin' from just appearances. Guess ya have to wait and see."

"Wait and see what?"

"Don't know. Imagine ya *will* know when it happens."

"When what happens?"

"It."

"Ara, what do you mean by 'it'?"

She looked away. "Don't really know if anythin's goin' to happen. Have to ask an older Minnawickie. Fire's gettin' low."

He stoked the fire and tossed in a few additional logs. The flames danced anew and he kept worrying it with the poker. It gave him time to decide whether or not he wanted to probe more deeply into what she might know. Something told him to drop it right there, for even though his face was not a foot from the stove there was no heat playing on it. Rather, it was as if a cold breeze was coming out at him. He closed the stove door to deflect the icy draft, and he turned back to Ara, who wasn't where she had been a moment before. She was at the door, holding her jacket.

He went to her and took her jacket from her hand, gently but emphatically, letting her know that the dialogue had not quite ended, that the audience she had granted him was not quite over. "When Maynard was killed, this house became mine."

The gray eyes came up at his. "A-yuh."

"He said he left his dogs with a couple of kids. Is that you and Froom?"

"A-yuh. But they run off."

"Sometimes I think I hear them."

"They run off a long time ago."

"I still think I hear them."

"They couldn't live in the wild. Ya hearin' wolves. Maybe fox."

"I think they're dogs."

"Could be. But not likely."

"What were their names?"

"Hither and Thither. And that's where they went." Again the quick smile, just one side of her face—the other side stoical, almost mocking. "Can I go now?"

He wasn't ready to let her go. Nor was he all that sure she wanted to go. She had volunteered information and then backed off—why? She was a girl with a mug of cocoa one minute, and a woman with some loosely guarded secret the next. She was tweaking his nose with half-data, scattering breadcrumbs for him to follow, only to double back and pick them up—why? "The man who told me this was a witch's house was Jack Meeker. Do you know him?"

"A-yuh. Stationmaster at Belden."

"He didn't just sense it, he knew it. Does that make him a Minnawickie?"

"Don't much matter. Mr. Meeker's dead."

He went along with it. "Yeah, well, I *thought* he was lookin' a little peaked."

"He's dead."

"Must've been real sudden. I saw him less than two weeks ago. And he leaves packages in my postbox—which you peek at. Must've happened—like *that*."

"Day before yesterday. Whole Belden depot burnt down."

He looked at her, standing in half-shadow like the half-creature she was, her eyes two straight lines carrying their gray light into and beyond his own. And he felt disrupted. "Listen, I have to tell you. I'm not a big fan of the Maine sense of humor. You all seem to get a big charge out of puttin' on strangers. Between you and your brother, and that hilarious Benson the bear-burner, I got an act goin' up here that's funnier than the Marx Brothers. Only I'm the only audience—and I ain't laughin'."

"Mr. Benson's dead, too."

"And *that's* the funniest thing you've said so far."

"Tweren't funny. Bear got 'im."

"Serves him right. Sonofabitch was a lousy shot. Couldn't kill a bear unless it was in a backhouse."

She was neither frightened nor upset by his nose-out-of-joint attitude. "We don't have much experience with strangers up here. People don't usually *come* here—they just *leave*. So maybe we find *you* a little strange, too."

"Well, I may seem strange, but I don't go around tellin' people that other people are dead when they're alive."

"Ya told me *Maynard* was dead."

"He *is* dead."

"Don't see no tombstone."

"There was no next of kin to ship his body to, so he was buried in Vietnam."

"Were ya there when they buried him?"

"No, I was somewhere up the line, getting my ass shot at!"

"Then how do ya know he's buried?"

"Because I was there when he got *killed!*"

"Not what I asked ya."

"Listen—Maynard is dead and Jack Meeker is not. And as for

Benson, I don't much give a damn!"

"Then why ya so angry?"

"Ara—"

"And usin' bad language? I was just givin' ya the news. Ya don't want to believe it, that's okay."

"Ara, I'm not angry. I'm just tired of listening to stories and making stupid cocoa. As to my language, I'm sorry. Besides, if that's your idea of bad language—"

Something hit the side of the house. And Austin, off balance and preconditioned by combat, grabbed her, pushed her into a corner and reached for his rifle.

She was calm. "It's Froom. He's snowballin' ya house. He wants to go home. So do I."

Austin ventured a look through the window. It was Froom, all right, lobbing snowballs at the house as if they were grenades, pulling imaginary pins and counting before releasing them, a barrage of them.

Ara was in her jacket and by the door. "Sometimes I tell stories, but most of the time I don't. Thanks for the stupid cocoa."

She left, linking up with Froom at the sled. The sun was setting prematurely, loosing lavender shafts every which way from behind the only cloud to appear in the sky that day. Austin watched them haul their sled up a hill, where they disappeared within the folds of a peach-purple light.

His gaze then went to the snow just beyond his porch. There was a shadow even though there couldn't have been, all light that could cause a shadow having gone over the hill with the sled. Yet there it was—and it was of the witch's tree, lead-gray upon the lavender snow, even though the tree itself was three hills and a quarter of a mile away.

Austin didn't care for it, not for any of it. He shuttered his windows, and went back into his house to where his fire had died despite the fact that it had been burning brightly five minutes prior. Reaching into the stove, he found the charred wood to be days cold to the touch, and the house a hundred years that way.

14

Inside the house the fire was roaring and the coffee was on, Austin having rekindled the one and reboiled the other, while outside, the in-and-out yelping of dogs pockmarked the otherwise noiseless and curiously windless night.

Austin was not yet willing to accept Ara's opinion that the barking was being done by wolves or foxes. He knew a dog when he heard one—and those were dogs out there. How many, he couldn't be certain of. Two for sure. Still, if he was right, and if they were truly Maynard's dogs, why weren't they sniffing right up to the house in search of their master? The answer: they were wolves or foxes.

On the other hand, since it was far more comforting to believe that they were dogs and not wolves or foxes, that was what he did. They were dogs. And that was all the thinking that he cared to devote to the issue.

He sat at his table, Maynard's book before him, propped up between two kerosene lamps that tossed haphazard light every which way but up the chimney. And, as had been the case for the last few nights, as he read Maynard's words he heard Maynard's voice. It was a phenomenon of Austin's own creation, and he indulged in it for all the right reasons. It was as though he were recreating Maynard, bringing him back to life, at least for those moments when he sat down to learn from his friend's writings.

And even though the words were set on the page quite grammatically, with proper punctuation and without slangy contradictions, they didn't pass into Austin's brain that way. For they weren't so much going through his eyes as through his ears, in Maynard's own curious manner of speech, inflections, mispronunciations, folksiness et al. And despite the fact that the night was pressing darkly in on him from all sides, even the house seeming to lose its interior dimensions, Austin was neither alone nor apprehensive—for, as Maynard used to say whenever they were confronted with a sticky military situation. "Have no fear, Maynard's here."

"Life is frittered away in just doin' details. What ya have to do is drive it into a corner, like ya do with a fox. And ya got to keep it there, and break it, and make it do what ya want it to. Some men go out to take on life directly, like on a battlefield. I think that's wrong. Least it's not the way I see it. The way I see it, life should be dealt with from a base. Like a house."

Austin spoke to the book. "Yeah, I figured you'd say somethin' like that."

"A house is a place to go back to, to regroup in. A house is a kind of a special corner of the universe. It's a place where everyone whoever lived in it still does."

"What you're sayin', Maynard, is what I know. I got a lot of company here."

"That's the nature of a house. It absorbs its occupants, kind of keepin' them forever alive."

"Well, that's just swell, Maynard. That's just—"

"In particular, that applies to those who loved that house without reservation and stuck with it through whatever tests and obstacles arose."

Austin's heart came close to stopping, for those last words, coming in Maynard's voice, were nowhere on the page, the written diary ending with the words "keeping them forever alive."

Austin closed the book and pushed it away, almost off the table. "Maynard, I got to tell you—I think you left your house to the wrong boy. And I'll tell you something else, I'm beginning to lose that rich sense of humor of mine that I was never noted for in the first place."

He was tired. More tired than he had at first realized. He was drag-assed tired, fall-down tired, dead tired. That, added to the unsettling things Ara had told him earlier—about Jack Meeker and Benson—was causing his mind to function like a badly run motel. Room numbers were either missing or upside down. Telephone receivers were off their hooks, and no one was at the switchboard. Specters, arriving with no advance notice, signed in with invisible ink and checked out with no forwarding addresses. Sudden clouds, unsponsored shadows, suggestive noises and intimidating silences were the only permanent guests, and they skulked about the corridors with all the attendant freedom such privileged phantoms were invariably afforded.

A good night's sleep, followed by a good day's sunshine, would scatter those oppressors, but Austin wasn't sure he was in line for either. On balance, in this house, there were more positives than negatives, more reasons for running than for digging in. The dogs, the tree, the book, the fucking hoot owl—all the incipient terrors he was sparring with were laying siege to his sanity.

If it were Nam it would be time for rest and rehabilitation. But it wasn't Nam. And there wasn't any respite—or any chaplain to take his troubles to, or buddies to hoist a beer with. It was wilderness Maine and he was more alone and unruddered in it than if he were wandering wounded behind Charlie's lines.

He had a beer anyway. Dutch Courage. It was warm, because he couldn't keep it on ice without having it freeze. Even stored in his root cellar it never approached the cool temperature it was supposed to have on being consumed. But it did its job, loosening the bolts in his head, calming the furor in his chest.

He went to bed, allowing two kerosene lamps in his other room to burn. They would be as twin beacons against anything that hid from light. And if the light failed he had his artillery and his cutlery, guns and knives to take up against things that flourished in shadow.

Sleep fluttered in, vague and spastic in its getting there, but it did arrive. And if it did not blanket him thoroughly, it did provide him with enough cover to drift off under. In the beginning of it, and at irregular moments, his eyes would open, involuntarily, as if programmed to check the lamps in the other room, to see if they were still there, on the alert. They were. Not as small lighthouses but, rather, as ship's searchlights, semaphoring some message at him across the floor.

Actually, the lamps were bright and unerringly steady, the semaphoring flicker taking place only in his head, caused by Austin himself, by the erratic blinking of his eyes. But in his haze he could not know that, and, tired as he was, he worked at deciphering that message, for he knew his Morse Code. And it came across the room at him—Thoreau, though he had never read it—"To be awake is to be alive."

In the morning he would forget all of it—but the night was not yet over. And somewhere in the darkest, iciest low part of it, when even owls and loons were prompted to noiselessness out of either fear or respect, he slipped deeper into sleep, as deep into it as a man could go without losing all chance of coming back. Still, even in the pit of it, he could hear and identify the sound. The rocker, creaking.

It was possible to sleep. Even though the jungle grab-bagged a thousand ways in which a man could die, if that man was tired, so tired that "Frankly, Scarlett, I don't give a damn," sleep would come. Fear could delay it somewhat. Awareness could deflect it. Youth and strength could ward it off to a degree—but it would come. As sure as God made little eyelids.

Austin was asleep, the ground, damp and acrid, making a fine enough mattress, the trees, thick as flared umbrellas, switching off the light of the moon.

It had been a piss-poor patrol—they usually were—Charlie in his black pajamas using the night to slither about in as naturally as if he were one of the nightscape's true nocturnals. Still, Austin slept well because Maynard was on guard.

They worked as a team, everyone did—one man awake, the other asleep. That far away from base it made more sense to wait until daylight than to keep pushing on. Yes, they'd be written off as missing, because they had no radio, but it wouldn't be the first time. Nor would they be the first patrol to have operated in such a manner. It was accepted procedure, though no manual ever prescribed it. They would straggle in in the morning, make their report, the C.O. would put a line through "Missing," and they'd all get something to eat.

Austin heard the creaking rocker in his sleep and sat straight up. He picked Maynard out in the night and smiled at him. "I think you spent too much time alone in this house, Maynard. And now you've got me doing it."

"Shhhh. Keep ya voice down, Austin. Ya don't have to advertise our presence." Maynard was sitting against a tree, as were four of the others in his ten-man patrol, all of them fanned out like the points of a star, each of them covering the jungle from a different direction. "Ya supposed to be asleep, anyway. Ya want to stay up, Austin, ya can stand my watch."

"If I'd of thought ten minutes before comin' here—but no, there I was, runnin' through the snow like a drunken rabbit."

"I'm not sure ya cut out for this world, Austin. A man has got to know what he's doin' before he sets out doin' it. I mean, ya got to be careful ya don't commit to somethin' too soon and then find yaself outflanked." Maynard's voice dropped and hushed. "There's somethin' out there, ya know."

"I know."

"I don't know quite what it is..."

"Maynard, did you ever check out the people who lived in your house before you did?"

"I said, 'There's somethin' out there.'"

"I heard, and I agreed."

Maynard coiled and waited another moment, his head cocked, his ear focused. Then he eased. "It's gone."

"Good."

"But it'll be back, so stay ready. Now what'd ya ask me, Austin?"

"I asked if you ever checked out the people who lived in your house before you did."

"Well, I tried to, but the records were gone. All I had was this pine plank on the wall where some of 'em wrote what was on their minds."

"Didn't it seem to you they were just a little leery of this house?"

"Some of 'em."

"Most of 'em."

"I love that house, Austin. That's why, if I don't come out of this ruckus alive—that's why I want to leave it to someone I can count on. That's why

I'm leavin' it to you in my will."

"Why me? I'm unreliable—not likely to stay in one place too long. I'm the last guy in the world for the job."

"I think ya perfect for the job."

"Yeah?"

"Wouldn't leave my house to anyone else."

"What about Ara and Froom?"

"There it is again. Wonder what that is. Keep ya voice down, Austin."

"That Ara—she'd have me believe Jack Meeker's dead."

"Shhhhh."

"Claims to be a Minnawickie. Did you put that idea in her mind, Maynard?"

"It's some kind of light. Two of 'em. Close together. Somethin's out there, all right. Makin' some kind of signal. Wait a minute...It's gone."

"Do you think Jack Meeker's dead?"

"What?"

"Do you think Jack Meeker's dead?"

"I think people die only because they accept it. I think Thoreau said it best when he said—"

"Listen, fuck Thoreau, okay?"

"—'Time is but a stream I go fishin' in. I see the sandy bottom and detect how shallow it is.'"

"I said, 'fuck Thoreau,' Maynard. He's beginning to bore the crap outa me."

"There it is again. Those lights. Flickerin'. Can ya make it out?"

"And your witch's tree. What about your witch's tree?"

"'There are a thousand hacking at the branches of evil to one who is striking at the root...'"

"And your goddamn rocking chair! Tell me about that chair, Maynard! I mean—I can hear it! I can hear it right now!"

"'...I have three chairs in my house. One for solitude, two for friendship, three for society...'"

"Don't you hear it?"

"'...I hear beyond the range of sound, I see beyond the range of sight, new earths and skies and seas abound, and in my day the sun doth pale

his light…'"

"Jesus, Maynard! You keep it up and I'm goin' to stuff that book right up your escape hatch!"

"Austin, ya gotta pull yaself together or ya ain't gonna make it."

Austin was sitting upright in his bed. The kerosene lamps had gone out and the rocker had stopped creaking. Absolute silence ruled. It was his only companion in the aberrated night. His bed was drenched with jungle sweat, his hands so morbidly clammy that when he touched them to his eyes and forehead, to chase the demons, he was revulsed by them. Maynard, wherever he was, was right—he would have to pull himself together if he was going to make it.

What nagged at him most was that he had no true reason for *trying* to make it. No one would miss him if he stayed, and no one would miss him if he left. It was his usual condition—he could do whatever he damned please, and the world would go right on turning. And yet he felt very important. Very important indeed. He didn't know why. He only knew that if he were to leave he'd *never* know.

And so he sat there, in his bed, ridiculously singing the lyric from an old Jimmy Durante song—"Did you ever have the feeling that you wanted to go; did you ever have the feeling that you wanted to stay…"

He had no idea what he was going to do. Even the next day was up for grabs. He was playing Hamlet in snowshoes. He was unfamiliar with the script. And he had never been a critic's darling. So what else was new?

15

The next morning Ara returned, looking too pretty to classify as mortal. Austin was fishing, or trying to fish, when she stepped between him and the sun, her shadow preceding her voice, causing him to almost drop his line in the quick blackness.

"Didn't mean to startle ya." She was smiling mischievously, for she did indeed mean to startle him.

And Austin knew it. "Oh, didn't you?"

"Didn't."

"Okay."

"Catch anythin'?"

"Yeah. Pneumonia."

"I had pneumonia once. Came close to dyin'."

"How do you know you didn't?"

"Nobody buried me."

"Where's your stupid brother?"

"Other side of the hill."

"I miss his snowballs."

"Ya won't for long. That's what he's doin'. Makin' 'em. Think ya got a bite there."

Austin looked and his line was jiggling. "Sonofagun!"

"Careful. Don't want to lose 'im."

Austin played the fish deftly. It fought hard, and for a moment he worried that the hole he'd chopped in the ice was not wide enough to haul his huge catch through. That fear vanished when he reeled in a small trout that couldn't have weighed a pound and wouldn't have fed a cat.

"What a whopper, Austin."

"Think so?"

"A-yuh. Biggest sardine I ever saw."

"Actually, it's a small whale."

"Goin' to mount it?"

"I don't think I've got a wall big enough."

"In that case, best ya throw it back."

"Give it its freedom."

"A-yuh."

"Only if you come back to the house with me."

"Only if ya don't make me drink cocoa."

"Deal."

He dropped the trout back into the lake, and he and Ara started back for his house, the day deliciously new around them. She had that ability—to turn the day on. It had been goofing off until she got there, moving this way and that, indolently, no pattern to its flow, no special requests of cloud or wind. But with her arrival it snapped to. Sounds were sharper, the crack of old twigs beneath their feet, their own breath laying into the air like dragon steam. Sights were more vivid, rabbits quicker, treetops greener, mountains higher. Even the sun switched over to a higher-intensity bulb, illuminating the horizon, setting fire to the snowline.

Again she allowed him to hold her hand. And again his blood responded by rushing to an immediate boil. He hoped that she was unaware of the effect she was having on him, but her sidelong glances told him that she knew. He wondered if he was affecting her similarly. If he was, he was courting big trouble, for she was far too young. It would be far more moral of him to throw her back, like the trout, and not mount her.

They came to the Devil's Dancing Rock. "You know what that is, don't you?" he asked.

"A-yuh."

"Devil's Dancing Rock."

"A-yuh."

"You danced on it."

"Who says?"

"You danced on it. You and Froom. I saw your prints in the snow."

"Who says?"

"And you left your names."

"Just to tell ya we were hereabouts."

"You didn't dance on that rock?"

"Bad luck to."

"Even for a Minnawickie?"

"Anyone dancin' on it's supposed to be in league with the Devil."

"Who says?"

"People. Folks."

"Then why'd you dance on it?"

She smiled. "'Cause I felt like it."

"Feel like doin' it again?"

She thought for a moment, looking first at the rock, and then at the sky, and then at Austin. "A-yuh."

"Then do it."

"Ya not to laugh."

"I won't laugh. I'll accompany you by whistling. What kind of music do you need?"

"None. Music's inside."

She stepped up onto the rock and danced. At first it looked to be the kind of dancing any kid might do. The frug, or the monkey— he couldn't be sure, because he wasn't up on that kind of thing. But whatever it was it soon slipped into something else, something distinctly serpentine and latently sexual, her arms curling about in the air, her fingers, even in their mittens, dancing singly and in sequence like miniature synchronized divers, beckoning to him no matter which way the rest of her turned. And all the while her eyes looked elsewhere, as if he weren't there at all.

She pulled off her hat and tossed it aside, and her black hair blew free, trailing her face like a comet's tail. And when she turned her head, quickly, in an opposite direction, her hair whipped on, veiling her features just below her eyes, making her appear as someone Eastern, foreign and headily forbidden.

Her hips and thighs, swathed in ski pants as they were, knew no bounds. Even her feet in those clumsy boots took to the slick rock as if belonging to a mountain goat. Every part of her moved independently and on its own, yet the sum total of her was of a choreography that would have goggled Terpsichore. She was seductive and endearing, swept up in a music that only she could hear—and Austin went all dismantled because little girls didn't dance that way.

Then, turning to him for the first time in her dance, her gray eyes filled his and he was pinned like a butterfly in a display case. Her hands, stretched toward him, were there for the taking, all ten fingers making come-hither bumps in the mittens. He filled his hands with hers and she drew him up onto the rock beside her.

"There'll be the Devil to pay," she said, not waiting for his response, leading him about on the rock instead, dancing him to a music he only faintly began to hear—church bells and strings, too distant to comprehend.

He held her hands and she spun him as in a child's game. Faster and faster the music folded about him, until he was as wrapped up in it as a papoose—until he was no longer moving of his own volition but of hers, his feet no longer feeling the rock beneath them, his eyes no longer seeing anything but her eyes, everything beyond being unfocused and ill-defined.

She laughed and he did likewise. She changed direction and he changed with her, the pair of them seeming to turn on the same axis, blown by the same breeze, provoked into the same laughter on the same musical scale, hers an octave higher, his a heartbeat faster. And cell for cell, blood for blood, he felt himself going into her, swallowed up by her.

A salvo of snowballs ended the devil-dancing. It came in silently, looping at them from over a hill—the infamous Froom unleashing another of his perfidious attacks.

Still laughing and still holding his hand, Ara led him out of range and on again toward the house, stopping only to rescue her hat, which hung playfully on a bush. Single file through the trench they ran, Froom racing alongside them but through the higher snow, which slowed him perceptibly. When last seen he was up to his knees in it, throwing snowballs and cursing rancorously, falling on his face in it while lobbing his last snow grenade, which fell pitifully short.

Breathless from running and laughing, Ara and Austin swept into the house and bolted the door. They laughed for minutes, holding on to each other, her hair forest sweet and soft on his cheek. She was remarkable, so much the changeling that it would not have surprised him if she sprouted wings and took to the beams.

He cupped his hand to her chin, raising the dear face to his, sighting it for a kiss. But the eyes looking up at him were so filled with cold and withering hate that the kiss never came to pass.

It lasted for but a moment, that look, but all the same it struck with the thin rage of a stiletto, inflicting no wound yet inferring a bloodless and incredulous death. He stepped back from her, three steps, before sagging into a chair, his breath coming hard, as if someone else were breathing for him and none too well.

She looked at him, as pretty again as she had been prior to demolishing him with her eyes. "What's the matter, Austin?"

"Nothing."

"Run too much for ya?"

"No."

"Ya got heart trouble or somethin'?"

"No."

"Want me to make ya some stupid cocoa?"

"No."

"Well, ya don't look too good."

"Why'd you look at me that way?"

"What way?"

"Come on, Ara."

"I didn't look at ya any way."

"I was going to kiss you."

"Ya were?"

"And you knew it."

"Didn't."

"And you looked at me like you wished I was dead."

"Didn't."

"Why?"

"Didn't."

"Who are you?"

She turned petulant and put on her hat, pulling it hard down over her ears as if preparing to go out into a blizzard. "Never goin' to dance with ya again if that's the way ya goin' to behave."

"Ara—"

"And who said ya could kiss me?"

"Ara—"

"Good thing ya didn't. I'd of bit ya nose off." She was leaving, had the door open and was halfway out when she turned to look at him, no humor in her voice. "I thought we were friends."

"We are."

"If I want to be kissed, I'll let ya know."

"Okay."

"And ya don't go doin' anything on ya own, if ya value ya nose." It was a smile that she tossed at him, fickle and Giaconda-like, but it was a smile. She was still funnin' him and he was still set off balance by it. And when she had gone, and was on the sled with her brother, coasting down a hill and laughing out of sight, he was still sitting there, in abject disarray, knowing that something was very wrong, but not knowing what.

He didn't like it. He was not in charge. Something else was gradually asserting itself, coming on the scene to call the tune and pull the strings. Something calculating and chilling, and he wanted to go home. And that was what the trouble was—he had no home other than the one he was in.

16

The night passed, Austin becoming accustomed to the amorphous haunts that populated it. His house, for some time, had been schizoid. By day it was as bright and inviting as a house could be—a Christmas card, a Robert Frost poem. But by night it was Edgar Allan Poe and Nathaniel Hawthorne, a foreboding thing of shapeless terrors and casual shadows, a cold place where no lantern lasted the night and no fire emanated any warmth. And none of the predatory beasts he knew to be outside came close to matching the fear he had of the apparitions he knew to be inside his house and his mind.

But it was morning, and after firing up his stove and drawing up some water for coffee, he glanced through his window and saw her, not ten yards from the porch, feeding his private deer. And the animal was eating right from her hand. Austin was amazed at how it allowed her to pat its muzzle and stroke its thin flanks. And when she no longer had food for it, the deer still would not leave, staying close by her side, as if on a short leash. She could have climbed up on it and it would not have objected. She could have ridden it to Londontown and back, whipping it all the way, and it would have been grateful.

Austin opened his door, silently, he thought, but the deer bolted and ran off in terror, leaving Ara facing the house, hands on hips in a gesture of no small disapproval.

"Scared him off, ya did."

"I didn't mean to."

"He don't know that."

"How'd you do that?"

"Do what?"

"Get him to eat out of your hand."

"It's a power I have."

"You have a power?"

"A-yuh."

"What kind of power?"

"Raisin power."

"Raisin power."

"A-yuh. He likes raisins. That's what I fed him. Always keep a pocketful, just in case."

"Do all deer like raisins?"

"*He* does."

"Then you've fed him before."

"A-yuh."

"Here?"

"Everywhere?"

"You're losing me."

"That was Brownie."

"Who?"

"Everybody feeds Brownie. He wanders all over, and everybody feeds him. He'll eat right out of ya hand if ya don't let on ya nervous. 'Course, if ya not pure of soul, he'll have nothin' to do with ya. And, judgin' from the way he run off, I'd say ya soul was in trouble."

"Come on in."

"No kissin'."

"No kissin', I promise."

She breezed past him, entering the house and going directly to the stove where the coffee simmered, and she poured herself a mug.

"I thought Minnawickies preferred tea," he said, baiting her playfully.

"They do."

"That's coffee."

"A-yuh."

"It's not tea."

"I can tell," she said, sipping it.

"Then how come you're drinkin' it?"

"I ain't drinkin' it." And she put it aside. "It's as bad as your cocoa."

"How come you always knock things?"

"Things that deserve knockin' get knocked." She took her jacket off and laid it aside.

"You're always knocking things."

"When it's called for."

"Anything else in here you care to knock?"

"Probably."

"Look around. Help yourself."

Austin sat down and watched as she moved through his house like an appraiser. She touched things, moved furniture, straightened one of his bearskin rugs. When she got to the trapdoor she studied it a shade too long before nudging the iron ring with her boot.

"Root cellar?" she asked.

"Yes."

"Right in the middle of ya floor."

"Square in the middle." It seemed to him to not deserve all that attention. What could be down there that was so important? "Care to see it?"

"Seen it."

"You have?"

"A-yuh. Seen one, seen 'em all." She moved on, checking the guns, the implements, the firewood—she didn't walk three steps without stopping to examine something. The utensils, the pump, the stove, the dry sink.

"Hey, I'm not plannin' on sellin' the place."

"Good," she said, looking at herself disinterestedly in the mirror. "No one'll buy it."

"Maynard bought it."

"A-yuh. He bought it."

Her comment required no comment from him. Maynard had indeed bought it. He bought it in Maine—and he bought it in Nam. Still, she was so certain of the ground she was on, so cocksure of all that she said, that he wanted very much to take her down a peg.

"What you just said—it was in very bad taste."

"Truth often is." She was looking up the chimney flue, checking his windows, studying his shirts, boots, towels, snow-shoes.

And he suddenly didn't like her. She was changing again, shucking identities—little girl sliding into bitchy broad. And she could do it just like that, without missing a beat. "Why don't you sit down and relax? You're making me nervous." There was an edge to his voice that surprised even himself.

And she sat down, contrarily, crosslegged in a corner, her usual Indian fashion, her hands in her hair again, straightening, fussing, an edge to *her* voice, too. "Found somethin' else to knock."

"Yeah, I figured you would."

"Care to hear?"

"No."

"Okay."

"I care to hear."

"Ya firewood."

"What about it?"

"Some is good. Some ain't. Some so full of dirt—it's why ya fire keeps goin' out."

"Who told you my fire keeps goin' out?"

"Nobody had to. More dirt in ya stove than ashes."

"I didn't see you look in my stove."

"Don't mean I didn't. Also, ya should mix ya wood. Not always use the same kind. Makes a better fire."

"I'll keep it in mind."

"I got a poem on wood. Care to hear?"

"A poem? On wood?"

"A-yuh. Care to hear?"

"Yes. I'd like very much to hear a poem on wood." He was being sarcastic.

And so was she. "Whatever turns ya on." She stood, walked to the center of the room, faced him, curtsied, and delivered her poem with all the innocence of a girl in grade school.

"Beech wood fires are bright and clear
If the logs are kept a year.
Chestnut's only good, they say,
If for long it's laid away.
Birch and fir logs burn too fast,
Blaze up bright and do not last.
It is by the Irish said
Hawthorn bakes the sweetest bread.
Elm wood burns like a churchyard mold;
E'en the very flames are cold.
Poplar gives a bitter smoke,
Fills your eyes and makes you choke.
Apple wood will scent your room
With an incense like perfume.
Oaken logs, if dry and old,
Keep away the winter cold.
But ash wood wet and ash wood dry,
A king shall warm his slippers by."

She curtsied and returned to her corner, where she sat again, crosslegged, reinserting her fingers into her hair, twirling a lock thoughtlessly, all as if she'd never gotten up in the first place.

Austin didn't quite know what to say. "That was very nice. Very educational."

"I know others, but I'm not goin' to recite 'em for ya."

"Why not?"

"Because we don't like each other anymore."

"I still like you."

"Ya don't, but it's all the same to me. I got better things to do than waste my poems." She stood up, slipped into her jacket and prepared to go.

He was at the door, blocking her way. "You're always leaving."

"Person can't leave more'n she arrives. Ain't mathematical."

"I'd like you to stay."

"Says who?"

"Says me."

She was squarely in front of him, her face not a foot away, her eyes softer than he had ever seen them. He had never been a ladies' man, not in the sense that he'd logged all that much experience with them. But he knew when a girl wanted to be kissed. And so he kissed her and she bit his nose.

"Jesus Christ!"

"Told ya I would." And she was gone. Out the door and into the lightly freckled snow, never looking back, going twenty or so haughty yards down the length of one of his trenches before climbing out to where Froom was waiting, though Austin couldn't see him.

His nose didn't hurt, not nearly as much as his ego, the bite she'd inflicted on it being the kind an affectionate puppy in a rowdy moment might bestow upon someone it liked. If she had really wanted to hurt him, she most certainly could have. It was a love bite, Austin reasoned. As such, unless he was completely out of his mind, it carried with it a definite invitation to try again.

He felt idiotic and enlightened and destroyed—and he loved it. His equilibrium was upset, his sanity threatened, his wagon fixed— and he loved it. He was holed up in the frozen silence of dead- center Maine, scared to shivering every night, his house filled with witches and goblins, his head filled with far worse than that—and he loved it. Funny what a bite on the nose by a pretty girl could do.

Later, having completed his morning chores, which included knocking the dirt from his firewood and sweeping a ton of it out the door, he headed out to his postbox to see what goodies, if any, Jack Meeker might have left there at some time during the last few days. Though Ara had shaken him with her flat pronouncement of the big man's death, he didn't really believe her because, by her own admission, Minnawickies were known to lie. And, if it turned out that Jack *had* left some foodstuffs in the postbox, meat in particular, it wouldn't be a bad idea to get there ahead of Brer Bear or Brer Wolf or Brer Benson, because that man, if still alive, could very easily shoot the postbox full of holes, killing the salami within and selling its pelt to some firewater-soaked Comanches.

He was feeling good, the bite on his nose coming almost as an injection of toe-tapping vitamin B. He knew that he was susceptible to Ara's charms, fair game for the gray-eyed huntress, if for no other reason than that she was the only game in town. Still, he had never been an itinerant tail-chaser. Any girl able to raise his hackles had to have something more going for her than merely being the only target in his sight. It had always been that way with him. He had always been discerning and particular, choosing the company of just himself over the debatable attractiveness of some handy lady. Even in Nam, where the females toppled like fir trees in lumber country, he had never been interested. No—Ara was different. Ara was worth his attention and his yearning. Even in crowded Cincinnati or steaming Saigon she'd have been a standout. The only thing she wasn't that he wished she was—was older.

He thought he was shot. He never heard it. It simply came out of nowhere to strike him squarely in the heart. It splatted, broke into powder, dusted his boots and lay there—the residue of another insidious Froom-ball.

Austin kicked it off and looked ahead, in the direction the missile had come from. And there he was, the Minnawickie kid himself, standing astride the crest of a small hill, hands on hips and a curse on his lips. Austin resumed his walk, heading toward the boy because that was the direction in which he originally had been going.

Froom loosed another snowball at Austin, and while it was still in the air, and before it had even reached the height of its parabola, the boy loosed still another snowball, the second one more of a line drive, calculated to strike its target quickly while its intended victim was looking skyward at the first one.

It was a fine strategy and it might have worked had Austin not been so combat-wise. He sidestepped the line drive and ducked the Texas Leaguer, and continued to advance on the Philistine.

Froom jumped and swore and dropped back to where he had a cache of snowballs piled like small cannonballs in the town square. He fired them all at Austin, but Austin kept coming, dodging most, undismayed by the few that did strike, because they were not life threatening.

Froom dropped back farther to where he had stockpiled yet another pyramid of snowballs. These too he fired at Austin, who continued to advance, fascinated at the boy's tactics, wondering why he was doing it and where it would stop, sensing that he was being sucked into an ambush but walking into it anyway.

The contest continued for three more stockpiles, and when it finally did stop it was only because there were no more stockpiles. That was it. Froom had used up all of his snowballs, perhaps a hundred of them, and that was all he had. He was plumb out of ammunition.

Austin had been hit perhaps fifteen times, none of the hits of a disabling nature, and still he had no idea as to why Froom was so determined to egg him on—over that small hill, into those few birches.

The boy was reduced to running large circles around Austin, like Indians circling a dug-in wagon train. Only this wagon train wasn't dug in, it was moving on, and not even the last desperate tosses of the tiring attacker were going to deter it.

On more than one occasion Froom darted in close enough for Austin to have grabbed him. But where, in the beginning, Austin would have been delighted to get his hands on the mad Minnawickie, he was by then far more interested in discovering just what it was that Froom was so intent on drawing him into.

And so, with Froom sprawled on the snow, his energy and his ammunition spent, nothing coming from him but a few rasping epithets that the wind stole long before Austin could be offended, the way was clear for Austin to see what he could see.

He walked up and over the small rise, down the other side, and on to the sparse birches that stood motionless until he reached them; after which they whipped and bent in a fresh-boiled wind, as if trying to hit at him as he passed. They creaked and groaned, and whistled and stabbed, sending dead twigs flying and deader leaves dancing—and whatever birds there were roosting in them at the time, they all took to flight as if flushed by hounds and harried by hunters.

Austin picked his way carefully between the snapping trees, ducking the grasping limbs whenever they swept down at him. He bobbed and weaved like a boxer and sidestepped like a halfback, but was unable to avoid all of the cutting edges—for they came at him without design, and no amount of anticipation on his part could enable him to predict just when they would strike.

He had walked through those birches before, for they were only slightly off the path to his postbox, and never once had they behaved in so unruly a manner. Rather, they had been a picturesque bunch, black, white and gray in their markings, more evocative of Currier and Ives than of such dark doings as they were then involved in. He emerged on the other side of them pretty much unscathed, except for the one long scratch that had drawn blood from his left cheek.

At first glance he saw nothing there, save a few trees and bushes, a few rises and falls. It was the same open expanse that led circuitously to the road, featuring the same small path that Austin had stamped out in it, for there had been no appreciable snowfall since the last time he walked it.

He looked again, shielding his eyes from the late-day glare with both hands, searching the horizon from left to right, like a maximum-security prison guard. And there *was* something out there, something pressed against the lowering sun and therefore silhouetted to his eyes. It had a shape that was of human dimension, and something about it was fluttering on the wind, flapping and billowing like the wings of some prehistoric bird.

A scarecrow, he thought. But why in winter? And how without his knowledge, since it hadn't been there before? And who? And when? The only question that brought an immediate answer was "Where?" There. Out there perhaps a hundred yards across the level snow. And he continued toward it, wondering how it was that he never had a gun when he needed it.

And with each step he took the wind built further, the birches behind him giving up *all* their old leaves, every dead one, shooting them at him, climbing them up his back, against his neck, the loud rustle of their last fury filling his ears like a necklacing explosion.

But he was not frightened and he was not deterred, for it was his land, his snow. The wind too, that was his. And the dead leaves shouting, those too. And the red sun setting. And the hard snow packing beneath his boots as he kept walking toward whatever it was out there. And the cold spearing up through his boot soles, and the strangled sound of his own breathing. And then the witch, its cape flapping, its laughter demonic. And its coal-black eyes and toothless maw, and hooked nose, and tall peaked hat, and frazzled broom—that too was his, and it froze his heart close to stopping.

And as he raised his hand to ward it off, making a noise that he had no sense of and could never identify as his own, she jumped out from behind it. Ara. And, as if to announce her appearance as the culmination of her trick, she thrust out her upturned palm at him while singing, "*Ta-da!*"

He sagged and almost fell, so close to dying on the spot that all his muscles went soft, all his bones going to wet spaghetti.

"What's the matter with ya, Austin?"

He could only look at her.

"Can't take a joke?"

The power of speech had not yet returned to him.

"Shame ya can't take a joke. Me and Froom worked all afternoon on it."

Froom appeared from between the birches, dancing and laughing and generally having himself a bang-up good time, falling all over himself in thigh-slapping hysteria.

"It's a snow witch, Austin," said Ara. "Guess it really scared ya. Found this old blanket, and I made this old hat. Eyes are coal. Teeth too, what there are of 'em. Broom I found. Sure ya not havin' a heart attack or somethin'? Ya get somethin' like appendicitis out here, ya can forget it. Ya just blow up and burst. Austin?"

"Yes?"

"Ya okay?"

"Sure. Why shouldn't I be?"

"Ya face is cut."

"It is?"

She studied him more closely, her voice more sympathetic. "I guess we really scared ya. I'm really sorry, Austin."

"It's okay. You didn't scare me."

"Did."

"Didn't."

"Well, did or didn't, I guess maybe it wasn't such a hot idea." She came even closer, touching his cheek. And he had an image of the cut healing and disappearing on contact. "It's okay," she whispered. "Just a branch bite. Birches'll do that if a wind kicks at 'em." She looked deep into his eyes and said the next words innocently, as one might say "Nice day" or "Let's have lunch." "Ya can kiss me if ya like."

"You goin' to bite my nose?"

"Nope."

He kissed her and it was fine. No arms, no bodies pressing. Just mouths, just lips. His still cold with shock and fear, rigid and leathery, his physiology yet to catch up with the moment. Hers more malleable, moist and receptive, parting softly but not enough to give him entrance. And they hung there like that, the pair of them, like two kids playing Pass the Orange, no hands allowed.

But if she did not take his tongue, that was not true of his breath, for she inhaled of him, at first most delicately, almost imperceptibly, without his knowing it, until he felt himself snaking down her throat, sucked in as if by a vacuum, his entire soul losing its hold on the outside world, all of him seemingly stuck on something wet and reptilian and inexorably retracting.

He was as an insect, death-dancing on the point of a lizard's tongue, and if he could not break free of it he was doomed to whatever undefined inner recesses lay beyond the sweet red lips and the fine white teeth.

There was a roaring in his head, a wind of no return, as he felt himself being drawn right out of his boots, off the earth, his brain stammering, struggling to clarify the moment, to frame the question: Is this a young girl yearning that I am kissing—or a witch upon whose lips I am dying, my will shattering, my grave opening?

And he broke from her, pushing her aside in a gesture of consummate revulsion—and she fell to the snow, her face whiter than the white of it.

He left her there, making straightaway for his house, too unstrung to look back, afraid that she might have metamorphosed into something as horrifying as her kiss. He fled the snow witch, its cape still tripping on the wind, endowing it with another moment of corporeal life. He didn't look at that either, sensing that it would be wearing Ara's face, pushing out Ara's smile.

He passed between the lean torsos of the birches, where he saw Froom, hiding from him. And it crossed his mind that Froom might well be Ara's familiar, for witches traveled with familiars, a cat or a dog, why not a boy? In any case, there'd be no more snowballs from *that* Minnawickie this day, Austin thought, as he made his way up the hill and down the other side, the sun behind him throwing his shadow before him, gargantuan and black and malevolently awesome, though proper for such a low-angled sun. He wouldn't catch it until he reached his house—if indeed it was his own.

17

That night, fortified by two beers, and having dined on tunafish and mandarin slices, with a box of Lorna Doones as a chaser, it occurred to him that he never did get to see what might have been in his postbox, if anything. He laughed, chiding himself for having overreacted to everything, Ara included. The poor girl, aroused and inexperienced, had no doubt been going for a soul kiss, and he had responded like Captain Virgin. He'd straighten it out the next day. Hopefully, the girl would still talk to him. And, actually, it *was* funny. They *had* scared him. As to Froom's being a familiar, the boy had more chance of being a full-blooded Minnawickie, with a touch of Apache, than a familiar.

He spent some time with Thoreau, whom, if the truth were known, he was becoming quite taken with. "When the playful breeze drops in the pool, it springs to right and left, quick as a kitten playing with dead leaves." That was nice, and it almost seemed to describe nutsy Froom.

As to Ara, Thoreau had captured her too: "I saw a delicate flower had grown up two feet high between the horse's feet and the wheel track. An inch more to right or left had sealed its fate, or an inch higher. Yet it lived to flourish, and never knew the danger it incurred. It did not borrow trouble, nor invite an evil fate by apprehending it." That surely described Ara—a delicate flower, flourishing and never knowing danger or borrowing trouble. Just a beautiful innocent. Surely, Thoreau must have had her in mind when he wrote those words—or someone like her, since he wrote them in 1850, more than a hundred years before Ara came to be.

He heard the dogs again, faint but audible—and spooky. And

he smiled because it struck him that it might just be Ara and Froom, the two of them, doing the dog bit, still trying to frighten him. If he was correct in that suspicion, it meant that they were out there in blackest night, in subzero temperature, a helluva way from home. So he didn't think about it anymore.

His fire was good, oak and pine and a variety of twigs for kindling. And the house was talking, its usual soft babble whenever the heat came out to expand its beams and floorboards and lay a coat of mist on all its windowpanes. And he felt the urge to set down some thoughts of his own, for he was feeling better about things and reasoned that it was time to add his own observations to those of his predecessors—about the house and the "fun" he was having in it. Ha-ha.

He searched for a pencil and, after some ten minutes of scrounging, realized that the house did not harbor any. It was perhaps the only item that it did not stock. No matter, for he found the nub of one in the bottom of his duffle bag, though he could find no paper there. Nor could he find paper anywhere in the house, unless he cared to write his observations on the back of a cracker box or on the label of a can of beets.

He found that odd and somewhat premeditated, as if someone or something was against his setting down any of his own impressions of the house. The more he thought about it, the less he cared for it. It was arbitrary. Too many things in and about the house were arbitrary—and seldom in his favor.

In any case, there was nothing for him to write on, unless there were some pages left empty in Maynard's notebook. He went to the table and to the book, which lay passively between the two kerosene lamps, both burning brightly, dutifully pumping much light into the house. He found no empty pages, not a one.

Jack Meeker had left pencil and paper in the postbox for him to use in their little correspondence. Well, he'd pick them up in the morning and that would be that. He'd begin his own notes, his own composition, first thing in the morning.

Still, he had his pencil nub in his hand and he wanted to write that night, and he was growing as stubborn in that desire as the house seemed determined that he not write. Again he thumbed through Maynard's book, and again he could find no page upon which he could scrawl as much as his name, unless he cared to write on the inside back cover, which, under the circumstances, he did.

As with many such looseleaf notebooks, the inside covers were of a kind of fabric, in this case light blue in color, a surface that could take a pencil imprint and still be reasonably legible though somewhat mottled. The inside front cover Maynard had already written on, utilizing that surface for his index. But the inside back cover was clean, and though it offered an area that was only eight and a half by eleven inches, to Austin it suddenly loomed as spacious as an empty billboard.

And so he started to write, perhaps a bit too forcefully, for his pencil point snapped immediately. Using a knife, he inflicted a new point upon the pencil, but it wasn't easy, either the knife being too dull or the pencil too hard. Still, he had his new point and once again he addressed the inside back cover. And once again the point broke.

The pencil did not have all that much length to it that he could continue to so abuse it. He would have to be more careful in fashioning the next point, and he was. It was more blunt than its ancestors and did not break upon making contact with the book. It merely grew hot to the touch, so hot that he could not hold it.

Annoyed more than alarmed, he picked up the thickest, most heavily insulated glove he could find, slipped his hand into it and went again for the pencil. Because the pencil was small and the glove bulky, he could not readily pick it up. And all the while he fussed with it, he could hear it hissing, burning easily into the leather of his glove so that, when he finally had it ready to write, the damned thing had burned right through, searing his thumb and forefinger, and he had to drop it.

"Fuck you, house!" He roared, smacking the pencil nub and sending it cartwheeling across the room. "What the hell is this! What the hell is going on here!"

It took awhile, but finally he rediscovered the pencil. It was cold. But when he put it to the book to write again, it had no point.

In frustration, he flung it across the room again, he didn't care where, and he stormed about the house, his words vibrating pots and pans and causing all underfloor life to scurry for cover. "Whoever the hell you are in here, I don't scare, okay! You don't want me to write—fine! You don't want my fires to burn—fine! You want to send bears after me, and snow witches and bullshit—fine! But you better get used to me, because I ain't leavin'! You don't like it, *you* leave! Pack up your spooks and piss off!"

He stood in the middle of the floor, allowing silence and sanity reentrance into the room. He was half surprised that he hadn't been struck dead as a result of his challenging words. But still he seethed. He had rights, damn it. He was a person, an entity. He was legal on the premises. First thing in the morning he would go out to his postbox, pick up the pencil and paper there, and write anything he goddamned pleased, and to his heart's content. And he would mail it to the D.A. in Millinocket, with instructions that it be opened and read upon his death. That would be first thing in the morning. He still had to contend with the night.

He read awhile, something other than Maynard Whittier because that writer was fast becoming a pain in the ass—and something other than Henry David Thoreau because, entertainingly informative as it was, it was also rooting him too firmly in the very ambience he was trying to escape. What he wanted of a book was an opportunity to check his brains, to fly, to cut out, at least for a few hours. Somerset Maugham's short stories filled the bill. They were lousy with jolly old England, but he preferred that to jolly New England any old day, old top, what ho.

He went to bed with all lamps blazing and all guns loaded, his usual after-dinner deployment, and he slid beneath his quilt with his shotgun lying lengthwise beneath his pillow, his hand on the stock. He didn't trust the night. The day he didn't mind, but the night, and the house, and the dogs, and the dark, and the tree, that hideous malignant, lifeless tree—he didn't care for it, any of it.

Somewhere near midnight he fell asleep. And somewhere

beyond it, in both time and clutch, he awoke, as alert as if he'd never been asleep, his eyes and ears straining, his mouth as dry as salt. Something was amiss, the night wriggling like a rained-up worm. Outside, in and about the snow and the dark, where fancies dangled and fear hung over the starched snow in rolling mists, something was coming to pass.

He threw off his quilt, both his feet hitting the floor simultaneously, never feeling the cold, his finger dislodging the safety on his shotgun, freeing both barrels to blow if but an ant breathed upon the trigger.

He went about extinguishing every lantern, the darkness offering no obstacle to his movements, his memory of every item's placement in the house serving him as effectively as radar. He bellied across the floor to a window too frosted to allow him vision until he rubbed a clear circle on a center pane and peeked out, like an urchin nose-pressing against a rich man's Christmas window.

It was a bear, the biggest he'd ever seen in any zoo, book or dream, standing straight up in the blue-gray nether fog, looking squarely at him, measuring him, staking him out. Austin immediately assumed it to be the mate of the bear that Benson had dispatched, and he wanted to tell the bear of his innocence, that it wasn't he who had done the killing—he had only done the running.

It crossed his mind what Ara had told him about Benson—that "a bear got 'im." Had she been anywhere near the truth? Was this that same bear? And could a bear think like that, and search out the very people and the very place implicated in the killing of its mate? Worse than anything else was Austin's sudden stark realization that none of his windows was shuttered.

He estimated the bear to be eight or ten feet tall, okay for a kodiak or a grizzly, but how in hell could a brown or a black grow so large? Considering the beast's size, he didn't want to rely solely on his shotgun. One of his rifles would serve him better, the .30-.06. No, the Winchester. No, both of them—and he removed them both from their pegs and held them alongside his shotgun. He had three guns at the ready and wondered how to position them. Should he take them out onto his porch and start shooting, not waiting for the bear to make its move? Or should he sweat it out and hope that the bear would go away, because perhaps it was a different bear, or an indifferent bear, or a stupid bear with a lousy memory. One thing it wasn't was a hibernating bear. It wasn't asleep and it wasn't drowsy. Austin looked again and it wasn't even there.

He went quickly to a window on the opposite side of the house—it wasn't there either. He looked through his remaining windows, all of them, and the bear was nowhere in sight.

And then he heard it. The bricks in his fireplace, trembling and complaining as if in an earthquake, chunks of dislodged mortar spewing and scattering about his hearth. The bear was on the roof. It had gone up the small hill behind the house, and from there it was an easy enough matter for it to rumble over onto the roof.

And it was up there like Kong, shaking the chimney while bellowing its displeasure, the roar coming loudly into the house, magnified a hundredfold by the flue which served as a megaphone. The chimney was breaking apart, the entire house vibrating around it, smoke and dust curling across the floor. The beast on the roof, if unchecked, was going to bring everything down.

Austin moved quickly, forgetting even to slip into his boots. Opening his door slowly, carrying his shotgun and both rifles, he ran into the shifting mists, leaving his house far enough behind so that when he turned to look he would have a good enough angle of his roof and his chimney—and the bear.

The light was not good, the moon showing no interest in that particular night. Still, he could see the bear throttling the chimney maniacally, swatting at it, knocking the top row of bricks every which way, like dominoes. And he could hear it roaring, though it didn't seem a noise that a bear might make. It was something else, some kind of bestial caterwauling, more in tune with a nightmare than with reality.

Positioning himself too quickly, he half knelt and fired the Winchester, the recoil knocking him flat on his pajamaed bottom. The rifle shot exploded the night, blowing it apart as if it had body, and a thousand birds, dislodged from their nests, screamed at the intrusion, and God only knew how many animals were triggered into frantic running.

He threw the Winchester aside and grabbed the .30-.06, firing it quickly, for the bear was still a standing target, though it couldn't be counted on to stay that way for long. The discharge of that weapon, as loud and as offensive as the first, did not cause nearly half the hubbub, the night creatures already jolted from their activities apparently not anxious to reveal their hastily sought-out hiding places.

The bear was still on the roof, still upright, turning its massive head this way and that, making its calculations as to how it was going to deal with whatever was out there in the snow. If either of Austin's rifles had hit home, it had done so with little effect, and he shuddered at the consequences of such a result.

The light was miasmic, endowing nothing with an outline that could be properly defined against the wallowing mists. There were no straight lines, no crisp silhouettes, just an absence of specificity, even trees and hills merging in a soft-focus shroud, even the sharp geometry of the house rounded off like an igloo. But he could see the bear, for it was the only thing other than the fog that was rolling. It had dropped to all fours and was barreling down the sloping roof, making straight for him.

He reflex-fired his shotgun, emptying both barrels at the catapulting form that passed over his head. And in the same instant, in the same motion, he raced back for his house, across the porch and through the open doorway. Bolting the door and standing with his back against it, he braced for the bear should it be of a mind to follow. And even as he did he wondered how many times he would have to play that scene before the big director in the sky would yell, "Print!"

But the bear did not come, and outside it turned silent again, not even the nagging owl wishing to announce its presence from a safe limb above it all.

Austin felt a sliver of fear, for he had left all his weapons out there in the snow. He still had his .44, but a fat lot of good that would do him against a creature still alive after having been gunned by two rifles and a double-barreled twelve-gauge shotgun. He was certain that he had hit the bear all four times he pulled the triggers—with the shotgun for sure, in the underbelly, since the bear hadn't cleared his head by much more than a foot. As to the quality of his marksmanship, in service he had consistently won sharpshooter medals, and if he had missed the bear with one of the rifles, there was no way in which he could have missed with both.

He looked through one of the windows flanking his door. And there was no bear. Nothing out there in the snow but his three guns. But that had to be impossible. If the bear had been hit even slightly, he'd have been so enraged that he'd have ripped off the front door or come crashing through the window. And if he had been wounded more than slightly, he'd still be out there, lying in the snow. And if he had managed to dodge both bullets and all the buckshot, he'd be out there ready to do what he'd come there to do in the first place. And yet—no bear.

One thing was certain, Austin was not going to be suckered into going outside to look. A bear might be churlishly benign at first glance, cute and cuddly; but wounded and angered, it was an adversary that even a pack of wolves might steer clear of. As to his guns, he'd get them in the morning—after first making certain that the bear was nowhere around, and that included the roof.

He lit a lamp and checked about the house. It was a mess around the fireplace. Soot, stones, rust, bits of brick, chunks of mortar all lay about the floor as if a boulder had struck the roof. He'd clean it up in the morning. He'd do everything in the morning. All he was going to do that night was what he usually did at night—not sleep.

18

He did sleep, not a helluva lot and certainly not well, but he did manage to crank out enough of it to not die from the lack of it. And in the morning, upon breaking free from Morpheus, he found his room sunstreaked and warm, the sun having rediscovered his windows and the fire having lasted the night.

But the room looked to have been bulldozed, its fine oak floor strewn with unidentifiable debris that the chimney had upchucked the night before. Austin rather liked it, for the sight of it was evidence that the bear *had* happened, that it had not been something he had fantasized like so many other off-center events of the last few days.

No matter, it all had to be cleaned up and set straight—and that included his bearskin rugs, which then housed more dirt than the bears themselves had accrued in their lifetimes. He found it upsetting to look at the lifeless hides, so thin and worn, and torn in spots and crackly dried of animation, for those same skins, motheaten trophies of some long-forgotten hunt, had once hosted tons of power, had encased a menacing combination of anger and sinew the likes of which, all too recently, Austin himself had seen in terrible action. How placid and feeble the once beasts, how pitiful an end—throw rugs for puny man.

The morning birds were at it outside, picketing his house, insisting on crumbs, scolding squirrels. It could only mean that the bear was gone, off on some windy ridge or foraging about in some deep hollow, scrounging for nuts, nuzzling for insects.

Austin dressed and went out to gather up his guns, which lay in the snow like remnants of Little Big Horn. He cleaned them and oiled them, and saw to it that they were properly loaded and hung ready on their pegs. That done, he tucked the .44 inside his belt and, as he had intended to do the day before, set out for his postbox. He went back for the Winchester because, in light of everything that had happened, it seemed prudent to have it with him always. Hanging from his hand, it made a straight line with the snow as he walked.

There was blood in the snow but no bear in the area because rabbits and partridge would know of such a presence, and the ones he saw were clearly undisturbed, though eye-dartingly alert.

The bear was wounded, that much was apparent. How badly wounded and how soon it might return he had no way of knowing. Soon enough was a fair enough guess. The blood appeared at imprecise intervals, spotting over half the length of one of his snow trenches before angling up and out. From there it trailed up a rise that led unerringly north. That was where the bear had gone, north, over the hill behind the house. And somewhere beyond the limits of his vision, Austin could almost see it—licking its wounds, harboring its rage, biding its time.

He semicircled the witch's tree, for he didn't want to see it or mess with it. In so doing he found himself passing through the birches to where the snow witch stood. He angled away from that too, sidestepping the wicked animation of its flapping cape and the evil fascination of its sightless eyes.

He wondered why he had gone that way at all, since it was hardly the most direct route to the road—probably some lunatic compulsion to frighten himself. All he wanted to do was get to his postbox and back to his house, and in record time. He'd rather not be doing it at all, but he wanted that pencil and paper, and if there was something from Jack Meeker he wanted that too.

The postbox stuck up out of the snow sea like a buoy, Austin able to pick it out long before reaching it. And all the way to it he was aware that it wasn't the pencil and paper he wanted, or a package of assorted foodstuffs with a chummy note attached—it was some evidence, some proof, that Jack Meeker was alive and well and living in Belden.

He had been suppressing that lingering "on-the-edge" feeling since Ara first told him of the big man's death. He had deliberately not thought about it, purposefully avoided tackling it—because he suspected that it might be true. And if it were true, it could only portend further bad news for Austin Fletcher, who was, frankly, not making it—not really, not alone in the wild, brother to the wind and cousin to the sky. He was more a stepchild to the loon and an orphan of the storm.

It went beyond apprehension. It went all the way to terror—and never, not even in combat, had he ever known terror. He wanted Jack Meeker back on the scene because he needed him, as an aide and a confidant and a bulwark. And if he couldn't get it, then "To hell with you, Maynard—I'm leaving."

He set his rifle against a tree, removed his glove and reached into the postbox. It was like plunging his hand into a mausoleum. It was that damp and dreadfully moribund.

"Nothin' in there."

He wheeled to see her standing not ten feet away. Ara. How could he not have noticed her?

She was smiling, so pretty in her woolen cap, her hair spilling out from under, her hands on her hips as she scolded him sweetly. "Gonna shoot me, Austin?"

His rifle was leveled at her. It had done that by itself. He lowered it sheepishly. "Where'd you come from?"

"I *been* here. Behind this tree."

"Hiding?"

"I guess. Wasn't sure ya'd be happy to see me."

He was so glad to see her that he could have swept her up, carried her off and holed up with her till Easter. "I'm happy to see you."

"Nothin' in the box, Austin." She had said it again, reiterating, making her point all too plainly.

"You looked."

"A-yuh."

"You knew I'd be coming here."

"Sooner or later."

"Wasn't there a pencil and a note pad in the box?"

"There was."

"What happened to it?"

"Froom took it for his mathematics."

Austin looked off and saw Froom, on a snowy rise, holding the reins of his sled, mercifully calm. "Well—I'm sure he'll give it back to me if I ask him."

"No, he won't. He never gives nothin' back. Anything he takes, he keeps. That's his way."

"Someday somebody's goin' to punch him out."

"Have to catch him first."

"Oh, I'll bet he's not so fast without that sled."

"In the summah we use a wagon. What're ya expectin', Austin? In the box, I mean?"

He didn't want to answer. Answering would involve him in a subject he plainly didn't want to discuss with her. "Oh—I just come by as a matter of course. Part of my routine."

"Ya lookin' for a package from Mr. Meeker."

"Right. Did you take it?"

"Nope."

"Froom?"

"Nope."

"Well, it doesn't seem to be here. Maybe tomorrow—"

"Won't be there tomorrow, Austin. Won't be there ever."

"You're sure of that."

"A-yuh."

He became immediately annoyed, as if she'd pressed a button that said, "Annoy Austin." "Listen, Ara, don't you think it's time you—"

She didn't let him finish. Instead, she thrust a newspaper into his hand. The weekly, from Millinocket. "Best ya read it."

He didn't want to read it. He wanted to hand it back to her because he knew what was in it. And he was right. It was the headline story and had a photo of Jack Meeker to it, the big man at his desk, on duty, serving the people of Belden, proud and pleased to do so.

JACK MEEKER DIES IN FIRE
SUDDEN BLAZE IN BELDEN DEPOT HOUSE
CLAIMS LIFE OF STATIONMASTER

On Saturday last, Jack Meeker, a town fixture as both Stationmaster and postmaster, lost his life in a flash fire that swept through the Belden train station, leveling it to the ground and...

"Sorry, Austin."

There was more to the story, the details, but Austin couldn't bring himself to read it, his hands so unsteady that they could barely hold the newspaper. "How do they know it was him?"

"It was him."

"Bodies get...charred. Sometimes beyond recognition." He was grasping at straws, pushing away the truth. He knew it but had to give it a try, it was all so awfully unacceptable.

"It was him."

"How do they know?"

"Because he wasn't burnt. Beam dropped on him. Norm Parker pulled him out, but his back was broke. It's all in there, Austin. He was already gone. I'm really sorry."

Austin was not surprised at the news. He had expected it. No, he *knew* it. "He was my friend." He knew it when she first told him, all his protests at the time being tantamount to a blind man insisting that he could see.

"Kind of was everyone's friend."

"He saved my life. He got me here. I'd never have made it without him."

"Ya would've."

"No. I don't think so."

"Ya would've."

He flared. "How come you're always so goddamned certain about everything? You're always so certain!"

"I'm only certain about things that're certain. You'd've made it."

"There a funeral?"

"Funeral *was*."

"Things sure happen fast up here."

"A-yuh."

"Seems they buried him almost before he's dead."

"Seems."

"Okay—now tell me about Benson. How come *he's* not written up in the paper? Didn't you tell me he was dead, too?"

"A-yuh." She took the newspaper from him and turned it to a page more nearly in the middle. Then, pointing to where he was to read, she handed it back to him and looked away, kicking snow with her boot tip, trying to not be there.

It was a much smaller article, smaller news, Benson not being as important to the community as Jack Meeker.

BEAR KILLS HUNTER

The mangled body of Merriwell Benson, a hunter and trapper, was found in the dense woods two miles east of the Great Northern Paper Co. dam. Forest Ranger Ed McAfferty made the initial identification even though the body had been rendered close to unrecognizable.

"It was a bear," McAfferty said, "and a big one. And judging from the tracks, the bear was hunting Benson. It's still out there and I'd advise everyone to take special precautions. Burn all refuse, don't leave any food around."

Austin handed the newspaper back to Ara. "If the body was so mangled, how could they make an identification?"

"Was a chain around his neck with his name on it. Time ya started believin' people, Austin. That paper don't lie."

"Just the same—"

"Just the same, they're both dead. Like I told ya."

He looked at his postbox, smiling sorrowfully, all the fight going out of him, all the heart, all the fun. "I never got to put my name on this."

"Ya still can."

"No. I don't think so."

"All ya need's a little paint. Blue'd be nice."

"No, Ara." He smiled at her, half in defeat, half in relief. "That's it for me."

"What do you mean?"

"I'm leaving." Saying it aloud, to someone else, made it more definite and most irreversible.

She stiffened, her face wreathed in surprise, a nervous smile forming as if to put the lie to his words. "Really?"

"Really."

"Just because some people died?"

"They didn't die, they were killed. There's a difference."

"Die or killed, they're dead. That's no reason to—"

"It's weird, but they were the only two people I knew up here."

"Ya know me and Froom."

"Do I?"

"A-yuh. I'm Ara. He's Froom."

"I'm goin' home, Ara—wherever that is. I'm goin' home."

"Ya quittin'?"

"I guess so. But I'll tell you something—I've been gettin' a lot of encouragement to quit. The most recent being that bear. He paid me a visit last night."

"A-yuh. He'd be in the area."

"He was ten feet tall on his hind legs and came close to knocking the chimney off my house."

"A-yuh. Bear that big could do that."

"Ara, he damn near killed me."

"Nope. If he wanted to kill ya, he would've."

"He's wounded and he'll be back."

"Nope. If he was wounded and wanted to kill ya, he'd of never taken off."

"I *shot* the sonofabitch! He's got a bellyful of buckshot and, unless I'm wrong, he took two other hits!"

"Nope."

"Ara, I saw his blood in the snow! He's wounded!"

"Ain't arguin' that he's wounded. Only arguin' that he won't be back."

"Jesus, you are the most—I swear, talkin' to you is like, like…"

"I thought *this* was ya home."

"I thought so, too—but it isn't."

"Ya don't like it anymore?"

"I liked it better before I got here. I liked the idea of it."

"Don't ya still? Like the idea of it?"

"Yes. But it's not enough. I'm cut off here, kid. That's not new for me, it's just that here I feel more cut off than ever. Like I'm floating around, like I have no weight. Like something's been keeping me here for some reason I'll never understand. And now, with Jack gone…"

"*I* can bring ya packages and write ya notes."

"Ara, at night, that house—there's noises I can't figure. Lanterns that keep goin' out. My fire, it can have flames as high as a mountain, but it's not always hot. There's an owl whose only job is to keep me awake. I hear those dogs, goddamn 'em, all the time. And a rocking chair, squeaking on its own. And now there's a bear out there that can kill hunters! I mean, Jesus!"

"I'll get Froom to give ya pencil and note pad back."

"Ara—"

"Else I'll buy ya new ones."

"Ara, the truth is—I mean, now that I think about it, the truth is, *you're* the only thing keepin' me here."

She took a moment before speaking, and when she did speak she doled out her words very carefully and most perceptively. "That's no good."

He smiled and touched her face, wanting to drown himself in her eyes. "I know. Jesus, don't you think I know?"

"I think ya know."

He looked around, at the fluffy whiteness of the land, at the sweet sky and quiet hills. "I wanted this place to be *my* place, because of Maynard. But also because of *me*. I mean, I never really had a place and I want one. But this isn't it. It just isn't it." He turned back to her. "And neither are you. You're just a baby."

"When ya leavin'?"

"I don't know. First chance. Tomorrow morning."

"What'll happen to ya house?"

"I wouldn't care if it burned to the ground."

"Won't burn."

"How do you know?"

"*Can't* burn."

"Ara, how do you know that? Why do you say that?"

"I know it because it's true. And I say it because it's true."

"Baby, I'm goin' to miss you like crazy, but what I *won't* miss is the way you talk sometimes. Saying things with such a certainty. Changing subjects whenever you feel like it. You do that, you know. Do you know that?"

"Shame is, I'm doin' better in school now. Lots better."

He shook his head in smiling resignation, joining her in the new subject. "Been goin' every day, like you should?"

"Not every day, but—more'n before."

"How much more?"

"Even Froom's gotten to like ya, though he don't like to show it. He hardly likes anybody. *Hates* me."

He could see the tears gathering in her eyes. "Ara—"

"Ain't ya noticed how he don't razz ya all the time? How he likes to play with ya if ya let 'im?"

"Yeah, like with that snow witch when he bombed me like I was Hanoi."

"We both like ya, Austin. So it's not like ya don't have anyone."

"I think you're tellin' me to stay."

"Nope. Just tellin' ya ya'll be missed."

"If I am, it'll be the first time."

"First time for everythin'."

"Ara, I have to go."

"No skin off me."

"Will you and Froom help me? I've got no transportation into
Belden. Maybe, with your sled…I've always wanted to ride your sled
with you."

"Ya got ya own sled."

"I guess I do, but—I don't know the way."

"Ya can ask a traffic cop."

"Ara—"

"Ya got here without my help, ya can leave the same way." She
turned and walked away, as icy as the snow underfoot, her chin
farther out than her nose, so apparent was her annoyance. Halfway
up the hill to Froom she turned and shouted back at Austin. "And
ya a lousy kisser, Austin!"

"Ara!" he called. "I love you!"

"Fat chance!"

She was over the hill and gone, Froom, faithful chauffeur,
steering her home on their obedient sled—and Austin felt a
wrenching in his gut like a bayonet being twisted. He loved the girl
but hated the house. The girl was too young, not to be tampered
with; the house too old, not to be endured. It was a dilemma and a
paradox and a pain in the ass. Everything was wrong that could be
wrong. His old luck was coming back—like swallows to Capistrano,
like the proverbial bad penny. He felt star-crossed, snake-bit and
faked out. He was the *Flying Dutchman* and there was no friendly
port. And the sooner he lifted anchor and shoved off, the sooner he
could try his luck elsewhere.

He picked up his rifle and trudged back toward his house,
stopping at the snow witch to tell her off. "Listen, you ugly mother,
I know you don't like me and I don't like *you*. But I'll tell you a secret,
okay? Come next summer, I'll be around, somewhere. You? You'll be
melted into nothing but a broom and a hat and a couple of lumps of
coal. How do you like *them* apples, Miss Maine of 1640-whatever?"

At the witch's tree he stopped again, addressing the skeletal
abomination with the contempt it deserved. "As for you, tree, I
don't know who they hung on you, but don't get any ideas about
me because I ain't hangin' around. Get it? And if you give me any

more crap with your no-show shadow, I'm goin' to come back on Washington's Birthday and chop you into kindling with my little hatchet. I cannot tell a lie."

He gave the tree the old "fuck you" half of his arm and stormed off. He had had enough of all of it and he was checking the hell out. As to paying the bill, he wouldn't. He hadn't had a decent night's sleep since arriving, it was noisy, the heat never came up, the food was lousy, the room was not comfortable and there was no room for him to sign the register.

The house was in sight and the bear wasn't, and that had to count as a plus in his then state of mind. If Jack Meeker was dead, Austin Fletcher was alive. And if the sun had ducked in at the witch's tree, it was on in full as he passed his woodshed. And if he felt bad about leaving Ara, he felt good about leaving Maine—and that went triple in spades for his chimney, and quadruple in clubs for his backhouse.

Feeling headier than he'd felt in days, he sucked in huge drafts of blessed winter air, clearing his mind, adding length to his stride and determination to his gait—and all was well with him except that something was behind him.

He didn't see it, he felt it. It didn't touch him, but he knew it was there. He couldn't hear it, because it made no sound. But it was there and he ran for his life, and the screaming in his head he recognized as his own.

Whatever it was, it was low, down around his ankles—and he kicked his feet high as he ran, like a strutting drum major, afraid to let his rear heel linger too long on the snow, for fear that it might be snapped at. He was Achilles on ice, terror gnashing at his heels, and his house seemed farther away than ever.

It touched him, grazing his ankle, and he kicked higher, almost falling and caused to veer slightly from his straight-for-the-house course. And he saw it, conical and black, the high-pointed hat of the snow-witch, rolling erratically after him though there was no wind to so propel it. It bounded over the snow at him, like a bloodhound with a scent. It pursued him frivolously, funny in its tumbling because its shape inspired no grace. Still, it was a hateful thing in concept, clinging to his ankle as if on an invisible thread, changing its course as he changed his, vexing him, plaguing him, frightening him to yelling out loud—and he ran all the way home.

19

It snowed. Late that afternoon the sky turned dull gray and released flakes the size of nickels, a million dollars' worth piling up in his trenches, quilting his roof, dusting his sills. It was a holiday snow, picturesque, descending slowly like small paratroopers. The wind slackened and the air warmed and animals ducked predictably into their lairs, birds tucking their heads under their wings, deer taking shelter in safe caves and covering bushes, while in his house daffy squirrels dug into the food hoards they had laid in for just such weather, and in his ceiling and below his floor he could hear them at their banqueting, singing songs and telling stories, happy with their host who had so beneficently turned up the heat.

He kept his stove door full open in hopes of coaxing even more heat out of it, and the light of the fire projected lazy shadows upon the walls—of beams and buckets and of himself, and of his Boston rocker which he disdained sitting in, its silhouette magnified to such a degree that a giant could have occupied it and not have felt cramped. The shadow did move, but only when provoked by the dancing flames, the chair itself remaining motionless and certainly not creaking.

He was trying, hard, to gather his capacities, to think, to judge, to act, for what had happened couldn't possibly have happened, and his sanity, sorely tested, was up for grabs.

Earlier, the witch's hat had stopped upon reaching his door, not of its own choice but of his, for he wouldn't let it in, clubbing at it with his rifle, pulling the door shut before it could gain access, stuffing a towel at the base of the door to prevent its sliding under.

From his window he had watched as it thrashed angrily about

on his porch, making a scoop of itself, filling itself with snow and hurling itself at his door. Twice it had flown at him, as if to crash the window, but, lacking a weight to match its temper, it succeeded only in denting its crown.

For a time it had hung on the sky, assessing the situation like an oversized hummingbird, after which it flew straightaway up to where he heard it on his roof, squeezing itself into a bundle and inserting itself into his chimney. He heard it funneling down the flue, causing the damper to rattle like a rock in a tin can. He heard the frustrated thumping as it came to realize that the flue was blocked. And he heard it whoosh back up the chimney, where, resuming its natural shape, it fluttered down again to his porch to flagellate itself further before tumbleweeding off to whatever hell would give it haven. And in its leaving it seemed to have punctured the sky, causing the big snow that came after, first as a trickle but soon as a flood, flake after flake of it, nickel after nickel. And, watching the snow, he had the feeling that he was watching his brain, shredded and tossed and coming down like confetti. And he knew that if he could not gather it all up and roll it back into his head, and soon, he was psycho ward bound and Section Eight doomed.

He was shaken, as close to flipping as he'd ever been. Two men had been killed in the action, Al Obermeyer and Jimmy Schaefer. And they lay there, side by side under the unperturbed sky like newly felled young trees, each with his dogtags in his mouth.

It was some kind of ritual that he never did understand. All he knew was that dogtags came notched so that if you were killed and still had a face, the metal tags could be slotted over your front lower teeth, holding your mouth open as if you were a baby bird waiting for Momma to come feed you. Why the Army wanted your mouth open in death was beyond him. Was it to let your soul out? Was it to let you look as though you were having the last word? Was it so that the flies could go inside you and do their work there, rather than work on the outside and make newsreel photographers ill?

"It's so Graves Registration can get at ya dogtags easy, Austin, and make a quick identification." Maynard had the answer. Maynard had all the answers all the time.

Austin felt an airiness, a lack of ballast, as if the death of the two soldiers had stolen his weight, making him too light for the world, a proper wind or a quick spin able to send him spinning into space.

Both men had been his friends, as much as he had friends. Both were younger than he was, were better people, and had more to lose. Obermeyer was married, was a college grad with a degree in sociology and had volunteered. Jimmy Schaefer had a football scholarship to Tennessee which was his for the asking as soon as he got out of the Army. Austin Fletcher had nothing, was nothing, and knew nothing. Why, then, had he been spared? The shell had landed right in their midst, killing the pair of them outright, yet not so much as scratching Austin or even slightly ruffling Maynard. Why?

"Hard to answer that, Austin. Maybe it's best we don't try. 'Specially since ya don't look so steady to me."

"I think we should try. How come they're dead and we're not? The four of us were in the same high grass—Obermeyer, me, Schaefer and you, in that order. How can a shell explode, kill one and three and miss two and four?"

"Well, ya might call it luck."

"Luck, my ass."

"Okay, then—design. Will ya accept design?"

"I don't know."

"Luck or design, Austin. One or the other. Can't be both. Not at the same time. Be a contradiction in terms."

"I don't know. I was hoping you'd know."

"You a fatalist?"

"I'm a nothing."

"Fatalist thinks when ya number is up it's up. Fatalist thinks things come to pass by design and can't be changed no matter what."

"I don't believe that."

"Then ya not a fatalist."

"What's the other again?"

"Don't know any word for it 'ceptin' luck. They had bad luck. We had good luck."

"What do you believe?"

"Well, I guess I believe in design."

"A fatalist."

"I guess so. I think what's goin' to be is goin' to be. I think the cards are dealt out a long time ago and all we do is ante up and play out the hand."

"You think they were supposed to get killed?"

"A-yuh."

"Today?"

"A-yuh. Guess I do."

"Isn't that cuttin' it pretty close? I mean—to the day?"

"Well, if things are scheduled, why not? Why allow any leeway? Only get people to bouncin' into one another. I mean, if a reservation's made ahead of time, no sense in not showin' up on time."

"And you and me—we didn't have a reservation?"

"Seems not. At least not for today. Maybe tomorrow. Maybe never."

"You think you'll never get killed?"

"Well—I think I'll die, one day. But, no, I don't think I'll ever get killed."

"Why don't I feel that way?"

"I guess because we're different."

"Do you think I'll get killed? Come on, give me a fast answer with none of your deep thinkin'."

"Well, I think you stand a better chance of gettin' killed than I do."

"Why?"

"Because ya believe it about yourself, and I don't."

"What's goin' to kill me?"

"I don't know."

"A bullet? A grenade? How about the food?"

"Don't know. Could be anythin'. Now, calm down, Austin. I know ya upset, but don't go loony on me."

"How 'bout the weather?"

"Weather could do it."

"How about a hat?"

"A hat?"

"Yeah. A hat."

"Austin, I want ya to hold yourself together till we can get a doctor to

look ya over."

"How about a hat comin' at me and killin' me?"

"Like in James Bond? That Chinese fella who used to flip his hat? That kind of hat?"

"I don't know. A hat."

"What kind of hat?"

"I don't know. Pointed."

"Pointed? Like those old German hats?"

"I don't know. No. Older."

"Like a Roman hat? One of those helmets?"

"I don't know."

"Well, if ya don't know…"

"A dunce hat. How's that?"

"A dunce hat?"

"Right."

"Ya think a dunce hat can kill ya?"

"I don't know. That's what I'm askin' you."

"Well, I suppose if it came right at ya, it could. I mean, it's got a point, don't it?"

"Yes. It's definitely got a point. A very sharp point. As I recall, a very sharp point, indeed."

"Then it could kill ya."

"It got away."

"Good. Ya better off without it. Come on, Austin, keep movin'."

"It blew away."

"Austin, when we get back to whatever town we're nearest, I'm goin' to buy ya a beer and we're goin' to get ya head on straight again."

"It blew all over the place. Across hills. Over roofs. Over snow. You should've seen it."

"Let's keep movin', Austin. One foot, t'other foot—"

"It was very angry with me. Madder'n hell. Real pissed off. Chased me half a mile, snappin' at me all the way."

"I know ya liked those two boys, Austin. I did, too. But ya can't let it get to ya."

"It tried to break my windows. It tried to come under my door, down

my chimney."

"Why would it want to do that?"

"I don't know. That's what I'd like to find out."

"Yeah, well, I should think so."

"Why'd they die?"

"Obermeyer and Schaefer?"

"No."

"Obermeyer and Schaefer died because a Charlie shell came over that ridge and—"

"No. Wrong. You got it wrong, Maynard."

"Hang on to me, okay? I got ya rifle. You just hang on to me."

"One by fire and one by bear. Helluva way to go, don't you think?"

"Gotta be a medic up here somewhere."

"I got hit a hundred times, Maynard."

"Come on. One foot, t'other foot. Ya doin' fine."

"A hundred times. Snowballs. Snowballs and hats. Fire and bears. I tell you, Maynard, you don't give me some answers real soon, I'm leavin'. AWOL. Over the fuckin' hill and outa sight."

"Sure, Austin. I understand."

"I mean, old buddy, I'm leavin' tomorrow. Crack of dawn. I'm goin' to pack up my duffle and make tracks. I mean, fuck this, Maynard—who needs it? Hangin' around, waitin' to get killed, that's not smart."

"Don't seem much we can do about it."

"Not much you can do, because you're dead."

"Me?"

"Me, I'm still alive. And I plan on stayin' that way."

"When'd ya find out I was dead, Austin?"

"Wouldn't you like to know?"

"A-yuh. I would."

"Hah!"

"Who told ya?"

"A little bird told me."

"Nice of 'im."

"Actually was a big bird. An owl."

"Said I was dead?"

"Says it every night. Tells everyone. Has a big mouth. First he asks, 'Who?' And then he says, 'Maynard.'"

"Well, I'll have to have a little talk with 'im. Keep walkin', Austin. Ya doin' fine."

"It was a pointed hat, Maynard—but it wasn't a dunce's hat."

"No?"

"It was a witch's hat."

"A witch's hat, ya say?"

"Yeah. Wicked witch of the fuckin' north. Has a big bear for a familiar."

"Ya don't say."

"I do say. I also say it's time for me to get outa here."

"Hey—let me help ya."

"You helped me enough, Maynard."

"Austin?"

Watching the snow fall and pile in the encompassing dimness, his sanity pressured by things monstrously beyond his ken, his equilibrium provoked by a conversation with Maynard that could not possibly have taken place except as a distortion, he knew that staying just one more night in that house would cause him to cross over completely—to a never-never land where nothing had a shadow, where memories were marbles and thoughts chewing gum, and people but tenpins in the gutter of the gods. He had to get out, make tracks, leave dust. Snow or no snow, wolves, bears or ducks, midnight or Mardi Gras, he had to go. He had come by lantern, he would leave by lantern, for, as the man had written on the fine pine plank, "This house is not fit."

He found his duffle bag and began to stuff things into it. All things, anything. Socks, beer, towels, ammo, crackers, underwear, salt. Whatever his fingers found, whichever they closed about, he took. He was like an amateur shoplifter, sweeping over every shelf he passed, shoveling into his duffle guns, knives, candles, coffee, soap, cigarettes and an ashtray.

He filled his biggest kerosene lamp and slung it over his shoulder. Over his other shoulder the .30-.06. In his jacket pocket the .44. The duffle bag, full to bursting, was so poorly packed that sharp things protruded from within, like poles under a collapsed tent, like porcupine quills inside a cocoon.

He dragged it all to the door, and, opening the door, he saw that it was darkest night and most foreboding; not a time for casual trekking, more a time for staying home and hiding beneath the bed. But he was committed to leaving, driven to it well past the point of reconsidering. He would go down the trench to his woodshed, to where his sled sat waiting. He would load his duffle upon the sled and move out—Jack London on the half shell, Admiral Peary on the floe. And he would not stop at Belden, or at Millinocket. He would go on to where there were no more tracks. And from there to where there were no more roads. And he would find himself a river. And he would make himself a raft. And he and Huck Finn would take themselves a trip, down the Mississippi to Mexico, Peru and Timbuktu, and—

Two yards off the porch he stopped, the night coming up to bless him, splendid and tranquil and inky, more stars in its tapestry than ever it had hung before, all of it occurring so suddenly that it was as though a page had been turned and the earth flipped onto its other side.

And he thought that it had to be on such a night that Christ was born, all life holding its breath, a beauty so rare and infinite upon them as to stop all men and all thinking, and make of time a fool, of death a caprice, and of life a new beginning.

She was bewilderingly lovely, immeasurably so, the light around her playing almost as music. Hatless, her hair flew loosely. Smiling, she did seem to glide across the snow, the cool gray eyes of her triumphing over the night's black velvet. Still the young girl, in the same thick jacket and the same sweet mittens, she was all the same something else, something astonishing and unexpected, paling the delicate snowfall, stifling the Jack Frost wind.

Her black hair, lost as it was against the night's dark canvas, framed her face like an ivory cameo, and she was with him. Ara. Slung ahead in time enough years to match his, arriving as intensely beautiful as ever God dared make a woman, taking his hand at a time when he was certain that he had used up all his luck.

She kissed him, finely, a child's kiss, lighting on his cheek, then sliding into the kiss of a woman—on the lips, the ear, the neck. A woman's eyes on his eyes and the marrow of him caldroned. A woman's arms around him and the soul of him shook free. A woman's touch, a woman's breath, a woman's voice saying his name—and the kiss that should not happen happened, and the bargain thus was sealed.

An effusion of stars accompanied them, writing their names on the frosted windows and in the stove fire's slow dancing. And nowhere did so much as a night bird comment, not an owl and not one loon. Though somewhere, in the very fabric of the house— in the beams perhaps, or possibly the cellar—a laugh occurred, tremolant and fleeting, passing over them as if on the motion of a wand, before disappearing as a vapor on the wind. And, as it always is with all doomed lovers, Austin never heard.

20

At a place in the onyx night where the hour of the wolf takes hold and all time stops though man never knows it, Austin awoke. She was gone, as he knew she would be. Even as he felt himself dropping into sleep, he knew she'd be gone when he awoke, for that would be in keeping with the way she had arrived, unexpected entrances begetting unanticipated exits.

He lay in the dark and spun it all back, how avidly the girl had made love. How knowledgeable and sweetly aggressive she had been. How demonic even, lost in her own pleasure while sponsoring such exaltation in him as few men would ever dream of.

It had occurred to him, even in the soft frenzy of their lovemaking, that the girl could not have been the sixteen years of age she had earlier claimed to be—not if she were to be judged by the way in which she was directing the trysting. She would have to have been older. How much older, to have behaved in so experienced and expert a manner? Five years at the least. Ten to be sure. A hundred would have been believable, though the young body, feline and willing, belied such an estimate.

The compelling thing, though, now that she was gone, was his certainty that she was not a child—not that he would have been all that troubled at having offended the law, for better men than he had locked horns with younger girls than she and lived to boast of it outside prison walls and inside confessional booths.

So it was not chronology and it was not the law that was troubling him. It wasn't even his own pristine upbringing, which, when examined alongside that of other men he had known, was considerable indeed. It was Ara herself and that fluctuating child-woman aspect of her, enabling her to appear as a temptress, yet preventing her from harboring or verbalizing a single licentious thought. And though she might well have gone to his bed willingly had he asked her directly, the having of her would have to have come under the broad heading of rape.

The way it turned out, however, rape was never an issue—unless it was his by her, for that was how magnificently in charge she had been and how happily helpless he had been, worshiping at her loins.

It crossed his mind that she might not have been there at all, that he had imagined her there or dreamed her there, for, Lord knows, the precision of his thinking those past few days had hardly been as a compass pointing unwaveringly north. It had been more like a weathervane in a tricking wind, signaling a dozen directions at once, as unerring in its pursuit of truth as a mindless mouse in an exitless maze.

The house had been deceiving him of late, lying low in the daytime and pouncing on him at night. Why could not the presence of Ara, at his side and in his bed—why could that not have been another errant fantasy cooked up by the house to further sport with him for whatever purpose it had in doing so all along?

He would have to check that kind of paranoia, of course, because it was precisely that kind of thinking that had set him to running from the house in the first place. And he would still be running had Ara not appeared in the night to lie with him and prevent his leaving.

Perhaps the quickest, easiest way for him to determine whether or not she had been with him was to look outside the house for her bootprints. If she had been with him, her bootprints would be there, in the snow, clear evidence of a human presence. On the other hand, if she had been conjured by him, or by the house, there would be no prints at all—for the girl, as light and lovely as she had been in her arriving, could hardly have flown there, or ridden the wind, or reindeered the roof there like Santa.

He got up from his bed and went to his door, and, opening it, he could see that it was still snowing, so heavily and incessantly that any tracks that she might have made had to lie buried well beneath the new fall.

So there was no answer to the riddle of her—not that he had expected one, for such an easy and irrefutable solution would have been inconsistent with the way things had unfolded thus far. Nor was there anything within the house that could speak of her having been there—not an item of clothing casually forgotten, or a word of hers clearly remembered, or a fragrance of her adrift in the room, conquering and occupying him with its dizzying dogma.

As to their names which he had clearly seen in the windowpane's frost, the spreading heat of the house had simply erased them, setting them to running down the glass as droplets before causing them to gather on the sill as a pool.

He dressed and ate, early as it was, for sleep was not of a mind to return, nor would he have trusted it if it had, for it had already fooled him enough times to no longer qualify as friendly—the best status it could aspire to under the circumstances being "nonbelligerent."

But if sleep was risky, catnaps were more so, for they were more vivid, with sharper images and colors less pastel, and when he awoke from them it was always with a start, his eyes cracking wide and his hands shooting out—sight and balance being continually compromised. At to the cast and conclusions of his catnaps, they were consistently terrifying: pain, fear and death the principal players; cold sweat and stifled screams the curtain-call survivors.

And so, with sleep and all its variations offering him small sanctuary, he turned to working by day and reading by night—light work and lighter reading, for he was conserving his strength, though he didn't know why, and keeping his mind clear for he didn't know what. He chopped wood and shoveled trenches and fished and hunted, the latter two with nonresults. And he read S. J. Perelman and H. Allen Smith, and perused the cartoons of Mauldin and the collected humors of Thurber. And all the while he did that, there was no sign of Ara, though he knew that she would return, because she simply had to—the only question being when. And for as long as it would take for that question to be answered, that's how long he was prepared to remain with the house.

He searched every horizon for her, and at night he would go repeatedly to his door, to look out over the blue snow for her, so hopeful of her returning that he truly believed that he could coax her into doing so. And more than once did he see her there, teetering on the mists—but as often as he saw her, that was as often as she failed to sustain.

As to his leaving—that became increasingly more impossible with each wending day. He could not leave, not without seeing her, talking with her, if only to establish whether or not she had lain with him in reality or only in his mind's creation. There was no avenue through which he could reach her. He didn't know her name or where she lived—though it did occur to him that, with Jack Meeker dead, a postman's job was open. He could apply for that job and take on its duties, traveling the countryside in a town-provided jeep, learning the names and houses of the area's citizens. Surely Ara's father received mail. Perhaps Ara herself received mail—*The Minnawickie Gazette* or *The Witch's Weekly* or *Seventeen.* By a process of elimination, sooner or later, he would uncover her, in some house, some school, though it would very likely take a year, and more likely two.

He had no idea as to what the day was, for he had lost all count. Perhaps it was a weekend and Ara was made to stay at home, or go to church, or sew some crewel, or make apple butter. Or perhaps it was a school day and she had exams and quizzes and homework and gym, things enough to keep her busy, preventing her from coming by. Or perhaps, just perhaps, he was plainly going nuts, no longer able to distinguish logic from lolligog and fantasy from flapdoodle. Better men than he had courted madness—artists, scholars, scientists, lechers—why not a rudderless veteran?

Each day shuffled by like its predecessor, gnawingly lonely, a circumstance that would have delighted Thoreau, though it merely caused Austin to feel sick at heart. The sun would rise, shine, wane and set—and another day would be gone, another night passing without her, another piece of his life lost to pointless pathos.

Four days passed in this manner, dragging off into history with nothing remarkable to take note of. Four days and four nights filled with the absence of her. Four suns going peach, to orange, to flame, to violet—and no Ara.

But on the fourth day, with evening telescoping into night, the sun dropping away like a red disk, Austin returned to his house, his sled loaded with pinecones to sweeten his fire, and he found there, sitting and creaking on the Boston rocker, the fire playing on his pixyish smile to such a degree that it almost endowed it with sound—Maynard, good-naturedly cross.

"Ya missed Christmas, Austin. And ya missed New Year's and almost half of January. What the hell ya been doin'?"

Maynard was not wearing army issue, which was the only clothing Austin had ever seen him in. Rather, he was wearing something from his own wardrobe, winter clothes and warm, a shirt and sweater that Austin himself had worn on occasion. And he was sitting there and rocking, while cleaning the .30-.06, pushing the brushrod up and back in the rifle's barrel.

"Ya got to do a better job on ya rifles, Austin. Wintah congeals the oil if ya don't get it all out. Good thing there's no inspection up here. Better thing ya don't fire this till ya sure it's clean. Bullet'd be so grimy, might just come back at ya and complain. Well, come in, Austin. Don't just stand there. And shut the door 'fore ya demoralize the fire."

Austin came in, shut the door, and found a place to sit. He also found a way to speak, for nothing that the house had tossed up at him of late could truly startle him. He would go along with it and contain his surprise. He would act as though it were a plain everyday thing that a dead man could show up in his house and make like nothing was unusual. "How long've you been here, Maynard?"

"Oh, awhile. In the woodwork, so to speak. A man don't leave his house just because he steps out of it."

"I guess not."

"No, sir. Always a part of him stays behind, to see to it the house don't go doin' anythin' foolish. It's as Thoreau says—"

"If it's all the same with you, Maynard, I'd just as soon you put a lid on Thoreau. I've had him up to here."

"That a fact?"

"It's a fact. He bores me. I find myself skippin'."

"'Books must be read as deliberately and reservedly as they were written.'"

"Don't tell me. Thoreau."

"On the nose."

"Look, Maynard, just so's we understand one another, I'm very glad to see you're alive. And I'm not goin' to get into any argument as to how you come to be here, but if you don't lay off Thoreau, I'm goin' to put you out into the night, and the whole reason for you comin' here is never goin' to get discussed."

"Ya think I come here for a special reason?"

"Let's just say I don't think you dropped in on me because you happened to be in the neighborhood."

"Suit yaself."

Austin wanted to get to the point, any point, as quickly as possible, for he didn't trust the situation and was leary of being manipulated by Maynard, the house, the night, and his own susceptibility to all of them. So he took the initiative, bringing up an issue that was of some importance to him. "Tell me about Ara."

Maynard looked up from his brushrods and oil patches and laughed, not a mocking laugh but a simpatico one. "Well, I can't do that, Austin."

"Why not?"

"'Cause I never told ya anythin' about her before."

"Yes you did. You told me you left your dogs with her."

Maynard seemed genuinely concerned about Austin's not becoming confused. "Austin, ya got to try to understand. I mean, what I'm about to say is pretty tricky and'll take some followin'."

"Go on."

"Well…everythin' you and me are talkin' about now we have, in one way or another, talked about before—in Nam, when we were both alive and kickin'. That's why we can talk about it again—the dogs, for example. But what you want to talk about now, well, we never talked about that ever—which makes it off limits because there's no credibility to it. Don't look at me so funny, Austin. I don't make the rules."

"That doesn't make any sense."

"Nothin' makes any sense. Gettin' killed doesn't make any sense. I wish it hadn't of happened."

"You sayin' you're dead? A minute ago you said you were alive."

"No. A minute ago *you* said I was alive."

"Well, you didn't deny it."

"No matter. Dead is dead, like it or not—take it or leave it."

Austin felt his hold on his patience slipping. He had wanted to scream in fright at seeing Maynard again but had held on, kept his cool, maintained his poise. But he didn't know how much longer he could practice such restraint. "Maynard, you are really beginnin' to get to me."

"Well, I'm sorry about that—"

"I mean, I've been up here all this time, I don't know how long, in a very unhappy house. A house that don't particularly like me or anyone else who ever lived in it, except maybe you. And what I don't need is an old friend comin' to call and makin' things worse."

Maynard softened. He looked at Austin, seeming to appreciate his friend's dilemma. "Austin, ya the nicest guy I ever met. I mean that. The best instincts and the truest heart. My closest friend ever, anytime, anywhere."

"I know. You told me that in Nam, when we were both alive and kicking."

"Right."

"Which is why you can tell it to me again, right?"

"Ya catchin' on, Austin. Ya surely catchin' on."

"Stupidest thing I ever heard of! I mean, Maynard, that is *stupid!*" His temper was flaring, but there was little he could do about it. Maynard was advancing illogic with logic, and Austin was powerless to stop him.

Maynard reassembled and laid aside the .30-.06 clickingly. Then he got up and walked about the room, touching things—his books, his chair, his clothes, all the articles he had always loved. "Ya carried me back, Austin. All the way. All the way to the aid station—thinkin' I was alive. *Hopin'* I was alive. True?"

"True. Of course it's true."

"I mean, even though ya knew ya'd be gettin' my house if I was to die, ya wanted me to live. Right?"

"Right."

"That says a lot about ya, Austin."

"I wish you *had* lived. 'Cause if you'd've lived I wouldn't be here now."

"Well, that's the way it goes, Austin."

"I mean—I *hate* this house! I hate it to hell! If you liked me so much, why'd you leave it to me?"

"You were the only one."

"The only one *what?*" He felt all rationality leaving him, going right out of his fingers like milk yanked out of a cow's udder. How could he be talking to Maynard when Maynard was ten thousand miles away and ten months dead?

"The only one who'd of come here. None of the others would've. They'd of sold the house sight unseen. Or waited for a sunny day to come up and take a look at it, out of curiosity, with their grandchildren. Then they'd go back to where they came from and make jokes about it."

"So what?"

"So I wanted someone to come here, to *live* here."

"How'd you know I'd stay? I wasn't plannin' on stayin'. Not when I first came up."

"I knew ya'd stay."

"Maynard, I hate this house so much…Anyone who comes in here seems to up and die. Jack Meeker. You know Jack Meeker."

"I know him."

"No, you *knew* him! He's not around anymore. He's dead."

"Austin, I have to invoke the rules—"

"Fuck the rules! *What* rules?"

"If Jack Meeker's dead, it happened after Nam. I can only talk about before."

"And what about Benson? Benson the bear hunter? Did you know *him?*"

"I know him."

"Wrong. You *knew* him! He's dead and in pieces! A *bear* got him!"

"Well, there's always a bear. If not in the woods, then in ya mind."

"This one's in *both!*"

"There's always a bear."

Austin was raging, all pretext of civility vanishing. He was learning nothing from Maynard that he didn't already know, and he was losing ground in the discussion, losing time as well. "Only ones still alive are me and Ara! You know about Ara, Maynard—and I want you to *tell* me!"

"I left her my dogs. Her and her brother. That's all I can tell ya, because, even if I *could* tell ya more, that's all I ever *knew* her. They were just two kids would come by. I swear it, Austin, on everythin' holy."

"You can tell me more!"

"I can't."

"You can, Maynard! God damn you!" And he went for him, to grab him and choke the truth from him. But Maynard either sidestepped or Austin's arms went through him, for he was grabbing nothing and was holding less.

"I'm sorry, Austin."

"You're not here, are you?"

"I'm here, but only for as long as you want me to be."

"Oh, it's up to me, is it?"

"I think so. I came here because ya kept thinkin' me. You can think anybody anywhere anytime ya want. Anyone can do it. Don't call for any great magic. A person can occur to another person, just like that. You can do it with a friend, a relative. You can do it with a bear. Any number of ways ya can do it, any number of times."

Austin felt that Maynard's explanation had gone on just a shade too long, just a hair, and he was getting a message. "That what you think, Maynard?"

"That's what *is*."

"That you're here at my invitation?"

"More or less, yes."

Austin knew that it went further than that, for the truth of it became suddenly and starkly apparent. He spoke deliberately, calmly, wanting Maynard to know that he wasn't fooled.

"No, Maynard, that's too easy. *I'm* not doin' it. Somebody else is doin' it. And we both know it."

"Do we?"

"We do."

"Well—I suppose it's possible."

"It's possible. Very possible."

"If ya right, and I ain't sayin' ya are, because I really don't know—but if ya right, findin' out who and why, that's got to be a pretty big assignment."

"You and me have had tough assignments before."

"I'd like to, Austin, but I can't help ya with this one."

"I'm not askin' you to."

"You want me to leave now?"

"Yeah. I'm through 'recalling' you. You can leave."

Maynard went to the door, where he stopped and turned back to Austin. "It's not up to me, Austin."

"I've been gettin' that message."

"I mean, I'm no surer of what I'm doin' here than you are. Less, maybe. I'm not consulted."

"Okay."

"All I know is, there's rules and that's the way the game has to be played."

"You think it's a game?"

Maynard seemed truly upset, standing there between leaving and staying, like a sailboat awaiting a breeze. "Austin—I don't know *what* to think. I don't like comin' here, because it stirs up memories.

And I don't like leavin', because it reminds me of the last time I left, which was very sad indeed. All I know is that I got nothin' to say about it."

"You take care of yourself, Maynard. I'll let you know when you occur to me again. I'll be in touch."

"Okay, Austin. Ya just take care, okay?"

"Maynard?"

"A-yuh?"

"You goin' to go out that door or pass right through it?"

Maynard had to smile. "You mean through it without openin' it?"

"Something like that."

"If I do that, ya'll think ya crazy."

"Excuse me, but isn't that what I'm supposed to think?"

Maynard shrugged and opened the door, and walked out into the night—a nice gesture if it was intended somewhere that Austin feel sane. But Austin, too clever for so simplistic a ruse, and not biting at the embarrassingly obvious bait, deliberately chose to feel and act otherwise. He chose to feel and act bonkers and crackers and proceeded to high-step around his house like a banshee on a hot prod—happy with himself because he had outfoxed the dead man, who also happened to be his best friend as well as an honored war hero, and a helluva backwoods philosopher to boot.

But—after watching from his window Maynard vanishing in the dusk, he quickly saw through the deception and slapped his forehead in realization because it was all so suddenly transparent. For how better to disarm an intended victim, and set him up for defeat, than to get him to believe that topsy was turvy and Minneapolis St. Paul?

And so he ceased his frantic Frooming and, becoming immediately sane, sat back in his rocker like some Grecian oracle, calmly quoting Thoreau—"It is characteristic of wisdom not to do desperate things"—and feeling as clever as shit.

There was a battle of wills taking place in his house and Austin was determined to stay very much on his toes.

21

He slept well, going to bed happily, almost giddily. The combat had begun, whatever it was, and the ultimate confrontation was not far off, hovering in the air, electrifying the night

He had no idea, not the foggiest of notions, as to what he was contending with. He only knew that, somehow, it had begun, and all the frightened anticipation, all the nervous marking of time, was over. He was into Phase Two, whatever it was, and the sooner the better. He was ready. As ready as Freddie. He was also as dizzy as Izzy and as wacky as Jackie, but there was no place in his war for defeatism.

The remarkable thing was that he felt invincible. He knew that he would survive whatever conflict was building. He knew that, come what may, like the song that rallied England against Hitler, "There'll Always Be an Austin."

He laughed as he breakfasted, certain of his cause, confident in his ability. He checked the guns that Maynard had oiled, and they were in perfect firing condition. Still, for all he knew, he had oiled them himself, for who could remember so mundane a thing as cleaning a gun, or sweeping a floor, or polishing up the handle on the old brass door? And who cared whether Maynard had been there or not? As long as Austin thought he'd been there, then he had been there—and was like to be there again, fighting under another banner, a darker master, no friend of England he.

The house was so filled with half-truths and semi-lies that it would have taken an Alvin Feinstein to separate fact from fiction, willy from nilly, Murray from Christmas—all of which made the upcoming battle seem all the more promising. *Anything* was better than the boredom he'd been contending with. More men went ape in service from doing nothing than had flipped out in combat. Check the figures. Don't argue, just check 'em.

He contemplated his sanity. It didn't bother him. Maybe he was crazy and maybe he wasn't. It didn't matter, because it was all relative. A man can be crazy only if there's someone around to tell him that such is the case. The wonderful thing about being isolated is that, whatever you do, you're right. And if you're not, then neither are you wrong, because there's no bigmouth around to throw it up to you.

Maynard's appearance in the house—that had been the trigger. It was the first time that that had happened. Prior to that, Maynard had confined all of his appearances to Nam, which was okay, because that was where he belonged. That he had shown up in Maine, in the house, was a straw in the wind not to be ignored. It indicated that things were closing in, time growing short, sides being taken, and woe to the soldier who, noting such a thing, chose to slumber in his pup tent rather than stand ready on his ramparts.

The fire was dandy and obedient. He cracked the whip, and the flames jumped so high up the stovepipe that he couldn't see the logs that were husbanding it. His kerosene lamps were full. If the attack came at night, he'd have them if he wanted them—though most likely he'd be better served if he kept the fort dark. In any event, the choice would be his—a step forward from his usual lie-back-and-wait situation.

He moved about his house like a man possessed, like Sergeant Markoff in *Beau Geste*, shouting orders to Legionnaires who were not there, cursing them for their cowardice, admonishing them for their decadent drinking habits...Something was coming. Something sure as hell was coming. If it wasn't Arabs, then it was bears, a flatulent flotilla of them. And if it wasn't bears, then it was Huns, or Japs, or Greeks, or Charlie—screaming over the sand dunes, climbing out of the muck, singing in the rain, fuck a rubber duck. Sons of bitches, they would not catch him napping. Not him, not England, not Belden.

He cleaned all of his windows, spankingly. There'd be nothing on them to obscure his vision. No grease or grime, no bird turds tossed and caked. No spiderwebs or moth corpses. Every panel was lint-free and squeaky clean. Visibility perfect. Up periscope. Lay on, Macbeth.

All his guns were on the table, every ammo box torn open for easy access. And if his ammo ran out he'd use his rifles as lances. And when *they* went he'd have his knives, a butcher-block flock of 'em. Carving knives and ice picks, all laid out like a surgeon's cutlery. And if the enemy still came, he'd pick up a flat knife and butter 'em to death. And after the knives, the forks. Fork you, Charlie. Take that and that and that. And after the forks the spoons. He'd use them as catapults to shoot sugar cubes up their noses, killing them with sweetness, like his mother had always advised him. And then his ladles, which he'd wield as battle-axes. And his cups which he'd throw as grenades. And his toothpaste which he'd squeeze up their asses to fight cavities. And toilet paper to remind them of home.

He went outside with a shovel and he worked on his trenches, laying pine sprigs across the tops of them, then sprinkling them with snow—creating in such a manner a long series of sneaky elephant traps, knowing full well that there were no elephants around, but, what the hell, maybe he'd catch Tarzan.

He took all his nails and sprinkled them around his house like grain. If the Fuzzy-Wuzzies blew in barefoot, their footsiewootsies would pay the price.

His backhouse door he left open, like a huge Venus Flytrap. Anyone fool enough to trespass there could do so at his own risk, especially with the Sears, Roebuck catalogue down to just its Scout-knife ads.

And on the roof of his house he placed his faithful sled, tied to the chimney by a slender cord. If the battle went unfavorably and the cry went up to "Abandon house!" he'd climb up there, leap into the saddle, and fly off the roof like the Light Brigade—one last charge into the enemy's midst; a battle flag, a bugle call, a jug of wine, a load of shit.

He was exhilarated as he scouted the further reaches of his territory, putting all in order that he could set in order, avoiding his witch's tree and his snow witch, since they could hardly be counted as allies once the battle was under way.

And because it was, by then, a time of day when evening was trying on night, he didn't see her at first—only the sled on the summit of a hill, Froom standing guard, stoic and alert, like the point man on a patrol.

But he saw her soon, snug in her woolen cap, a little girl again, looking at him as if he were crazy, wondering just what in the world he was doing.

He determined, immediately, to play it cool, for it was four days since he had seen her, four days since they had made such perfect love, and he observed little in her expression or in her actions as she walked toward him that might indicate her acknowledgment that they had been lovers at all.

She came closer, looking hardly sixteen, more like thirteen, and his sanity hung on a bombsight thread, for, judging from the questioning innocence swimming about her, the girl remembered not a thing.

"What ya doin', Austin?" she said, removing her hat, stuffing it into a pocket and freeing her hair, which she shook like a filly.

"Oh—straightenin' about."

"Can't tell whether ya diggin' *in* or diggin' *out*."

"Little of both."

"Sure doin' some funny things."

"You been watchin'?"

"A-yuh. Me and Froom."

"What'd you find out?"

"That ya left ya backhouse door open."

"You been watchin' *there* too?"

"Well—if ya leave it open…" She smiled, again that unfathomable smile. "Free show." And she laughed, a child's laugh, and it threw him further because he didn't want her to be a child.

"Where've you been?" he asked.

"Me?"

"Yes, you. Of course you. Who else could I be talkin' to?"

"Don't know. Ya can be a strange man, from time to time."

"What do you mean?"

"What I said. I find ya strange. Froom finds ya *nuts*. Oh, well." She bent down, scooped up some snow, made it into a snowball, tossed it underhanded into the air and allowed it to descend upon her head, a puff of white on her jet-black hair, marshmallow topping for a chocolate sundae. "Direct hit." She smiled. "Pow!"

She was twelve years old, Austin thought. Maybe ten. They could not possibly have made love. "Do you do that a lot?"

"What?"

"What you just did."

"What'd I just did?"

"Hit yourself with a snowball."

"Oh, that? I do it whenever I feel like it. If I want to be real dangerous, I make it bigger and throw it higher. If I throw it too high, I can't always get under it. Then it's just wasted. Froom can throw it up a mile and get under it every time. Once almost busted his nose. Another time almost choked. But he keeps on doin' it. Says he's an expert." She did it again, sending up another snowball, allowing it to land upon her head. "Pow!"

"I asked you where you've been."

"I know."

"You goin' to answer?"

"Sure."

"When?"

"How's about now?"

"Fine."

"Been in school."

"Four days?"

"That what it's been?"

"Four days."

"Felt like four hundred. Ya'd been proud of me, Austin. I think my grades are gainin' ground. Even geometry, if ya can believe it.

Even isosceles triangles, which I'm gettin' to know 'most everythin' about. 'Specially their sides, which are equidistant from somewhere as well as equally lateral—from somewhere else."

"I missed you."

"I wanted ya to." She did the snowball thing again, playing it like a child but looking at him with a woman's eyes, eyes that came at him from left field—gray, unavoidable, sidelong and promising. "Wanted ya to get used to not havin' me around, which will be the case when ya leave."

"Ara, why would I want to leave *now*?"

She rolled another snowball. "'Cause ya *said* ya were leavin'." And she tossed it into the air over *his* head, and he made no move to avoid it. She laughed as it crowned him. "Pow!"

"But how could I leave you after…" He allowed the question to hang in the air, just as he allowed the snow to remain on his head.

"Ya look pretty funny, Austin. Ya look hit by an eagle." She brushed away the snow, her little mittens flying. "Goin' to freeze there. Freeze ya brains."

"You don't want to talk about it, is that it?"

"We already talked about it."

"About *what*?"

"About ya leavin'."

"That's not what I'm talkin' about!"

"Well, that's what *I'm* talkin' about."

He felt it come over him again, dusting him as the snowball had dusted him—the fleeting suspicion of his own fading sanity, fitting over his head like a hat, and just the right size. "Okay—let's start over, okay?"

"Okay. Start over what?"

"Ara—the last day I saw you, I said I loved you."

"A-yuh. I heard ya."

"And what did you say?"

"I said, 'Fat chance.'"

"And what did you mean by that?"

"That I was angry."

"At what?"

"At ya leavin'."

"Ara—you came back that night."

She looked at him squarely, surprised at what he had just said. "No I didn't."

"You did."

"Didn't."

"Jesus Christ."

"Jesus Christ might've, but I didn't."

"Hey—I can understand your not wantin' to talk about it."

"Ya can?"

"Yes. Of course. And I'm sorry you feel that way, because I don't. Because I think it was...the greatest thing that ever happened to me."

"Ya do?"

"Yes."

"*What* was?"

"Ara! You came back that night and we made love!"

Her face blanched, all color and expression flying, even the pink from her cheeks taking flight. Only her eyes, gray and searing, continued to function, fixing unblinkingly on his, accusingly, as if to say, "How dare you!" then looking away, as if to say, "True, it happened, it truly happened," and then back into his, and then once more away. "Guilty. Not guilty. Maybe. Perhaps." A whole range of reactions played in her eyes, from clarity to confusion, to anger, to bliss. And Austin could see, his own eyes not stupid, that the issue was unsettled, the truth, elusive, the girl close to panic, the tears soon to come.

He pulled her to him and she allowed it, pressing herself against him as if to fuse herself there, her hair rife with winter, pine and balsam—clean, fresh drifts of it, blowing the thought into his head, hammering the words home as with chisel to marble: I love this girl, this Minnawickie, this sprite. God forgive me, but I love her and all that comes with it, all the jumble and all the pain—and, yes, death too, if it must. But I love her, Lord, and what the hell do I do about it?

"Look, Ara—tell me you hated it. Or that you're sorry we did it. Or that your father's coming to shoot me. But don't tell me you don't remember it."

She said nothing, choosing to stay as she was, clinging to him hard, like a marsupial in a pocket or a child in a quandary, snuggling for protection or buying time to frame an answer. With her head down as it was he couldn't see her face and couldn't guess which.

"Ara—I wasn't sure myself, that it happened. I went outside, looking for your bootprints. They weren't there, but that could've been because the snow covered 'em over."

She stirred in his arms, pushing herself from him lightly, unraveling from him as it were, but not with coquetry or anger— with sublime gentleness. She looked up at him, and the eyes had indeed been crying, and could have cried more but for the fact that she would not allow it, running her irresistible mittens across them, stopping the tears dead in their ducts. "Maybe it *didn't* happen, Austin."

"It happened."

"Maybe it didn't." She dropped back a short distance and picked up a few years, no longer the girl with a snowball on her head, more the woman with a problem on her mind. "I *wanted* to come back. That very night. I *wanted* to. And almost did. Almost ready to walk the whole way."

"Maybe you did."

"Didn't. Later, after some dreamin', I *thought* maybe I did— because it was so strong in me. But I didn't. I didn't, Austin. I didn't."

"What kind of dreamin'?"

"Nice dreamin'."

"No. Specifically. What kind of dreamin'? Ara?"

"Nice dreamin'...Naughty dreamin'."

"Strong dreamin'?"

"A-yuh. It was strong."

"You and me?"

"A-yuh."

"Ara—"

"And that's all I got to say on it. That's all the answer ya goin' to get."

He would be inductive, working toward a solution rather than from a hypothesis. "That day, Ara, the last day we saw each other, you didn't want me to leave, right?"

"A-yuh."

"So you came back. To my house. To make certain I wouldn't leave."

"No."

"Ara, there's no shame in that. There's a naturalness in it."

"I don't care what ya say, Austin. I didn't come back. Not until now."

"Okay. Then how come, if I said I'd be leaving the next morning, and you believed me, how come you come back today, four days later, and you're not the littlest bit surprised to see that I'm still here?"

"I don't know."

"You don't know."

"No. I just knew ya wouldn't be gone."

"*How* could you know?"

"I don't know. I just knew. Austin, ya goin' to make me cry."

He hugged her tightly. "No, we don't want to do *that*." And he took her mittened hand, all roly-poly and babyish. "Come on, it's gettin' cold. Let's go back to the house and I'll perk us up some coffee."

She balked, looking at him disapprovingly.

"Ara, you don't have to be afraid. I'll behave. You can ask Nutsy to come along. He'll protect you."

And still she didn't move. She just stood there, all of her pretty weight on one foot, her chin jutted out, her eyes narrowed, her hands on her hips like a schoolmarm who had just been crossed.

"Ara? What's the problem?"

"Problem is, it's Penobscots what like coffee. Not Minnawickies."

"Oh—I forget. I'm sorry."

"Minnawickies prefer *tea.*"

"Right. Right. I should've realized."

"Passamaquoddies like cocoa. Wabanaki like milk. Abanaki'll drink anything. But Minnawickies like tea."

"Right. Well, then, I'll make us some tea."

"Best ya do."

They walked back to the house and she was young again, making him walk ahead while she hung back, lobbing snowballs into the air in hopes of their coming down upon his head. Once or twice they did and she'd shout, "Pow!" and would laugh, while he wondered how the girl could change the direction of his emotions so quickly and so easily, giving him a distinct lift where, but a moment ago, he was half out of his mind with depression. Make that *full.*

It pleased him to be having tea with her, it was like old times. Though they had not known each other two weeks, Maine winter and Maine isolation had a way of moving things along, accelerating such natural phenomena as late-migrating birds, underground streams, hungry rabbits, and human relationships. Even the cloud-struck sky outside was beginning to whip by as in time-lapse cinematography.

He saw how she held her tea mug, not as a woman with pinky extended—but as a child, both hands wrapped about the mug, all ten fingers clutching as if to plug a leak. Her eyes peeked out at him from over the rim—and the high part of her nose, and the forehead, and the fine black hair—and the rest was steam, encircling her face like a halo, and it was as though he were looking at her in a morning mist when no girl looks prettier and no forest creature more fantastic.

He had calmed down by then, his lunatic war preparations retreating once the girl arrived to make of the battlefield a meadow, and of his heart a sponge that absorbed the sight of her, storing it for that future time when he might wish to drink of her again. "You know I love you, don't you?"

"A-yuh. That's what ya said."

"I still do. Always will."

"Whatever turns ya on."

"*And you* love *me.*"

"Ya got no proof."

"I know. I knew you couldn't have walked across the night like you did."

"It'd be eight miles."

"I think I knew it then, but I didn't care. Real or imagined, I wanted you. Anyway I could get you—it didn't matter."

"Still of been a long walk."

"You were in your house and I was in mine, yet something made us both believe we'd made love. Why?"

"Maybe 'cause it'd of been wrong for us to actually do it."

"You're talkin' conscience, and I'm talkin' something else."

"You're *always* talkin' somethin' else, Austin. I'd have to take a whole extra course in school to understand ya."

Austin was arriving at something. Slowly. But he was getting there. "Ara—something either sent you here, which is what we both felt—or made me believe you came here to…keep me here, waitin' for you, for these four days."

She had nothing to say on his last point, no pithy rejoinder, no off-center observation. She simply looked at him, silently, not even pretending to sip at the tea which, but a moment before, she had been consuming so happily. But in saying nothing she said it all, and Austin was quick to see that she was as confused and troubled by the event as he was, and that no amount of hiding behind her little-girl veneer could disguise that fact.

"There's something about this house, isn't there?"

Her voice was small, her words, aimed down into her mug, hollow and distant. "I don't know."

"I felt it the first night. I figured it was the power of suggestion— all those things Jack Meeker was fillin' my head with, plus all the things Maynard'd told me." For the first time he noticed the sky, the clouds seeming to rush over it like sheep to a barn; cold-colored streaks of it threading across the heavens at such a pace as to appear like all the colors of death, gathered upon one enormous brush before being hurriedly slapdashed across the world's last canvas.

Ara noticed it, too, though her reaction was more passive, her eyes simply taking their cue from his, turning to the window and looking out, almost casually, at the strangely motivated sky. She didn't blink. She didn't speak. She just looked.

"Ara, what is it? What's going on?"

"Don't know."

"A blizzard?"

"No call for it."

"It's beginning, isn't it?"

"What?"

"Whatever's goin' to happen—it's beginnin'."

"No wind. No cold. No snow. It'll pass."

"No."

"It'll pass, Austin."

"Yeah, and me with it." He grabbed her jacket. "Well, whatever the hell it is, you don't want to get caught in it." He helped her into her jacket as if she were an infant, handing her her mittens and her muffler. "Eight miles to your house. Better get movin'."

"A-yuh."

Through the window he could see Froom signaling wildly, throwing snowballs at the house like a baseball-pitching machine. "Your brother's gettin' nervous."

"Looks that way." She allowed him to hold her mittens as she thrust her fingers into them, like a surgeon about to operate. Then she put on her muffler, twirling it with such a practiced quickness that it went twice around her neck and once across her wan smile. Next came her hat, and she looked like a little woolen teddy bear, her hair redolent as she tucked it under. Never in his life had he been exposed to such simple beauty, to such a fine winter creature, to such innocent sensuality. And he wondered if he would ever see her again, and he panicked at that disquieting thought though he struggled not to show it.

"I don't suppose you'd care to stay," he said, "and wait it out with me."

"Can't."

"Froom could stay, too. I've got a good fire, lots of wood, lots of food."

"Can't, Austin."

"I know. Just thought I'd ask."

"Ya shouldn't of."

"I know. Think you'll make it?"

"A-yuh."

"It's eight miles. Whatever's comin' out of that sky, it's eight miles, Ara."

"We can travel fast."

"It's a hundred hills."

"Half of 'ems down."

"No. It's a hundred up and a hundred down."

"Right. Guess I'm still not all that good at mathematics."

"Will you come back tomorrow?"

She cocked her head, giving the matter thought. "Tomorrow? What day is tomorrow?"

"I don't know. I don't even know what today is."

"Well…" She smiled, figuring it out rather philosophically. "Tomorrow, today'll be yesterday, and the rest'll kind of just follow." She went to him, stood on her toes, and gave him a kiss. A little-girl kiss, dry and pure and soft, but on the lips all the same, and he drew her closer, looking into her eyes, into the deep gray depths of them.

"I love you, Ara."

"I guess I know."

"Do you love *me*?"

"A-yuh."

"Will you come back?"

She thought about it, again for too long, and it shook him. "I will if you will, Austin." And she pulled free from him, turned away, and went out.

He held the door open and watched as she walked out to where Froom was twitching like a live wire, anxiously motioning her on. Their sled was waiting. Soon they'd be gone—over the hill to Grandmother's house, laughing all the way. He was only twenty-three. Still he wondered if he had ever been as young as she. Endearingly young. Eternally young. Peter Pan young. Would she ever grow old?

The door flew from his hand, as if it were alive and had gotten away from him. It slammed shut with a finality that surprised him, and he couldn't get it open. That too he accepted as a signal that it was all beginning and that he'd better get ready.

He went to his window to watch as Ara and Froom pulled their sled to the top of the hill and mounted it. Ara turned and waved and he waved back. And then they were gone, the sled nosing over the hill and tailing out of sight, the last thing he saw of her being the fringe of her bright muffler, flapping gaily—farewell and goodbye, sweet girl, till we meet again.

The sky was driving, whipping furiously over the far horizon, more of it ribboning in from the opposite direction to replace it. Faster and faster it unraveled, until he wondered if gravity hadn't lost its mind and if he wouldn't be tossed off the earth and spun into infinity like a top, or a crumb, or a fleck of dust, or an Austin Fletcher, anonymous child of the Midwest. Who would miss him, who would kiss him?

He looked at the sky from each of his windows, and in each window it was off a different hue, the colors stabbing separately into his house, pinning him within their crisscrossing center so that, once again, he saw himself as crucified. And once again it lasted for an incalcuable moment, like a flash camera taking your picture when you weren't quite ready, causing you to wonder if your mouth was open, or your fly, or if there was any film in the camera in the first place.

He wasn't frightened, for he knew that it had all been coming, everything in and about the house being a harbinger of its arrival, a precursor of the eventual. The only thing he did not know was *what* was coming and *why* it was coming. Time would tell. And time, at the time, seemed in quite short abundance.

He picked up his Winchester, and the heft of it gave him security, the kind of security he was familiar with: lodge the stock, sight the target, pull the trigger, and the enemy is wasted. But what enemy? What was out there in the vaporous gloom beyond his windows, setting the snow to swirl like a smokescreen insidiously laid down to mask someone's movements?

Things were in motion, floating toward the house. Forms and shapes, amorphous and quivering at first, but gradually assuming the filmy silhouettes of men as it all drew closer. There were twenty of them, maybe thirty. It would be difficult to estimate their number and even more difficult to sight any one of them over a rifle barrel.

The sky drew darker as it slowed and settled on the land like a shot-down balloon, the principal color of it being swamp green. It was no color for a sky, though it did suit a jungle.

It would be a siege and then an attack. That was Charlie's usual pattern. He'd circle and probe, trying to figure how many of you there were and how you were deployed. He'd taunt you with his shrill laughter and pigeon-English threats. There'd be silence—and then'd he'd be there, all over you, on top of you and in back of you, his black pajamas and sneakered feet covering his skulkings and muffling his sounds. Austin knew it all. In that sense he was on familiar turf. The bitch of it was that the rest of the patrol had vanished. Lost or picked off. And he was out there alone, bellied down in the fog, trying to focus his ears like a deer fixing the location of whatever predator was out there. He sniffed too, because sometimes he could smell Charlie. Charlie didn't know from deodorants, and often, upwind, his scent would give him away.

"Austin?"

"Yeah. Who's that?"

"Austin, ya got to get out of here."

"Maynard?"

"A-yuh."

"Maynard, where the hell you been? Where the hell *is* everybody?"

"Austin, ya don't belong here."

"Helluva time to be tellin' me that. There's a couple dozen Cong out there."

"Austin—"

"And they know we're in here. Who's left in the patrol? Who do we have?"

"Austin, it's my fault and I'm sorry. I never should've left ya this house."

"Where's Cunningham and the flamethrower?"

"Austin, listen to me—"

"You don't keep your voice down, Maynard—. I swear, everytime we need him, that idiot Cunningham..."

"Austin—"

"Shhhh! Be quiet. They're all over the place. In the trees, in the river. Jungle's crawlin' with 'em."

"Austin—"

"Please shut up, Maynard. Some of 'em ain't ten feet away."

Maynard lay still on the floor of his house, craning his head up so that he could look out through the window, across the snow, at the encirclers not of this world. He could see their capes and their high Pilgrim hats. He could see the occasional flash of their square-buckles and their white collars and cuffs chalking the gray dimness. He resented having being used as a pawn and bristled at still not knowing what the eventual outcome would be. And he worried about the safety of his friend, who, obviously, knew less than even he did.

"They set down some kind of smokescreen, Maynard. You can't see 'em, but they're out there. Does Battalion know we're here? Maynard? Does Battalion know?"

"Nobody knows. I been tryin' to tell ya—"

"Well, another fine mess you've gotten us into, Stanley."

Maynard tried to think. The sky was turning black, serving as a deadly backdrop for the gray figures lurking in the obscure swirl. They were about to make their move—lighting torches, dotting the darkness they inhabited, spreading out into a huge semicircle some two hundred yards from the house. It was horrifyingly quiet, the torchlight playing against the windows on all sides, the mists spiraling, the mumbled voices becoming more and more audible as the semicircle slowly closed, like a noose being drawn about the house.

He looked over to where Austin was as intense as a mongoose, no sight or sound eluding him. It was his conditioned response to imminent battle. It was what had always made him so good at it.

"Hear 'em, Maynard? Must be about thirty of 'em. Comin' from the river, from those rice paddies. Maynard? You still there?"

"I'm here."

"Got any grenades?"

"Austin, I didn't want it to be this way."

"Tell *them*, not me. Now, do you have any grenades?"

"No."

"Jesus, you really come prepared."

"For Christ's sake, Austin! Can't ya see what's happenin'?"

"Not too well. It's a little dark out there. But I can see that *you* ain't goin' to be much help."

"Please listen to me. I think ya can still get out of here."

"I know. There's a bus every ten minutes."

"They're out there, Austin, but—they're *not*. All ya have to do is get out of the house before they get in. If ya get out, they can't hurt ya. Make a run for it. You can do it."

"Listen, Maynard, it's a helluva time for you to go psycho on me."

"No, *you* listen! You're not in Nam, Austin! You're in Maine!"

"That's good to know, Maynard, but—"

"In *my* house!"

"Tell you what, Maynard—you just lay back and let me handle it. You just give me whatever weapons you got and I'll fix up a nice welcome for 'em. Then we'll get outa here like we always do."

Maynard looked through the window again, into the protracted dark. They were closer, much closer. The torchlights brighter, the grumble louder, the semicircle tighter. It would soon strangle.

He looked over at Austin, who was standing, a rifle in each hand, unafraid, steadfast, not backing off an inch—so typically Austin that Maynard could almost have cried. "They'll get in the house, Austin." He said it dully, knowing that it would have no impact on Austin and that it would shortly be too late, but saying it all the same. It was all he could do. "I'm sorry, Austin. Sorry for the whole thing. It wasn't up to me. Never was."

Austin was not listening. He had more important matters to attend to. And, planting both feet firmly on the old wooden floors, he broke one of the windows with a rifle butt. "Okay, Charlie! You want it so bad?"

And Maynard knew that it was over. Still, he wanted to make his explanations, as best he could, for the record. "It was a setup. I didn't really know it till now. You were the perfect choice and ya walked right into it."

Austin fired, both rifles, from the hip and out the window. Then the shotgun, and then the .44. And then he set about reloading them all, coolly, like the good combat soldier he was. "You say somethin', Maynard?"

"I said ya were hand-picked."

"Correct. I do *not* remember volunteerin' for this shit detail."

"I just want ya to know that if I knew what was goin' to happen I wouldn't of named ya in my will."

"Oh, piss off, Maynard. I got work to do."

He was on his feet and firing again, through another window. Through *all* the windows, the glass shattering, his guns blasting point blank at the fog—and still they came. Maynard could see them, floating across the snow, stepping over the window ledges, sifting into the house. Faceless and dead, their capes undulating like manta rays, there were twenty of them, thirty.

"They're in the house, Austin." He said it unfeelingly, just reporting the news.

Austin fired everything he had, his rifles steaming hot—but the attackers did not disperse. "They're in, Maynard! Let 'em have it! Cunningham, you moron! Flamethrower! Flamethrower!"

Maynard watched helplessly as the torches bobbed and as Austin blazed away at everything in the room, at the old Boston rocker, at all the books, Thoreau included—all of which were summarily obliterated. Even the pine plank with the names disappeared in a splintering of wood and a showering of pulp. And Austin was every soldier who ever lived and ever fought and ever died.

"Fire! Fire! Fire! Cunningham, you——. Fire! Fire! Fire!" Denied the time to reload, he was using a rifle as a club, swinging wildly at all he thought to come within its perimeter. "Come and get it, Charlie! Step right up, folks!"

Maynard watched, and still the dark figures came, pouring through the no-more windows, their capes flapping, their torches fluttering like flaming birds, Austin swatting at them with his rifle, creating wicked arcs but inflicting no harm upon the inexorable specters.

"Attaboy, Cunningham, you sonofabitch! Maynard—where the hell are you?"

"I'm here, Austin. Right here."

"Fire! Fire! Fire!"

The kerosene lamps exploded, adding to the hellishness, and Maynard watched as Austin fell into the embrace of the consuming flames and the billowing capes. Maynard had done all he could to alter the unalterable. He had stepped in where he had no power and interceded where he had no rights. He had crossed borders and run boundaries on Austin's behalf but had failed, as he feared he would, as he knew he must. Whatever trickery had been launched two years prior, it was all about to culminate. There was nothing more he could do other than wait and see—and from where he sat in that cold, damp house on that fog-drenched night, it certainly looked to him that Austin was as dead as *he* was.

22

Austin lay on the cold rock that constituted his cellar floor. It was hard and irregular and sharp, and his right ankle throbbed hotly. He had obviously injured it when dropping through the trapdoor, landing on it unevenly with his full weight, twisting it unnaturally, and it hurt. He hoped it wasn't broken but wasn't quite ready to test it, especially in the dark where his footing, at best, would be uncertain.

His head throbbed, too, not from the fall but from something else, and he was trying to sort it out, trying to pick his way through the night's events and emerge with some vestige of rationality.

One minute he had been in the jungle, in the hot thick mists of Nam, spending his last breath, the Cong coming at him as liquidy shadows, black-garbed and quick, wrenching his rifle from his grip, and he was going down. And the next minute his fingers found the iron ring, dislodged the trapdoor, and he dropped into New England—just like that. Miracle or madness? More likely it was something else, something terribly in between. Something he had better decipher or fall into something far deeper than his cellar.

He didn't move. Movement would be anathema, an impediment to thinking, if for no other reason that that it would require a decision (move to where?). Movement too would sponsor pain (his ankle). Pain would divert thought (how badly am I hurt?). And he could not allow thought to be diverted, not then. Thought had to be mustered and concentrated, like the rays of the sun converging on a magnifying glass, for he desperately needed some flash-fire answers.

It was filling in, albeit slowly. Jigsawed pieces and scalloped fragments—diverse puzzle scraps sliding about on their own because their owner, confused and hurt, was of no great help.

They maneuvered, turned, navigated and addressed one another, struggling to link up, to slot in, to cog, to mesh, anything that might result in a totality that, though imperfect, Austin might understand and accept and soon, before his own mind split into Humpty-Dumpty shells that all the King's horses...and all that.

Maynard seemed to be one of those pieces. Maynard had been with him. In the house, yes. Talking to him. But not about the same thing. How could Maynard have been with him, yet be so wildly out of sync with the circumstances? Austin had been fighting Cong, and Maynard had been talking house. Therefore, no, Maynard could not have been with him. Extension of thought: Maynard had never been with him.

Oh, in the beginning, yes, Maynard had been with him, via simple recollections and reconstructions of events and conversations that had taken place in Vietnam. It was all right to think back on those, for they had occurred, and were real, and were thus allowed. But Maynard's *later* appearances—they were highly suspect. They wrung time and logic all out of shape, braiding twisted dialogue with incredulous ramblings. As such, they were not pieces to the puzzle, they were imposters, red herrings flaunted to confuse the issue and hinder the solution. They did not belong and had to be discarded. Final hypothesis: Maynard *had* been with him, so to speak, and for much of the time—but not all of the time, and certainly not that night.

Other illuminations were skinnying in. Illuminations, realizations and self-recriminations, all of them firing fitfully like a berserk Gatling gun, some hitting home directly, others ricocheting to target, still others missing altogether though the spent cartridges, to be found later, would eventually serve to complete and fasten the puzzle.

For example: There had been no Cong, and that stab of reality warmed him and he felt his senses rushing back to their posts and his intellect taking heart. There had been no Charlie on the night, overrunning him and burying him. He had imagined them. They had been a sometime recurring dream since the first time they happened to him, in Nam, over a year before. And from then on, frequently, whenever he was at low ebb and vulnerable, they could come at him again, at whim, fancifully and ferociously. Yes, there had been *something* out there in the night, some movement, some life, the bear perhaps, monstrous and mauling—but no Cong. For there had been no jungle, and no patrol, and no last stand—just snow and mist and cold and fear and imminent death, but no Cong.

So—two tricks played on himself *by* himself he was onto and had trumped. What else? What else had seemed but wasn't? The fire? No. The fire was real. The fire had encroached and driven him to the floor, where, in the white smoke and coughing blindness of it, he had found the trapdoor and dropped through.

As to how the fire came to be: He had fired all his weapons, destroying the Boston rocker, and the pine plank, and all the windows, and everything within the house. Still, that act in itself had not caused the fire. Nor had the reluctant Cunningham and his long-awaited flamethrower caused that crowning inferno, for that man was still in Nam. It was himself, Austin Fletcher, who had caused it by shooting out his lanterns, the kerosene spitting up the walls as liquid flame, dousing the beams and ceilings with dripping fire, the entire structure immediately set to drowning as in a blazing sea.

And, looking up, he could see that the fire was still there, stretching across the open trapdoor square like the full-on jets of a gas stove, blue and hissing and licking. If he were to stand up, he would lose his head to it.

He continued to lie where he had fallen, the fire above him being all the light he had to work with. It hung above his head like a malignant blue moon, no longer an issue, since it would eventually run its course.

The issue was that the fall had jogged his objectivity and the pain had sharpened his awareness, and he was able to place time and events in sensible perspective. He had all of his answers.

Well, almost all. One of them was still outstanding, lying like an unclaimed body in the morgue, unidentified and with few distinguishing features, i.e., if it wasn't the Cong he had been fighting off, who was it?

The answer to that question would have to come later, because the smoke, instead of rising and billowing up and out of whatever was left of the house, was descending, choking blankets of it fingering down through floorboard cracks as well as from the trapdoor opening, while above and beyond it he could hear the freight-train noise of the fire still roaring through his house.

Not only was the smoke coming down—the fire was, too. The flames oddly more green than orange, more cold than hot. Well, he laughed, you burn down a witch's house, what do you expect? "The Star-Spangled Banner" on a hot summer's night?

The flames squiggled down farther than they had a right to, defying all laws of physics in that flames should rise and not fall. They pressed through crevices and vacant knotholes like snake tongues—flicking, darting, as if trying to reach him. Some of them almost doing it, chilling him with their reptilian proximity.

Breathing was becoming a problem. What oxygen there was hovered at ground level, and he had to lay his face into it. Everything above that six-inch layer was of a cold and translucent green, a gaseous yet gelatinous lime. And above that—the still visible tentacles of fire. And he knew that if just one of those tendrils were to touch him, or even barely graze him, he would freeze in time where he lay, like that ash-covered Pompeian at the foot of Vesuvius.

He could feel the temperature dropping, plummeting. And the six inches of breathable oxygen was quickly three. It was time for him to move on—and he did, dragging himself across the rough rock, his ankle suddenly alive with glass-chip pain, the green light following him like the eye of some omnipotent Cyclops.

He was not all that familiar with his cellar. He had seldom spent much time in it, descending into it only to select some of the foodstuffs it warehoused. He didn't even know its dimensions—how far it extended and in what directions. He had never thought to explore it, assuming that it went no farther than the house's outside walls. Nor had he ever lingered too long in it, being unanxious to chance upon whatever damp animal life might abound in it, rats and such never being much to his liking. And so, in dragging himself along, he was moving into an uncharted area—not that he had much choice.

He bumped into it—his cistern barrel; and he stopped to contemplate it, at first reasoning that it was a wall and that he could go no farther, until he heard the sound—water, trickling. Through the barrel and on, coursing its natural way to somewhere else. To where?

He groped and found it, the stream, rushing. It had a destination. He did not. He'd follow it, his ankle hurting so piercingly that he allowed it to drag through the cold water as he crawled. It did little to lessen the pain.

He felt all coming apart. His mind was fine, functioning clearly, telling him where he was and what he was doing and why. But his body was failing him, his right leg already so useless that he'd have done better without it. His hands were burned close to skinless, the result of his having held hot rifle barrels too hard for too long. They were also cut and bleeding for a variety of other reasons—from having grappled with his shattered windows, from having dragged himself over the sharp rock ledge of his cellar, from having gotten his left hand jammed in the trapdoor when he failed to lift it all the way the first time he tried—and two of his fingers, he suspected, were broken.

His eyes were caused to tear by whatever gas the trailing green light was bringing with it. His lungs were straining, for there was less and less oxygen, and he breathed in all that was still available to him, like a kid sucking soda through a bent straw.

His heart was thumping and his head was ringing, and his knees hurt from his crawling, and his ribs felt pulled fleshless, and his stomach lurched, and the cold sweat ran, and the green light pursued, and he knew that he had to have gone well past the perimeters of his house perhaps by a quarter of a mile, though there was nothing he could do about it. He had to keep moving on because there was no turning back.

The stream would have to lead to somewhere, but its overhead clearance was shrinking with every yard he crawled, so that even if he were physically capable of standing he'd not have been able to do so to his full height. It was a narrowing, lowering funnel that he was passing through, and when the jagged rock ceiling was but inches above the stream he was forced to follow its descending contour and go with it into the water.

It was icy but not deep. He could walk through it and still keep his nose above it, but not by much—and still the green fog followed, barely an inch of air between its base and the stream's surface. But what deviled him more than anything, more than the grinding pain and the stalking terror, was the realization that he had no choice in the matter, that he was doing what he was doing because somewhere it had been *determined* that he would do it. Nor was it a case of right or wrong. It was do or die. Though, in the frightening final analysis, it might well be a case of do *and* die, for nowhere was it written that by doing it he wouldn't die.

The green light still trailed him, floating above him, dragging its noxious fumes like a rotting carcass, plugging his nostrils if he tarried, plunging down his throat when he idled to check his footing.

Though the stream still gurgled, he was aware that it had slowed, no longer urging him on insistently—rather, seductively coaxing him along; small eddies of it bubbling about his face as though the stream had run out of ancillaries and was unsure about where to flow next.

And then, as if the stopper had been pulled, it all trickled out, all the water, slowly disappearing under what appeared to be some kind of wall directly before him, wedged between two huge flanking rocks. And the stream drained off him, shimmying down from his neck to his boots, as if he were stepping out of a slithery chemise.

The green light hung back, blocking his return if that was his intention, sitting on the water like a huge hen. And so he had to turn his full attention to what was ahead of him—the wooden wall. He had no other option.

He examined it, balancing on one leg because the pain was still intense despite its immersion in the Novocaining cold water. It looked to be a door. It had the dimensions of a door, rectangular, higher than it was wide. He reached out to touch it and was immediately revulsed, his hand recoiling involuntarily from the moss-swathed green fungus that ran with slime and oozed with pustules that burst at his touch, releasing a smell of such decay that he came close to collapsing at the reek of it.

And something came with the choking odor—from beyond the door, which, in touching, he had apparently pushed open just enough for it to wander out. A sound. Voices. Throaty and whispery. Where had he heard it before?

He was, by then, almost fearless—various horrors having afflicted him so constantly and without killing him that the newer ones were bouncing off him with a reduced effectiveness. Instead of being frightened, he was curious, wondering what would come next. It was like wandering through a fun house. Nothing could scare you as long as you knew that you couldn't be hurt, and that it would all end soon enough, and that you would one day look back on it and laugh.

Bravely or stupidly, but certainly curiously, he pushed at the door again, with both hands—and both hands disappeared half a foot into the dripping moss of it, causing odors worse than before to explode at him, smells so foul as to be uncataloguable, for there was nothing that they could be compared with. But he hung on and continued to push, up to his elbows in the rancid muck before the door showed any sign of giving.

But give it did, and slowly it swung open on silent and unseen hinges, like some form of huge plant life able to think and plot, allowing an interloper easy entrance so that it might devour him just as easily.

All within the place turned to him, twenty of them, thirty, their voices a garbled babble, yet so arranged and rendered as to not be cacophonous; Austin hearing it all as a chant, Gregorian and judgmental and chillingly condemning, though none of the words registered beyond an occasional "thee" and an interspersed "thou."

They were draped in gray hues, these specters, with touches of pitch and dapples of white, dull flashes of light playing accents on their metal buckles, soft highlights of death wiggling blandly in their pupilless eyes, their tall hats and loose capes corrupting whatever true shapes they once might have possessed.

The air they stood in was equally muted, dull grays and flat blues silking in and out in movable planes, like microscope slides, coursing over one another to keep the colors murkily diffused. All of it slow, slow—no hurry in there where everything was, at minimum count, three hundred years dead.

Then the green mist that had herded him all that distance flew in from behind him, rushing up and overtaking him as if pulled in by the suddenly opened door. And it camped on his shoulders, endowing him with a cape of his own, as if it were a sacrificial mantle and he the chosen victim. At which point the murmur grew, a chord of angry satisfaction adding to the mix—and Austin knew where he had seen and heard them, and could guess at why Maynard had been so disturbed by his unwillingness to leave the house.

Two of them came to him, each taking an arm, the cold going through him like a spear, and he could hear his heart stop. He wasn't dead but knew he would be, the time, place and circumstances of that cut-in-stone fact about to be decided by the ungodly assemblage.

They walked him to the center of the place, where, almost directly above his head, hung a jangle of flapping roots that at first look appeared as whipping steel cables. Instinctively he jumped back from it, his captors giving him that leeway, though they held him fast at the spot to where he had retreated.

He looked up at it again and saw it for what it was: the dangling roots of a tree. It was as if he were in the earth, standing below it, loathsome abomination that it was—his witch's tree.

He had come that far from his house in following the random stream and was now standing beneath it as it slowly began to descend, like a sluggish elevator. And he could feel the consummate evil of it, crowding out all sanity—even his captors falling back from it, to allow it room, for its roots were as spastic ropes that could eat, and, thrashing about for sustenance as they were, anything might serve as fare.

The tree continued its descent, its roots reaching for and ultimately fixing on the smoky floor of the place, taking horrible hold there like a huge fist of many fingers, drawing in whatever juices it found there while making an inhaling noise like the death rattle of a beast.

And as it sunk its roots deeper it pulled itself farther down, and its trunk appeared before Austin, scaled and blotched and wretchedly petrified. And, unable to retain what its roots had leeched onto, it bled a dreadful sap that rivuleted down its bark to spill back into the place it had been sucked from.

Austin looked up to see the tree's mangled branches, rotted into a nightmarish crosshatch that no mad sketcher could have rendered. And there, on one of the limbs, her scrawny neck stretched like a chicken's, on a length of taut hemp—hung the witch, dangling and twitching, spitting urine and drooling feces, laughing hoarsely at her own never-ending agony.

Her face was as creased and as scaled as the bark of the tree she twisted on. Her black eyes sightless; her nose but a gnawed bone with parched skin stretched across it; her mouth screamingly open in perpetual rigor mortis; her few teeth, grown long in death, were as the teeth of a rake, inches apart and a half a foot long, curved down into inverted tusks that probed at her chest. And her toenails and fingernails were like the frozen flight paths of gnats, extending and curling every which way, some even returning to penetrate her body.

Hatless, her white matted hair hung down in tormented strands, more of it seeming to spring from the pits and valleys of her cadaverous face, and from her nose and her ears. Insects were visible in it, worms and slugs, touring their way in and out of her hornet's-nest skull which was of the consistency of papier-mâché.

And from every pore a yellow fluid oozed, even from her eyes, caking wherever it chose to on her shred of a black smock, the attendant odor causing Austin to wither and sag and drop to his knees before the eternally dying gorgon.

Death-dancing and swaying, slobbering and regurgitating, the grotesquerie raised one hand at him—a condor hand, plated and hooked, its spiraling nails straightening and pressing together so as to form a scimitar. Long, sharp and wicked, the thus fashioned blade was ready to decapitate—and Austin, like a dumb animal, stood there, awaiting his own beheading.

The two specters holding him stepped sideways so as to allow the witch proper room in which to perform the scheduled execution—but she did no such thing, choosing instead to make of her fist a hand again, her nails curving under and retracting to accommodate the act. And, holding it to Austin's face, she counted silently with it, unfolding three fingers one at a time, each finger whipping a nail close enough to his forehead to inflict there three separate cuts, none of which he ever felt though he bled profusely, a ribbon of blood flowing down into each eye, the third blood ribbon coursing over his nose and into his mouth.

One—two—three!

23

Clump—clump—clump!

The footsteps were heavy on the floor above his head, but they penetrated enough to bridge the gap and bring him back, though not all at once, and not with the clarity of thinking necessary to complete the journey.

He was exhausted, squeezed dry of all energy, his brain close to absent. Still, some thoughts began to diligently filter in.

In was dark. Cellar dark. He was in his root cellar. The fire was out, the green mist gone, the trapdoor in place. He reached down to touch his ankle. It didn't hurt. There was nothing wrong with it beyond an inconsequential twist. He was not wet. Wet with perspiration, yes, but not stream wet, not wading-in-the-water wet. He touched his forehead. No cuts, no bleeding. He was intact.

Again the footsteps above his head. Clump, clump, clump. Three times. The witch's count. He inhaled, half expecting her acrid breath to again offend his senses. It didn't. It wasn't there. Only the damp smell of his cellar, ringing with the fragrance of wet earth, hung with the clean, clear promise of life.

He found matches in his pocket and struck one, bestowing a light upon the darkness that was immediately picked up by the running stream. It illuminated the entire cellar, and he could see where the little stream ran lazily beyond the cistern before trickling away into the dark, ducking under and between mossy rock walls that invited speculation but not passage. The match spent, it went out, burning his fingers, but that was good. It meant that feeling was straggling back into formation as well as thought.

All manner of frightening recollections vanished with the light of that one match. He was alive and well. He had survived the house's most powerful trick. It also had to have been its last trick, for it could never top it, nor would it be likely to try. The nightmare was over. The spell broken. He had won.

"Anyone down there?" Somebody was standing on the trapdoor directly above his head. "Hey—time to be goin'."

He was not yet ready to deal with whoever it was up there. Other things had to be wrestled with first. Other images had to be set straight, evaluations made, reality and fantasy separated and kept apart, before he could go up into the charred remnants of his house.

He remembered shooting it up, causing the fire and dropping into the cellar. He remembered, too, reaching up and putting the trapdoor back into place. Still, much of what had happened continued to dodge dissection. *Why* had he done it? What forces had driven him to it? Fear? Isolation? Susceptibility? Where did Ara enter into it? And had he struck his head somewhere along the way like in so many old movies? And if so, was all that business with the witch and the tree and the specters a result of that injury? Concussion. Concussion could do that. Concussion, even a mild one, could cause a man to lose his memory and his rationality. It could cause and sustain such a condition for a split second, for minutes, for hours or for days. How long had been *his* trauma? How deep his jumble? And was he, at the root of it, dealing with a journey that, though clearly remembered, had never been embarked upon?

He heard the heavy wooden square being dislodged from its position. He heard the scraping of it and the clang of it, the iron ring of it slapping back into place as whatever hand held it released it. He looked up, his eyes taking some moments to focus, and he saw, standing there in a halo of diffused and dusty light, his huge hands spread over his knees as he squinted down into the cellar—Jack Meeker.

"What're ya doin' down there? Ya goin' to miss ya train if ya don't get movin'."

He didn't move. He tried to get a fix on it. Jack Meeker. Dead Jack Meeker standing up and talking down at him. Or was it just a trick of sight and sound? With the light behind him as it was, the man could be anyone. And the voice, nasal and drifting, could be the voice of any state-o'-Mainer. He looked up again, into the light, shielding his eyes with a salute, cocking his ear, the better to hear that voice again.

"Come on, Maynard. Stop sportin' with me and come on up outa there."

He had called him Maynard. It was definitely Jack Meeker up there, and Jack had definitely called him Maynard. His stomach quickly bore the brunt of both of those lunacies, a straight-line pain shooting up his middle from his rectum to his navel, the tip of it probing further, out to get his heart.

"Maynard, time and tide ain't goin' to wait." And the big man moved away from the trapdoor, a sharp light sliding in to fill his place.

Uncertain and shaken, he suspended all judgment, at least for the moment, though the suspicion was fast taking hold that the house was not yet through with him. He pulled himself up and out of the cellar, and, with his legs still dangling, and with only his torso in the room, he balanced on his forearms and looked around, like a groundhog for its shadow—and almost let go at what he saw.

The house was whole and cheery, the room untouched, sunlight streaming in from its morning windows. The fire? What fire? There was no sign of it ever having occurred. The shattered windows? Hardly. They were all in place, frost-covered and merry. The Boston rocker? Right where it had always sat. The books, the stores, the fine pine plank, all as they were supposed to be. As were his guns, all hanging on their respective pegs with nothing to indicate that they had recently done battle. Everything was neat and tidy and parked right smack in the middle of a fine winter morning. And Jack Meeker was at the stove, feeding it a log, prodding the fire with a poker, and he was as big and as real and as motherly-concerned as he had always been.

"Got to respect fire. Else it can jump up and grab ya." He turned and smiled, the crinkly eyes positive proof that all was well in Maine. "One hour to make that train. This the bag ya takin'?" He picked up a small overnight bag that lay on a table. It was vinyl and new and had a name inked onto its plastic-covered card marker: "Maynard Whittier."

He pulled himself the rest of the way into the room, feeling the floor beneath his boots firm and real. It was *all* real. It was all happening. Either that or he had gone mad—which might well be the case, since he'd been flirting with that prospect almost from the day he arrived.

"Hope ya got a couple sandwiches in here, Maynard. Have no idea how long it'll take ya to get to Fort Devens." Jack zipped open the bag and examined its contents. "A-yuh. Two sandwiches. And an apple. And what's this? Cookies. Even a couple napkins. Ya did good, Maynard. Good thinkin'."

His head ringing, he walked over to the pine plank that was still there, still nailed to the wall, all the names and comments carved into it still legible. He knelt to look at the last legend on the plank, and, running his fingers over it, he could feel that it had been freshly carved, the wood light and splintery as compared with all the other words, which were dark and smooth with age. There were even wood chips on the floor, fresh shavings of pine. And a small knife next to it. And the implication was all too clear. The words were newly carved.

Maynard Whittier took occupancy of this house on October 7, 1968. He left to serve with the U.S. Army on January 14th, 1971. I fear that I may not return.

"Left a little mess there, Maynard." Jack was leaning over him, and then, kneeling alongside him, he picked up the small knife and simply blew away the residue of shavings. "Just about run out of room on that wood, ain't ya?"

He walked as far away from the plank as he could, his ankle hurting just enough to keep him aware of it. Then, leaning against a wall at the other side of the room, he asked Jack, "What day is it?"

"Day? Thursday."

"No. I mean the year."

Jack looked at him curiously. "Nineteen seventy-one."

"And the date?"

"January fourteenth."

"Which is why I wasn't allowed to leave five days ago, when I wanted to."

"How's that?"

He smiled knowingly at Jack. "A witch has a sense of orderliness. Things happening on specific dates, by the numbers, according to schedule. Didn't you tell me that?"

"Never had to. Figured ya always knew it, Maynard."

"And why do you call me Maynard?"

Jack was no longer smiling, the question so puzzling as to make him wonder why it had ever been asked. But the answer came soon enough, and without a word from Jack. Shifting his weight because his leg was still nagging him, he was aware that something was behind him, emanating cold, and he wheeled to face it. It was a mirror.

And though he knew his own face to be bearded and grimy, the face in the mirror was not. It was clean-shaven and youthful, with hair the color of wheat and pale eyes that riveted, and a quizzical smile that ingratiated. Maynard.

But though the face was Maynard's, its emotions were quickly Austin's, for it immediately mirrored Austin's panic, its eyes widening, its mouth grimacing, its hands reaching up to touch Austin's hands, all four hands meeting at the mirror's surface—two in reality, two somewhere else.

And a sound came out of the twisting mouth as it struggled to form words that Austin, on his side of the mirror, was not forming. And it was an awful sound, like the sandpapered whisper of a man without a larynx struggling to make himself heard across an abyss. Hoarse and harsh it pressed out, mouth straining, veins bulging, until the words passed through the mirror to fall on Austin's ear as a rasping contortion of five convulsive words: "I...told...you...to ...run..."

And he was stuck there, his fingers affixed to those in the mirror, and he could not pull free. And in the soul of him he knew that if he could not break the suction of those other hands, he was doomed to go flying beyond the looking glass like smoke up a flue, to somewhere from which he would never find his way back. So, balancing himself on his toes, he leaned forward, his fingers made to bend contrary to nature, building enough coil and strength to sever the suction and catapult himself away from the mirror and back into the room. He staggered backward as he broke from the mirror, his wheezing lungs struggling for any lumps of air they could sift past his gritted teeth.

Four, five reeling, gasping steps he took, his shoulders slamming up against the far wall, hard. He flattened himself against it, like a man trying to eliminate his shadow, half expecting to be boomeranged back into the mirror. But he was evidently far enough away from the detestable glass for it to no longer have any hold on him.

And he stayed there like that, pressing himself shadowless, for how long he did not know. Long enough to feel a part of that wall—until, finally, his body unclenched and proper breathing returned, and his ankle no longer hurt.

He looked over at Jack, who, apparently, had taken no notice of the incident. "Maynard, ya miss that train and ya AWOL ya first day in the Army."

"What if I don't go?"

"What?"

"What if I don't go?"

"Ya *have* to go. Ya know that."

"I don't know that." He could see his feet firm on the floor, yet felt himself slipping. He was still Austin Fletcher, but he was running out of identity. Even his voice, though familiar inside his head, seemed no longer his own.

"'Course ya do," said Jack, "It's ya duty."

"No. I don't know that." He was losing hold and he knew it, all life running out of him, as though an exchange of blood was being made, as in a transfusion, his going to somewhere else, someone else's pumping into him, his veins filling with another's genes and chromosomes, another's intellect and experiences.

"Ya all right, boy?"

"I don't think so."

"It's only natural. Happened to me in World War Two. Every man feels it."

"Feels what?"

"Fear, I guess."

"Tell me the day again."

"Thursday, January fourteenth."

"And the year."

"Nineteen seventy-one."

"Austin Fletcher."

"What?"

"Austin—"

"Who?"

"—Fletcher."

"Don't know him." Jack was at the door, holding it open. "Now let's go." He tossed the little overnight bag across the room, and the younger man caught it and followed Jack out onto the porch, stopping there to take one last look back into his house before closing the door.

"Ya'll come back to it, Maynard."

"A-yuh. I think I will."

"Goin' to lock it?"

"Nope. Never lock it."

They headed out across the snow, passing the witch's tree and the Devil's Dancing Rock, and the postbox with the name "Maynard Whittier" painted on it. And it occurred to the younger man that he never did get around to changing the name on the postbox. Change it to what? He couldn't remember.

He followed Jack to where the jeep stood idling, puffing exhaust smoke like a little train, and he ran his hands over his beardless face, though he couldn't for the life of him, remember having shaved that morning. And he heard a voice, not his, not anyone's he knew: "A house is a place to go back to, to regroup in. A house is a kind of a special corner of the universe."

"Ya say somethin', Maynard?"

"Nope."

They climbed up and into the jeep, and Jack threw the feisty thing into gear. It took to the road cruelly, as if on octagonal wheels, Jack mumbling something about rough spots, though the younger man wasn't listening, an earlier speech of Jack's rolling around in his head—"A witch can occupy a house and do things to ya if ya cross its threshold. It can be layin' in wait for ya, baitin' a trap....A witch can make ya wish ya never came near it."

They drove on down the company road to Belden, to where the train would take him to whatever adventures the U.S. Army had him scheduled for. He would miss his house, yet somehow knew he'd be back. In the meantime, he had left his icehouse stocked, his root cellar full, and a shovel leaning against the backhouse door in case of snow. The birds would miss him, for they relied on him so. Still, they'd adapt, as would the little creatures under his floors. It was Brownie who worried him. That crazy deer stood a good chance of starving to death if he couldn't get his regular handouts. Oh, well, he thought, nature will provide.

As to his dogs, he had left them in the care of those two kids. Ara and Froom, they said their names were, and they claimed to be Minnawickies. Minnawickies indeed. In any case, they promised they'd be looking for him and would hold on to his dogs until he came back.

He had been the perfect choice and he'd walked right into it, just as Maynard had said. Nor should it have come as a surprise, for wherever he went in life he was never missed when he left. He made no imprint, not in Cincinnati, not in the Army, and probably not in the snow. Like the witch's tree, he cast no shadow. No pencil would write him down. No girl would remember making love to him. No house would accept him.

The house had loved only Maynard. None of the others, for they had all feared the house, himself included. Whereas Maynard loved it. "It's the nature of a house to absorb its occupants, kind of keeping them forever alive. In particular, that applies to those who loved that house without reservation and stuck with it through whatever tests and obstacles arose."

Still, he had enjoyed it all, damn it. And given the same set of circumstances, he'd do it again. He'd walk over the snow, and contend with witches, and turn himself inside out for a girl with gray eyes—for he had pulled more living out of his dying than he ever would have harvested from the Biblical three score and ten. As such, his days had been well spent. As such, he'd do it again—somehow.

The jeep plowed along, leaving the house farther and farther behind. And he sat there, his overnight bag on his lap, unable to look back. But ahead of him, on the road and in time, he caught a fragile glimpse of someone else—a friend, who would come to the house from somewhere else and who, before leaving, would embrace Thoreau as would no other man...

"...I went to the woods because I wished to live deliberately, to front only the essential facts of life, and see if I could learn what it had to teach—and not, when I came to die, discover that I had not lived."

24

The train aimed itself devotedly along, nudging snow from the beckoning rails while the vanishing point ahead kept retreating like a playful Lorelei. On straightaways the engine displayed a joyful confidence, accelerating at times to ten miles an hour. But on turns it grew cautious, and in tunnels it groped, and on bridges it quite simply held its breath.

It was the Bangor & Aroostook Railway—hauler of potatoes and occasional passengers, picking its way over the little spur line that linked Millinocket with Belden, carrying its horizontal red, white and blue stripes into inexorable and wobbly extinction. In a few years it would be no more. All of this in Maine, in the winter of 1972–73.

Inside, turtle-sunk in the parka that had warmed him for one and a half Vietnam winters, Austin Fletcher amused himself by watching the steam of his breath disappear as soon as he created it. The train was unheated and no other passengers abounded. Nothing for companionship but his duffle bag: FLETCHER, A. G., US 51070406. It sat beside him on the seat, embracing everything he owned in the world. As such, and in more ways than one, it was all he had to lean on.

He was a young man, in his twenties, physically unremarkable and possessing no particular characteristic that anyone might notice beyond a certain impish smile that seemed never to fade. He had come a long way to this place so far from his native Cincinnati, but he had made a friend a promise and he was very big on keeping promises. Besides, he had always wished to be alone somewhere, and here was a perfect opportunity to do so.

He took the paper from his pocket, reverently, as if it were centuries-old papyrus. Yet it was only blue-lined notebook paper, dogeared and sweat-stained, hardly the kind one would choose to record his last will and testament on. Still, it meant that he owned a house, Maynard's house. And he owed it to Maynard to at least have a look at it.

The train slowly came into the station, and Austin looked out the window at the little depot. BELDEN, the sign read, and Belden it was, and he hoisted his duffle bag to his shoulder and made his way through the car to the exit door.

Stepping down from the train and onto the snow-shoveled platform, he saw only a handful of disinterested people milling about, mostly unloading freight, and mostly wearing plaid mackinaws as if that were the uniform of the day.

He peeked through the window of the depot house, where a big man in a shaggy sweater sat very officially at a desk, though it was apparent that the man had very little to do except keep his eye on the coffeepot and on the bacon and eggs jumping in the pan.

He found himself lingering on the platform, though not knowing why. It was not his style to linger. It was his style to find a local and arrange for transportation to Maynard's house, wherever the hell it was, and get on with things. And yet he was lingering, which he thought odd.

Disjointed thoughts shuffled about in his head, like memories not his own. They were there and then gone, in and out the window, never quite taking hold. It had been like that the entire way from San Francisco. Actually, it had been like that his entire life—nothing solid in it, anything of value he ever had being either borrowed or bestowed upon him, temporarily or against his will. Why should this house be any different?

He looked away from the depot, at the low snowy hills beyond, as though looking for someone but not knowing whom. And there, perhaps thirty yards away, atop a small hill and beside a strange sled, stood a boy about twelve, sullen and stolid, and a girl about sixteen, as pretty as a picture, with a bright scarf going twice around her neck. They were both looking back at him, each holding a leash that restrained a large dog—but not for long.

For upon seeing Austin, both dogs broke free, running directly to him, yelping happily and arriving heavily to jump all over him, almost knocking him to the snow.

Taking their cue from the dogs, the boy and the girl advanced, though more sedately, to where Austin stood patting both dogs. The boy was not special, he was simply a boy. But the girl looked at Austin with eyes of such a glittering gray that, for the longest time, he could not look away.

And while he was transfixed, no words coming to mouth or mind, the boy ran off, returning with the sled, upon which Austin knew to place his duffle bag. The three of them then hauled the sled to the top of the hill and climbed aboard, straddling the duffle bag as if it were a rocket. And down the hill they went, laughing and shouting, the dogs giving chase, never far behind.

A hundred hills they traveled, dragging the sled up and riding it down, before the little house revealed itself, tucked away as it was against a hill of its own, like a cat snoozing.

And they coasted down that last hill, right to the house's porch, the dogs giving chase, sliding and tumbling like seals in a barrel. And they entered the house, all of them, putting a fire into the stove and waking old beams, setting animals to scurrying in the ceiling and beneath the floors.

And once in the house, he sat down on the old Boston rocker and wondered—was there any ice still in the icehouse, and any crackers for the deer? And was the shovel still there at the backhouse door?

And outside, though none of them saw it as it ducked out from behind the chimney and scooted about on the roof, was a witch's hat, empty of everything save a small, tight laughing, which it indulged itself in—over and over and over.

SUMMER OF '42

Captivating and evocative, Herman Raucher's semi-autobiographical tale has been made into a record-breaking Academy Award nominated hit movie, adapted for the stage, and enchanted readers for generations.

In the summer of 1942, Hermie is fifteen. He is wildly obsessed with sex, and passionately in love with an "older woman" of twenty-two, whose husband is overseas and at war. Ambling through Nantucket Island with his friends, Hermie's indelible narration chronicles his frantic efforts to become a man, especially one worthy of the lovely Dorothy, as well as his glorious and heartbreaking initiation into sex.

A GLIMPSE OF TIGER

Tiger is a nineteen-year-old runaway who comes to the big city to start anew. There she meets Luther, a quirky con artist with charm to burn. Together they pull small scams and petty crimes on the populace of New York in the 1970s, making their money and falling in love. But a con artist is a con artist seven days a week, and soon Tiger finds herself wondering if Luther will ever be able to settle down and start building a life with her.

This mesmerizing, surprising novel explores two unforgettable people as they live and love in Manhattan—and enchants readers with a romance impossible to forget.

THERE SHOULD HAVE BEEN CASTLES

Ben is the writer who can't seem to make it; Ginnie is the dancer who can't seem to miss. In 1951 they are two scared kids in love—determined to hold onto each other no matter what. Together the world is theirs for the asking.

In the exhilarating landscape of 1950's show biz, from the neon glamour of the New York stage to the starry glitter of Hollywood, they have love and success—pure, intense, and perfect. It should go on forever, fueled by enough romance and glamour for all the record books and fairytales that ever were. But can their love prevail or will it all come tumbling down due to an unexpected twist neither of them could have foreseen?

Printed in the USA
CPSIA information can be obtained
at www.ICGtesting.com
JSHW031712140824
68134JS00038B/3642